## HEART TO HEART

Clementine surrendered herself to the warm, welcome shelter of Rand's arms. The fierceness of his kiss left her feeling light-headed. Frightened and emboldened. Eager and tentative. A tempest of conflicting emotions brewed within her, flowing warm, rushing hot.

She opened her eyes to the face imprinted on her heart. The striking face of her daydreams, the strong, angular face that invaded her dreams at night. Rand's face. From inches away, his breath tickled her cheek, teased her sensitive skin.

Narrow streaks of moonlight shot through his dark, coffee-colored hair. His locks had grown long and curled at the nape of his neck. The blue gaze that she'd come to know as well as her own fixed on her. Desire glazed his eyes.

Clementine ached for him. To have him and hold him until the tide came in and swept them from the sand. She needed his kisses more than her beloved bluebonnets needed the Texas sun.

# BOOK YOUR PLACE ON OUR WEBSITE AND MAKE THE READING CONNECTION!

We've created a customized website just for our very special readers, where you can get the inside scoop on everything that's going on with Zebra, Pinnacle and Kensington books.

When you come online, you'll have the exciting opportunity to:

- View covers of upcoming books

- Read sample chapters

- Learn about our future publishing schedule (listed by publication month *and author*)

- Find out when your favorite authors will be visiting a city near you

- Search for and order backlist books from our online catalog

- Check out author bios and background information

- Send e-mail to your favorite authors

- Meet the Kensington staff online

- Join us in weekly chats with authors, readers and other guests

- Get writing guidelines

- AND MUCH MORE!

Visit our website at
http://www.kensingtonbooks.com

# Kiss Me at Christmas

## Sandra Madden

**ZEBRA BOOKS**
Kensington Publishing Corp.
http://www.kensingtonbooks.com

ZEBRA BOOKS are published by

Kensington Publishing Corp.
850 Third Avenue
New York, NY 10022

All Kensington titles, imprints and distributed lines are available at special quantity discounts for bulk purchases for sales
promotion, premiums, fund-raising, educational or institu-
tional use.

Special book excerpts or customized printings can also be created to fit specific needs. For details, write or phone the office
of the Kensington Special Sales Manager: Kensington Publishing Corp., 850 Third Avenue, New York, NY 10022. Attn:
Special Sales Department. Phone: 1-800-221-2647.

Zebra and the Z logo Reg. U.S. Pat. & TM Off.

First Printing: October 2004
10 9 8 7 6 5 4 3 2 1

Printed in the United States of America

*To Dave Madden*
*for his unflagging support*
*and promotion!*

# One

"Do you, Clementine Rebecca Calhoun, take this man, Rand Jonathan Noble, to be your lawfully wedded husband?"

"Ah do." Clementine raised her chin a notch and attempted a smile, but the smile felt tight and untrue.

The solemn preacher turned to the stranger at her side. "Do you, Rand Jonathan Noble, take this woman, Clementine Rebecca Calhoun, to be your lawfully wedded wife?"

"I do." Oddly enough, Rand Noble's deep baritone conveyed an assuredness lacking in many bridegrooms with much greater cause for certainty.

A series of quickly moving events had brought Clementine to this, an arranged marriage in the Annapolis, Maryland home of Lieutenant Commander Rand Noble. Wealth whispered in the corridors of the grand old Georgian home. She'd never seen such high ceilings or rich furnishings, each tabletop polished to a high sheen. She'd been amazed to see a blurry reflection of herself in the elegant black-walnut side table. No boots she'd ever worn cushioned her feet like the thick oriental carpet beneath her. Most astonishing of all, her husband's grand house boasted an indoor privy. They called it a water closet.

A gentle breeze stirred the lace curtains; unfortunately, not enough air to actually breathe.

"With this ring . . ."

The bridegroom turned to his father. "Where's the ring?"

"Here, right here," he said, fumbling in his breast pocket before producing a narrow gold band.

Rand took the ring and slid it onto the third finger of Clementine's left hand. It stuck at the second knuckle.

"Ah believe it's too small," she whispered.

"I'll take care of it later," Rand whispered back.

And the ceremony continued.

Clementine waited in suffocating suspense for the moment when the preacher would ask if anyone present knew of a reason why she should not be joined with this man. She meant to holler "Ah do!"

But the moment did not come.

The Reverend Rowe eliminated what, to her, was the most important portion of the ceremony. Instead, while the blood drained from her body, leaving her numb, the preacher's voice boomed in dramatic conclusion.

"By the powers vested in me by the State of Maryland, in the year of our Lord eighteen hundred and seventy-eight, I now pronounce you man and wife."

A profound silence met his declaration.

Clementine's heart stopped. She died on the spot. If only for an instant. Thankfully, within seconds, her heart swung back into action, making a loud thumping sound.

She'd joined the legions of June brides.

Rand Noble had married her. A respected, wealthy naval surgeon, he'd married Clementine Calhoun, a poor tomboy rancher from Oddon, Texas. She'd counted on him backing out. She couldn't figure the handsome doctor would marry a woman he'd met for the very first time last night. Her lungs felt as if they were stuffed with cotton. In an effort to take just one deep breath, she gasped noisily.

Her broad-shouldered groom shot her a sideways glance, the concerned frown of a professional physician.

He'd married her. She silently repeated the fact to herself yet again in an attempt to make the moment real. The uniformed officer, splendid in blue and gold, oozing infinite charm and a breathtaking excess of male virility—which made it difficult to take anywhere near a full breath in his presence—had just become her husband.

Rand Noble towered over her as no man in her acquaintance ever had. Back home Clementine had been frequently teased about her height. Folks constantly told her she resembled a long blade of grass. But if she could be likened to a long blade of grass, her husband qualified as a giant oak.

Her husband. How odd that sounded even as it rolled around in her head where no one could hear.

His shoulders appeared strong enough to support an entire battalion of men. And, to Clementine's utter fascination, a permanent twinkle lodged in his sapphire blue eyes. The ever-present sparkle transformed the broad, friendly planes of his face into a remarkably attractive visage.

The preacher cleared his throat. Did he have more to say? She fervently hoped not. She'd never swooned before, but one more word from the Reverend Rowe might push her over the edge into oblivion.

Short of stature, the preacher nonetheless possessed the regal bearing of a bishop. He'd conducted the ceremony standing with his back to the fireplace in the intimate reception room.

She focused on the vase of wilted white roses adorning the mantle. Earlier in the day it must have been a beautiful bouquet, but now the roses looked like a sad afterthought. Clementine felt like one of the withering blossoms. Life as she knew and loved it, nipped in the bud.

With a smile that stopped just short of a smirk, the Reverend Rowe addressed Rand. "You may kiss your bride now."

Rand turned to Clementine, his eyes alight, eyes captioned by a fan of deep laugh lines, the mark of a man who enjoyed life. She had no idea what he could possibly find amusing about the present situation— unless he mocked her.

She stiffened. Faced with a kiss from a mocking stranger, she felt her courage slipping away. Back home she was known for her bravery. Why, she was recognized as the best shot west of Houston. More than one rattlesnake could attest to her aim. And then there was that thieving cattle rustler. He'd learned the hard way about her skills with a Winchester.

Telling herself she had nothing to fear here in the cozy chamber nestled in the heart of big-city civilization, Clementine squeezed her eyes shut. She puckered her lips and leaned in just a bit toward her husband. He smelled pleasantly of soap and spruce. Fancying the woodsy scent of him, she took her first deep breath. She expected a quick peck on the lips. But that's not what she got. Rand swept her into his arms as if he had been waiting all of his life for this moment.

Engulfed in his arms of steel, Clementine's breasts flattened against the muscled wall of her stalwart groom's chest. The steady rhythm of his heart thumped against her chest. Her heart skittered in response. Slightly.

*Dang!*

She opened her eyes just in time to see the playful gleam in his. Before she could yank herself free of his embrace, the polecat brought his mouth down hard on hers. He kissed her like she'd never been kissed before—not that she'd had much experience. Rand's warm lips took hers in a bruising, dizzying declaration.

An eerie light-headedness took hold of her. Clementine swayed in his arms. Her breasts tingled in some sort of sinful reaction to his wanton lust. But her shame had just begun. His tongue plunged deep into her mouth. A rush of blood spun from her head to the tumbling pit of her stomach. Emotions she'd never even guessed a body could feel careened through her like a Texas lightning storm until she became a quivering mass. Stunned, she had but one thought.

He'd tried to kill her!

For what other reason would a man push his tongue down a woman's throat? What manner of man was this who had the audacity to attempt murder in front of the preacher and his own father? She was doomed. Her throat felt drier than corral dust.

The preacher twittered, emitting an embarrassed choking sound.

Clementine wobbled on unsteady legs. Finally, Rand released her with what could only be interpreted as a triumphant smile.

"May I?" The Reverend Rowe stepped between Clementine and Rand to buss her lightly on the cheek. "Congratulations, Mrs. Noble."

"Th-thank you." *Mrs. Noble.* How grand, how respectful, how strange the sound. *Mrs. Noble.* She hated it!

Because her own pa had passed away years before, Jonathan Noble, Rand's father, had given Clementine to his son in marriage. Smiling broadly, he waited his turn before stepping forward and taking her hands in his. "It's a pleasure to welcome you to the family, my dear. May I give my new daughter a kiss?"

How could she say no?

His lips grazed her cheek softly and swiftly.

Clementine's pa and Jonathan Noble had been lifelong friends. Jonathan had been an officer and her pa just a sailor, but they became as close as brothers. During a particularly dangerous battle, the two young salts made a pact binding their offspring to a marriage neither man knew if he would live to see. Although she'd heard the story many times growing up, Clementine never actually expected that she would be asked to fulfill the arrangement.

Her pa hadn't lived to give her away, nor to witness her honoring his pledge. Roy Calhoun had died in the service of his country more than ten years ago. Not long afterward, Clementine's ma had passed from a broken heart.

Clementine lived with her older brother. Together, she and Roy Junior ran the ranch they'd inherited. One day she'd hoped to buy Junior out and take sole ownership of the cattle spread. Her dream ended the day Junior came across the ancient pact written by Jonathan Noble and their father. He regarded the document as a contract guaranteed.

Without her knowledge, Junior corresponded with the elder Noble, suggesting the marriage take place before Clementine grew any older. She'd observed her twentieth birthday without a single marriage proposal.

Junior wanted her gone from the ranch. He'd given up hope of finding Clementine a husband and taken himself a bride. Neither he nor his wife, Margaret, wanted his younger sister living with them. A woman who wore chaps, played poker and ate two helpings at every meal didn't fit in with their plans. She didn't fit in with anyone's plans. Seemed like she'd always felt alone, in the way or out of step. She didn't fit in anywhere, especially here in Annapolis.

Searching for solace, Clementine tried to imagine her pa's spirit in the room. But imagination failed her. Any number of women might build a shrine to a pa who had promised them to a man who looked like Rand Noble. But she was not one of them. She hadn't been draggin' her rope for a man, any man. But like it or not, she had one now.

"If ever my son says or does anything to disturb you even slightly, you just let me know, my dear," her new father-in-law advised, rousing Clementine from her musings. "I intend to see that you are as happy as Roy intended."

"You're mighty kind." She smiled but couldn't think of a thing else to say. Clementine could talk about horses for hours, but her father-in-law had already confessed to not even owning a horse.

Still a good-looking man at sixty years of age, Jonathan Noble tucked her hand into the crook of his arm. During the past twenty-four hours, Clementine had spent more time in his company than her husband's. Shortly after her arrival in Annapolis, an emergency case had called Rand away from their get-acquainted dinner to the academy's hospital. As the chief surgeon of the Naval Academy, he bore responsibility for a sizable hospital and the health of more than two hundred midshipmen.

A popping sound shattered the silence.

Clementine started. She swung around to see that Rand had wrestled the cork from a bottle of champagne, signaling the start of a small celebration.

Unwilling to lock eyes with her bridegroom after what he'd just done with his tongue, she kept her gaze on the fizzing bubbles. Just keeping her glass steady as he poured commanded a heap of her concentration.

"To a successful adventure," he said, gently clinking his glass against hers.

*Adventure?* He made it sound as if they were cowhands preparing to blaze a new trail together. Her parents' marriage had been a happy partnership of hearts and spirits. And that's what she was raised up to expect from marriage. Fact bein', after years of loneliness, Clementine longed for a warm corner in life. Her father-in-law raised his glass. "May you live a long and joyous life together and produce a dozen healthy children."

*A dozen children!* She'd landed in a den of madmen!

Declining a piece of the heavily frosted one-layer plain wedding cake, Clementine downed the contents of her glass in one hasty gulp and immediately held it out for a refill. The sparkling wine was much too sweet for her taste but went down easy and might deaden her brain if she was lucky.

"Whoa!" Rand appeared surprised as he glanced at her empty glass, but he quickly recovered, shot her a disarming smile and poured.

As she raised the glass to her lips, her dashing bridegroom sidled up to her, slick as a bobcat on the prowl. "Most likely you wish to retire now and prepare for your wedding night?"

The deep, smooth-as-syrup timbre of his voice caused Clementine to warm in unfamiliar places. "Ah-ah guess ah do."

"I have a special supper planned," he said, adding a slow, rakish wink.

Her light-headedness returned at the same instant a mass of butterflies took flight deep in her belly. In that moment Clementine experienced an epiphany. Any man who could make her feel like this with just a wink and a few soft words was a downright danger-ous man.

"Ah'd be right pleased to share supper with you," she replied, struck at the unexpected breathless qual-ity of her voice. She would agree to anything in order to leave his overpowering presence as quickly as pos-sible.

"I'll join you shortly." His lips curved up in a smile of seduction so plain and heart-stopping that even Clementine understood its meaning. "I shall not keep you waiting, darlin'."

*Dang.*

Again, Clementine drained her glass in one gulp. Slanting her bridegroom a tight, twitchy smile, she turned on her heel and fled to the wedding chamber.

As soon as Rand paid the reverend and saw him to the door, he returned to the reception room, where his father waited.

"Well, son, congratulations." He slapped Rand on the back in comradely fashion. "You have yourself a new bride."

"Yes, I do. The deed is done." Rand stood by the fireplace. He braced one arm against the mantle, star-ing into the empty grate.

He'd done it. He'd married Clementine Calhoun. He'd taken a deep breath and gotten it over with, much like a man faced with an abscessed tooth that needed to be pulled. "But tell me again, why did you ever make such a pact?"

"Good breeding. I knew Roy Calhoun better than I've known any man, before or since. There was no doubt in my mind, and I have none now, that Roy Calhoun's daughter was born to be the perfect wife for my only son."

"The perfect wife?" Rand turned to his father in surprise. "Have you taken a good look at my bride? She walks like a gunslinger."

*And has a figure of lush, womanly curves.*

"Clementine has a nice, determined step," his father agreed. "Shows there's nothing wishy-washy about the girl. That's a damn fine trait in a woman."

"She speaks with a Texas drawl," Rand countered, pushing away from the mantle.

*And each soft sentence charmed him.*

"A person knows that Clementine comes from the West the moment she speaks. A man can't do better than to have a hearty western woman at his side. You'll be the envy of all Annapolis."

Rand poured another glass of champagne for his father and himself. "The envy of Annapolis?"

Despite his bride's obvious attributes, the last thing Rand expected was for anyone to envy him. The old man was dreaming.

"Clementine is like an unpolished gem. Her value will become clear to you soon, son."

"She's tall—for a woman."

His father pursed his lips and dipped his head to the side. "I was taken aback at first. Roy wasn't quite as tall as his daughter. I asked her about her height.

According to Clementine, she only stands a little more than sixteen hands high—"

"Horse talk?" he interrupted. The more Rand learned about his bride, the more concerned he felt. Something similar to a lead brick settled in his stomach. But he could think of no medical explanation for the sensation.

"Sixteen hands translates into about five foot seven inches," his father finished. "It's Clementine's slim figure that makes her appear taller."

"Still, she doesn't appear to be fragile."

"Thank heavens. She's a woman who won't be blowing in the wind," his father said, once again rising to Clementine's defense. "She's obviously a healthy young woman, the type who grows more graceful with each passing year."

If anyone should know which type of woman improved with age, it would be his father. Jonathan Noble had possessed an eye for the ladies ever since Rand could remember. And the ladies vied for his attentions.

After being widowed early in life, his father never remarried or displayed any interest in remarriage. Rand was raised by a succession of nannies. Although he had inherited family wealth, Jonathan Noble chose to make himself useful. He earned an excellent reputation during his thirty years as a Navy surgeon. He'd also gained a certain amount of fame for having a woman in every port.

Rand had followed in his father's footsteps—in every way.

Jonathan raised his champagne flute once again. "To my extremely fortunate son."

Rand knew his father would never admit to having made a mistake. He'd inherited the same failing.

"Fortunate and a bit . . . frightened," he said, feigning apprehension by assuming a deep frown. "I've heard it said that redheaded women possess fierce tempers."

"Nonsense. A woman possessing red hair is known for passion."

Rand arched a brow. "You're teasing me."

"And with her flaming red hair, Clementine will always stand out in a crowd. You will never lose your wife."

"I fear not."

Jonathan Noble's silver-flecked brows gathered at the bridge of his patrician nose. "What was that?"

"A poor jest."

His father shot Rand a look of displeasure. When he had been younger, the look was often accompanied by a swat to his behind. "Clementine's hair is the fine shade of a copper penny," Jonathan intoned. "Fiery hair, fiery heart, Son."

"And fiery freckles as well."

"Your wife may have spent a bit too much time in the Texas sun, I grant you. But that small smattering of spots across her nose will fade away in no time, mark my words."

Rand grinned. In fact he'd rather liked his bride's freckles. And although her appearance really didn't matter, it had been Clementine's full, blush pink lips and soulful, wide green eyes that had earned his reluctant admiration the moment they met.

"You needn't defend your daughter-in-law. I'm sure that she and I will get along tolerably well. All I require from Clementine is a son."

"A son to carry on the family name." Jonathan nodded his approval.

Rand knew that his having a son was almost as important to his father as it was to him. In a past rebellious period, Rand had sorely disappointed his sire. Which is why, when Jonathan had approached him to honor the pact made with his old friend, Rand agreed without argument. This marriage with Clementine Calhoun would serve to heal the breach between him and his father and also give Rand what he wanted most—a son.

"You will have many sons," his father declared.

"I appreciate your confidence."

"You will have as many sons as you desire—if you ever get started." He gestured toward the door. "Your bride awaits you. Nervously, I expect."

"I expect," Rand murmured in agreement. Clementine had made her anxiety apparent when she tossed back the champagne he'd poured her and with a glazed smile immediately held out the flute for a refill.

He blew out a heavy breath, squared his shoulders and gave his father a knowing grin. "Duty calls."

His only parent raised a finger and issued a stern warning. "Move slowly. Assure your wife every step of the way. Her brother swore to me that Clementine is a virgin."

The last thing Rand needed was instruction from his father on how to make love to a woman. "Don't worry, Father. I shall manage."

"Very well. I'll show myself out."

A massive fireplace, delicately carved cornices and the color purple distinguished the master bedchamber. Purple. A color more suited for mourning, in Clementine's opinion. When she first entered the chamber, she felt as if she'd been swallowed by a giant grape.

In addition to the gas lighting, an array of candles glittered in the spacious room. The bedspread and thick brocade drapes were the shade of eggplants. Gilt frames surrounding three portraits of Rand Noble's long-dead ancestors provided the only other color, unless the gold fringe tassels that bedecked two deep violet velvet chaise lounges were considered.

Clementine had kicked off the high-button shoes that pinched her toes. Skittish as a newborn colt, she roamed the room in stockinged feet. The thick oriental carpet soothed the soles of her feet: ugly feet, granted, but feet accustomed to lizardskin boots. She still wore her wedding gown, the only nice dress she owned. There had been no time for shopping in her brother's rush to remove her to Maryland. Being wed in the old moss silk with the tattered hem didn't bother her. Removing it, however, distressed her mightily.

She'd grown up on a ranch. She knew what happened when horses mated. Before she left, her sister-in-law had hinted it was much the same with humans. And every man expected to mate with his bride on their wedding night.

A shiver ripped through Clementine as she gazed at the bed. It was four times bigger than her bed at the ranch and almost as high as the loft in the barn. A step stool or flying leap would be needed to climb into its downy folds. The brass headrails gleamed and the snow white sheets had been turned back in unmistakable invitation. A crop of fresh goose bumps prickled up on her arms.

Falling to her knees, Clementine retrieved her satchel from beneath the monster bed. Sitting Indian style, she pulled out her precious belongings. A red velvet pouch where her ma had kept a locket until they came upon hard times and the jewelry had to be sold. Now the pouch held Clementine's savings. She'd planned to put enough money away to get her back to Texas if things didn't work out between her and Rand Noble, but she was a little short.

Next she brought out the coarse swatch of hairs from her horse's tail. A tear slid down her cheek as she fingered the reddish-brown strands tied together with a blue ribbon. She sorely missed Bay.

Holding the things that were dear to her, and which took her home in spirit, brought a sense of comfort. With a deep, ragged breath, Clementine pulled out her banjo and placed it across her lap. Strummin' had kept her company on many lonely nights.

She reached into the satchel for her derringer. Roy wouldn't let her bring her Winchester. But if she ever needed to shoot, man or beast, this shiny little gun would do the job.

Buried in the folds of an inside pocket, she found her most prized possession, the small seahorse her pa had carved for her from the ivory of a whale bone. He'd spent the long, spare hours at sea carving. She brushed her finger lightly, lovingly, over the two-inch treasure. Pa told her that they shared a love for horses, the only difference being that her horses raced on land and his swam in the ocean with the rest of the wondrous creatures of the deep.

Clementine cherished the delicate carving. She carried it with her at all times, feeling that the tiny ivory creature brought good luck. He symbolized her pa's love and the only truly joyful Christmas she had ever known.

She raised the seahorse to her lips.

A sound in the hall brought her up short.

"Clementine."

Rand.

She hastily shoved her satchel under the bed.

He'd come for her.

Clementine married Rand to honor her pa's vow. She had loved Pa mightily and had done anything he asked while he was alive. But she wanted more than a marriage ceremony, a ring that didn't fit and too much champagne. She meant to win her husband's love or die a virgin trying.

# Two

Clementine stared in horror as the gleaming brass handle on the bedchamber door slowly turned. The door opened.

Her bridegroom paused on the threshold, tall, dark and devilishly handsome. Silver dust sparkled in the depths of his blue, blue eyes.

"Doc . . . Dr. Noble."

He grinned. A knock-a-girl-from-her-saddle grin. Clementine's blood warmed.

"Rand," he corrected.

"Rand," she repeated.

He strode into the room with cocksure confidence. No longer wearing his uniform jacket, her husband was dressed for comfort. The collar of his white shirt lay open, exposing a glimpse of dark chest curls. He'd rolled his shirtsleeves up to the crook of his elbows. With these minor changes, the officer had become a man. A man on the prowl.

For a fleeting instant, Clementine knew just how buzzard bait felt.

And the buzzard was her husband.

His smile hinted at pleasures only a man experienced in the art of making love could offer. Masculinity radiated from Rand like the hot rays of a summer sun. Blinding. Immobilizing. If she didn't act quickly to save herself, she would melt in his path. She would be his to do with as he pleased. There could be worse fates, unless he still had murder on his mind.

Mercy, no! She could not think like that.

He raised the tray he held. "Champagne and oysters, our wedding supper."

Clementine didn't care for the sissy champagne drink. The bubbles tickled her nose, and the alcohol had failed to provide a soothing effect on her ragged nerves. At least, not that she could tell. She felt a bit muzzy-headed, but she laid the blame on this whole fool wedding thing. Her insides had gone all haywire.

"Them oysters look raw," she said. Although she'd never seen an oyster before, the slimy gray blobs lying on half their shells didn't appear the least appetizin'.

"Raw is the best way to eat them. These oysters are Annapolis's finest, fresh from the dock. They'll slide right down," he assured her with another heart-stoppin' wink.

"Ah'm not hungry."

"You don't need to be hungry to enjoy nature's best aphrodisiac." Her groom proceeded to demonstrate, sipping one raw oyster straight from its shell.

Chills skipped down her spine. Clementine wasn't exactly sure what an aphrodisiac was, but she had a good idea. She considered it one more good reason not to swallow the slimy things.

"Mah stomach is a bit unsettled."

"Ah, the doctor has a remedy. Champagne."

He handed her a glass filled to the brim with light, dancing bubbles. How her lips found the rim Clementine would never know. Unable to tear her gaze from her new husband's blatantly seductive smile, she feared he'd hypnotized her. In that fleeting instant, she understood quite clearly that Rand had conquered every woman he'd ever wanted.

Instantly on guard, she stiffened. The seahorse fell from her free hand. She'd forgotten she still held her treasure until it dropped.

Rand picked it up. "What's this?"

"A seahorse mah pa carved me for Christmas one year."

"Your father was a master craftsman," Rand said as he turned the seahorse over in his palm.

"We didn't usually receive gifts for Christmas—"

"Why not?"

Clementine lowered her eyes. "We didn't have much, tryin' to build a spread and all. But this one year was different. And Pa, he told me that seahorses mate for life. Did you know that?" she asked, grappling for conversation.

"No. But it's, ah, fascinating." He raised his glass. "To a wise master craftsman and a marriage made at sea."

Unable to claim their union had any heartfelt ties, she clinked her glass against his with more force than intended.

Heaving a sigh, she lifted her gaze heavenward and softly delivered her own toast. "Ah hope ah made you happy tonight, Pa." Rand hiked a startled brow but did not comment on her toast.

She finished the champagne in one gulp.

He reached for the champagne bottle.

She eyed the bottle with growing annoyance. Obviously, her husband operated in the belief that if she drank enough, he could have his way with her.

"Ah do think ah've had mah fill."

His wonderful melt-ice eyes met hers. A slow,

crooked smile spread from the corner of his mouth. "You've made the right decision, darlin'."

Beans. The polecat thought she meant to pass over the champagne in order to hop right into the bed with him. Well, he had another think coming.

"On second thought, ah might require a mite more of the bubbly."

The shadow of disappointment that fell over his face passed so quickly, a less sharp-eyed body might have missed it. Recovering swiftly, he poured. "You must have been nervous traveling so far to wed a man that you had never even met."

"Ah reckon so."

"You'll find that I'm an easygoing sort."

"Ah can't claim to be the same. According to mah brother, Junior, ah fly off the handle a mite too much. He says ah'm an uppity woman."

"I appreciate the warning."

"Mah pa promised me to you a long time ago, and ah aim to keep his word. Ah'm gonna make you the best wife ah know how to be."

"I couldn't ask for more. Except perhaps—"

"But ah don't like water." She thought he should know the worst right off. It was only fair.

Grinning, he cocked his head slightly to one side. "I don't understand. What water is it that you don't like, Clementine? Well-water? The ocean? The bay. . . ?" His voice trailed off.

"None of it. Ah don't even go too close to a well." She folded her arms across her chest. She hoped the defiant gesture would also protect her heart from Rand's smile, pearly white teeth and all. "Ah don't know how to swim, and ah ain't hankerin' to learn."

"Almost everyone who lives in Annapolis enjoys the

water. We're sailors here. I'll be happy to help you overcome your fear. Once you learn to sail, you'll—"

She cut him off. "Mah pa drowned at sea."

Her husband appeared instantly contrite. "I had forgotten. My apologies."

"Pa loved the navy life, so ah'm thinkin' he left this world the best way possible for a man of his kind. Ah reckon he's content on the other side."

"The other side?"

Sensing that this might not be the time to discuss her beliefs, Clementine nodded vaguely and yawned. To ensure she made her point, she yawned wider than the widest point in Dead River Gulch.

"Are you tired?" He inclined his head again. His smile seemed less confident.

On the chance that additional evidence was required, Clementine blew out a heavy whoosh of air. The tiny, tight curls, which had escaped their pins to fall haphazardly above her temples, blew in the warm breeze.

"Ah'm exhausted. It took a full week to get East. The stagecoaches rocked, the trains rumbled and spewed soot and you don't even want to hear about the places ah had to rest overnight."

"You shouldn't have traveled alone. It was a dangerous thing to do. If I had any idea you'd been sent without an escort—"

"Ah don't need anyone to coddle me."

"It's not a matter of coddling, Clementine. It's only proper for a lady to be escorted on her journeys."

"Escorts aren't always handy where ah come from. But that doesn't mean we're not ladies. Besides, all ah need to get back on mah feet is a week or so of hard sleep."

"A week or so?"

"Two at the most."

His alarmed expression gave way to a soothing smile and a soft, persuasive tone. "Tonight is the night we become man and wife, Clementine. And I promise, you will be amazed at how quickly your feelings of exhaustion will disappear."

Stretching, she meandered around the table to position the polished rosewood furniture between them. "Ah think you'll enjoy our first night better, which ah am real eager to have, if ah am fully awake and aware. Don't you?"

"Do you mean to begin our marriage by . . . denying me?" He sounded incredulous; the timbre of his voice shifted in midsentence to a croak. He sounded very much like a young man encountering a voice change.

"Oh, ah hesitate to deny you anything . . ."

Rand's smile returned. He advanced on her, reaching out as if to loosen the buttons of her bodice. "Then let's slip off this dress . . ."

Using the swiftness she'd learned tracking coyotes, she slipped out of reach. "But ah must."

His arms fell. A scowl of disbelief replaced his smile.

"And ah trust that a kind and sensitive man such as yourself would never force his attentions on a bone-tired wife who'd just traveled hundreds of miles to make him a happy man."

But Rand did not appear to be listening. His gaze skimmed her body, lingering on her breasts, waist and hips. His burning inspection extended clear down to her stockinged feet. During Rand's perusal, his disgruntled expression gave way to what appeared to be admiration.

Clementine had never been the object of such close scrutiny before. With just a glance, he'd made her feel

as if she stood naked before him. Her flesh alternately
burned with embarrassment and tingled as if awakening from a long nap.

"You're so beautiful," he said in a soft, hoarse voice.
"I don't know if I can help myself."

The man was full of horse manure.

"And you are the most handsome man ah ever have
laid these Texas eyes upon." That, at least, was true.
"Perhaps if ah had a small bite to eat—a piece of wedding cake, perhaps—then ah'd recover mah energy."

"Of course!" With lightning speed, the twinkle returned to Rand's eyes. He took to the idea as if it had
been his own. "My apologies. I should have thought
of cake and . . . icing myself."

He strode to the door, paused and raised a hand.
"Wait for me. I'll be back in time to help remove your
dress."

"Take your time." Clementine smiled as her hand
closed over the door handle.

"I'll be back in a flash."

"No need to hurry."

The second her groom cleared the threshold, she
shut the door and turned the lock.

A moment of silence passed. Clementine did not
hear Rand move away. She held her ear to the door,
keeping as still as a statue.

"Clementine, did you just lock me out?"

The undisguised shock in his tone brought up a
giggle that she blamed on the champagne and stifled
with both hands. Unable to answer, she silently
counted the seconds, waiting for him to leave.

"What the hell? Let me in, Clementine."

"Ah must retire now."

"Not yet, you don't."

"Ah don't wish to lock horns with you, Rand."

"Lock horns?" he snapped. "Is that Texas cattle talk?"

Rand's terse remark brought her up short. Clementine didn't know how the women in her husband's life spoke. She expected that they used fancy words and phrases. She hadn't been educated in the East. She'd had little education at all, except for what she'd picked up from reading. Still, she knew right from wrong, and it felt all wrong to spend the night with a man she hardly knew. Even if he was her husband. She required proper courtin'.

"Good night, Rand."

"You're locking me out of my own bedroom?"

"Ah reckon. A girl appreciates being courted, don't you know?"

Eventually, she heard him turn on his heel and walk away.

Just on the happenstance that he might not be as easygoing as he claimed, Clementine slept fully clothed. After blowing out the candles, she lay in the dark, staring up at a ceiling she could not see. And gave in to unbearable homesickness.

The pain of her loss had begun only hours after she'd left the ranch, the only home she had ever known. Now homesickness as thick as a buffalo hide engulfed her. The pining tore at her stomach and brought tears to her eyes. Warm, wet drops silently tracked down her cheeks and slid over her earlobes onto the pillow.

It hadn't taken long for her to miss the long, flat, grazing acres of Texas soil. Homesickness had set in by the time she'd reached New Orleans. Thanks to one of Pa's wild nights, which was all she could attribute this marriage arrangement to, she'd been forced to trade wide-open space for the town of Annapolis and wall-to-wall brick buildings.

Clementine yearned with all her being for the horse she'd had to leave behind. Her pretty Bay was the best friend she'd ever had. She could talk to her four-legged partner about anything. Miles away from the nearest ranch and the small town of Oddon, close friendships were difficult to establish.

Her pa had been unfailingly kind and loving toward Clementine. He'd only suffered one lapse of judgment that she could figure—a whopper of a lapse. He'd just about ruined her life by arranging this marriage to Rand Noble.

In the enormous bed, she felt as small and vulnerable as a child. Unfamiliar sounds surrounded her: the creak of a floor board outside the room, a branch brushing against the window. Was she doomed to die of homesickness in a strange city? Married to a man who didn't love her?

Unwilling to dwell on such an unhappy scenario, Clementine once more turned her thoughts to home and softly sang herself to sleep. "Home . . . home on the range . . ."

Rand Noble approached the dining room the following morning with his usual good humor restored. He even felt optimistic. He'd put aside his anger of the night before and rationalized the unfortunate outcome. He'd never been bested—no, the proper word was *tricked*—by a woman before. His pride smarted. But allowances must be made for the country girl. Once he'd calmed down, Rand realized that Clementine's stubborn refusal was due to normal wedding-night jitters. According to several Texas midshipmen that he'd treated as patients, everything was bigger in Texas. The rivers were wider, the sky higher and the grass greener. It only made sense that a virgin bride's fears would be greater too.

He'd finished his breakfast when his wife strode through the door of the dining room. She did not appear to notice him as her gaze went directly to the food-laden sideboard.

"Good morning, Clementine." Rand gave her a wide grin meant to dispel any fears she might have that he held a grudge. "Did you rest well?"

She stopped in her tracks. Her entire upper torso, shoulders and breasts, rose and fell with the heaviest sigh he'd ever heard. Her eyes, the shade of green crystal, widened with distress as they came to rest on his. "Ah-ah never sleep truly fine on the first night in a strange bed," she stammered.

"I'm sorry to hear that." More sorry than she could know.

Several months had passed since his father showed him the initial correspondence from Roy Calhoun, Jr. In no uncertain terms, Junior's letter proposed that the marriage arrangement made for Clementine by his father and Jonathan years ago be honored forthwith. To his father's surprise, Rand agreed.

In the years since Ellie passed away, he'd not met a single woman who had captured his fancy or his heart. But his desire to start a family had grown more urgent.

From the moment he agreed to marry Clementine Calhoun, he had not had another woman. Oh, he'd looked, of course. He possessed an innate appreciation of women. He was also a man who enjoyed his pleasures. Rand reasoned that by depriving himself of feminine company, he would be prepared to make love to his new wife with enthusiasm, even if, by chance, she should resemble Queen Victoria.

As it happened, Clementine looked far better in person than in the daguerreotype exchanged in the second piece of correspondence from Roy Calhoun, Jr. The blurred picture showed a figure sitting astride a large horse, wearing hairy chaps and an eight-gallon hat that hid her face. Rand couldn't even be certain the rider was a woman. He was certain now.

Her calico dress, fine for the West, unsuitable in the city, nonetheless displayed a curvaceous figure that tantalized the explorer in him. The rose-colored garment fit snugly through the midriff, emphasizing a child-sized waist and high, full breasts. He could detect nothing delicate nor fragile about her figure. Clementine possessed the trim lines of a swift, sleek sloop. If he wasn't mistaken, she was built for birthing.

While Rand considered the possible pleasures of making babies with her, his skittish bride had turned to concentrate on filling her china breakfast plate. She lifted the top of a silver tureen and beheld more oatmeal than the entire first class of midshipmen could possibly eat. Covered platters of scrambled eggs, fried, crisp bacon and plump, hot biscuits sat on the sideboard emitting mouth-watering aromas.

"Is there coffee?" she asked, eyeing his cup.

"I thought you might prefer tea."

The women of Rand's acquaintance drank only tea and champagne.

"Oh, no." She shook her head emphatically, bouncing the mass of tight, rusty-colored curls falling to her shoulders. "Tea is for tinhorns. Ah like mah coffee strong and hot."

What kind of woman was this? The woman who would be the mother of his children possessed an alarming ability to startle him. Wariness burned its way into the pit of his stomach.

"Exactly the way I prefer my coffee," he admitted with some consternation before ringing the bell to summon his longtime housekeeper.

Offering a curt nod of her head in thanks, Clementine then bestowed a smile that took Rand by surprise. A dazzling, warm smile, a smile reflected in her eyes.

Rand felt like a man who had been living in the dark and unexpectedly finds the sun parting the clouds to shine down upon him. He sunned himself in Clementine's light, knowing it would flicker out too soon. And it did.

She cast an apologetic glance at him as she scooped up a spoonful of fried potatoes. "Mah brother, Junior, told me more than once that ah was goin' to eat him out of house and home. But you know, a body works up an appetite working out on the range."

"Needless to say, you won't be working out on the range any longer."

In addition to the potatoes, Clementine piled her plate high with a hearty portion of eggs, six strips of bacon, and three steaming biscuits. Ignoring the place setting at his side, she sat at the far end of the table, opposite him.

He needed a telescope to see her. Suppressing his irritation, Rand gritted his teeth and smiled. Unless he put his wife at ease and made her feel at home, his plans were doomed.

Clementine chomped down on a biscuit. But then, seeming to remember herself, she delicately licked a residue of melted butter from her bottom lip. Transfixed by her dainty tongue and moist, buttery lip, Rand forgot to breathe for a moment.

"Ah hope ah don't get too awful homesick," she said.

"You'll be too busy settling into your new life . . . with me."

Clementine's gaze fell to her plate. "You're right about that. Ah'll need to keep up mah strength. Right off this morning, your father is escortin' me to the dressmakers. Ah only had but two dresses at home. This old calico is one. It was all ah needed. Ah wore jeans, work shirts and chaps around the ranch 'cause you can't rope and round up stray cattle in a dress."

"Heaven forbid."

Clementine ate quickly, as if she was afraid someone would remove her meal at any moment. Rand waited, eager to work the conversation back to life in Annapolis and what would be expected of her as his wife.

She looked up eventually, regarding him with wide-eyed curiosity. "Ah never did see a man who ate like a bird."

Rand felt yet another pang of anxiety. If he could not quickly curb her bluntness, he would never be able to introduce Clementine to his friends and colleagues at the Naval Academy. Attributing his wife's candid way of speaking to her Wild West upbringing, or lack of any upbringing, he resolved to give the rough stone he'd wed some polishing. Starting now.

"I don't eat like a bird. I've already had my breakfast," he explained with utmost patience. "On most mornings I leave for the hospital early."

"Don't let me stop you from leavin."

"You're not stopping me. I want to stay. I intend to spend as much time with you as possible, Clementine. We need to get to know one another and know what to expect from each other."

"Can't hurry things," she mumbled between bites.

If she referred to consummating their marriage, he certainly would do all in his power to hurry things along. Rand decided to launch what he hoped would have a snowballing effect, by clearing the air.

"You know, of course, that I've been married before."

Clementine nodded; her expression grew soft. "Ah'm sorry for your loss."

Could that be compassion in her eyes, the glint of tears? She sat too far away from him to be certain.

"I gained a great deal of experience before Ellie's untimely death."

"Were you married long?"

"Little more than a year. There was nothing I could do, nothing the doctors could do to save her from the consumption. I've been a widower for the past five years."

Rand had slowly come to realize that no one could take Ellie's place. After two years of mourning the loss of his fragile wife, he'd reverted to his bachelor ways. Once more he became the flirtatious, carefree man he'd been as a midshipman at the academy. He appreciated women, and, as before his brief marriage, he had no trouble bedding the most beautiful. But none had sparked his interest beyond a tumble of pleasure. He'd sworn to enjoy the ladies, but never, never to lose his heart again. His enjoyment ended the moment he agreed to marry Clementine. But Rand's vow to protect his heart applied to his bride as well. Although at present he felt he had nothing to fear on that account.

Clementine pushed her plate back, making room for the cup of coffee Rand's elderly housekeeper brought her. "You must have loved Ellie very much."

This is not where he wanted the conversation to go. "Yes. Naturally."

His green-eyed bride lowered her eyes. Wordlessly, without recrimination, Clementine reminded him that she was his second choice.

"But I believe a man has room in his heart for more than one love," he added hastily. He'd heard it said, and although the thought served him in this instance, Rand didn't believe it to be true. Besides, he'd sealed his heart. It was no longer available.

He didn't know how to explain the full truth to Clementine without revealing a chink in his knight-in-shining-armor. As a rebellious youth, it had seemed fitting to assert his independence by thwarting his father's pact with Roy Calhoun. He chose his own bride based on merits that had since escaped him. One fine spring day, he had eloped with the beautiful Ellie Tidwell.

"Reckon that would take a big-hearted man," Clementine said. "Ah can't even imagine a heart so big that it could hold two loves."

"But that's where men have it over women."

"Ah didn't know," she exclaimed softly.

Rand was feeling increasingly uncomfortable. "I was a mutinous youth," he admitted, changing the direction of the conversation. "Doing the opposite of whatever my father recommended. I drove him to distraction."

He caught a slight twitch of her lips as Clementine's gaze locked on his. "And now you are your father."

Her pronouncement brought him up short. "What?"

She grinned. "Ah like him."

"Uh, as do I."

Jonathan Noble was a rake, which made Rand the

son of a rake. Before he could regain his equanimity and lose the daunting thought that he'd become his father, a pounding on the door brought Rand to his feet. Such a pounding usually meant trouble. He would have to answer it.

He sprinted toward the front door, expecting to find a midshipman with a medical emergency. For everyday, mundane health problems, the students waited at the hospital.

The swish of skirts and the faint, fresh-scrubbed scent of chamomile told him that Clementine followed fast on his heels.

He opened the door to find a midshipman shaking with fear and bleeding profusely from a head wound. The crimson blood gushed from his forehead and down his face, splattering angry red splotches on the young student's white shirt.

"Doc . . . I had an . . . an accident."

"Head wounds are not as serious as they appear," Rand replied in a calming, reassuring tone. He reached out for the midshipman, but just as he took hold of the frightened young man's arm, he heard a thud behind him.

Clementine lay slumped on the floor, passed out.

"Millie!" he called to the housekeeper. "I need help."

# Three

"What happened?" Clementine rubbed her aching head. Somehow she'd landed in bed, fully clothed. A lump the size of a lemon lodged on the back of her head, and a particularly foul odor wafted beneath her nose. Smelling salts.

"You fainted." Her husband sat on the edge of the bed, regarding her with the professional scrutiny of a surgeon.

She was mightily embarrassed. "Ah always do that at the sight of blood. Don't know why. Can't seem to stop."

Rand chuckled, clearly amused.

It wasn't right. Clementine was in pain. She rubbed the knot on her head.

"A doctor's wife who faints at the sight of blood. That might be a first," he said, giving her a wry grin.

Her heart set to fluttering like a chicken being chased from the henhouse by a hungry coyote. "Ah reckon."

The blow had been worse than she thought. It was the only explanation for her strange physical reaction.

"I hope word of this doesn't get around," he whispered, plainly having fun with her.

Still, how was she to resist him when his twinkling

eyes and teasing smile could easily disarm even the most hard-hearted woman?

"No one will know if you keep this our little . . . secret." Clementine took pride in her reputation. Back home she was known for her grit. She'd be mightily embarrassed if word got out, in either Oddon or Annapolis, that she fainted at the sight of blood.

"All right. Your secret is safe with me. But in the future, you might want to run and stay out of sight if you hear a pounding on the door," he commented drolly.

"Do wounded boys come right to the door often?"

He nodded. "It happens when they're very frightened, or close by."

This wasn't what Clementine wanted to hear, but she needed to know more. "Will the midshipman who came by this morning live?"

"Yes."

"How did he cut himself?"

"He fell out of a young woman's window in his haste to return to the academy grounds before he was discovered missing. The lady in question lives just a block away."

"Why, that varmint doesn't deserve to live!"

Rand laughed. "Boys will be boys."

"Are you going to report him?"

"I bound the boy's wound, stopped the bleeding and gave him warning."

Clementine harbored a suspicious mind. "Did you disobey the rules when you were a midshipman?"

"Never."

She didn't believe him. "Never?"

He smiled, and again Clementine caught the devil lurking in those eyes. For a moment she forgot to breathe, was forced to smile. The virile doctor's bedside manner was unlike any other. Tiny, magical fairy wings fluttered within her heart, a heart about to take flight.

Rand rose from the bed. Standing above her, he gave her a sheepish grin, which was feigned, she felt certain. "I confess. I might have been guilty of a boyish peccadillo or two."

A world of danger lay in his grin. The rogue she'd married was capable of stealing her heart and more. How could a simple, crusty girl from the West, raised to have a hide thicker than a longhorn's, live in peace with a honey-tongued husband? She had no education, not a single bit of spit and polish. Even if she dreamed of it, she could never hope to earn the love of a man like Rand Noble.

Not unless she bushwhacked him.


Clementine enjoyed her morning sojourn at the dressmaker's with her father-in-law. Jonathan arrived not long after Rand departed for the academy hospital. The elder Noble had volunteered for and planned the excursion, which was fine with Clementine. All she knew about fashion was what she'd seen in the Montgomery Ward catalogue.

Jonathan appeared to be quite the fashion plate. He wore a top hat and a smart, dove gray double-breasted frock coat with black velvet facing on the collar and sleeves. Even if it were not his custom to walk with his head held high, the extreme stiffness of his shirt collar would have forced his chin up. Clementine especially liked his black brocade waistcoat shot through with silver silk threads. He seemed completely unaware of her admiring eye as he walked at her side, wielding a gold-crowned walking stick. At times she was hard-pressed to keep up with his jaunty step.

A warm sun and vivid blue sky conspired to win Clementine over to her new home. The elegant Georgian homes with their columned and intricately carved doorways awed her as she walked along Maryland Street with her escort. Oddon, Texas, could not boast of even one home as grand as these.

Maryland Street reminded her of a spoke in a wheel. The State Circle, site of the magnificent wooden-domed capitol building, sat at its hub.

"Annapolis has been the capital of Maryland since sixteen hundred and ninety-four," Jonathan told her, pride ringing in his tone. "Our fair city also served as the capital of our country during the Revolutionary War."

Clementine hadn't known. She possessed a heap more horse sense than book learning.

Upon reaching Main Street, her escort came to a stop. "Look down there."

Gazing down over the rooftops, Clementine viewed the spot where the Severn River met the Chesapeake Bay. The crowded city docks teamed with dock workers unloading barrels, crates and sacks of foodstuffs from a large oceangoing steamer. Fishermen tongued the oyster beds from flat-bottomed boats. Sailboats of all sizes bobbed at anchor; several headed out to sea with sails unfurled and flapping in the breeze.

Despite her fear of any body of water deeper and wider than what a bathtub could hold, the bustling port presented a picturesque tableau.

"It's mighty pretty, like a Currier and Ives painting," she said.

"This has always been a seafaring town. Rather like a Siren, Annapolis is, calling old sea dogs like me home." Closing his eyes, Jonathan Noble inhaled deeply, taking in the salt-laced air as if it were an invigorating tonic.

"Ah know when ah get used to it, ah'll like Annapolis just fine." She could never like Annapolis better than Oddon, Texas, but she wouldn't let on. Clementine had made up her mind to make the best of where destiny had led her. She had no choice. She couldn't go back home.

A few short blocks later, Jonathan opened the door to the dressmaker's shop, Adelaide's Alterations and Dressmaking. Her father-in-law, who seemed to know the eponymous broad-hipped dressmaker well, introduced the two women, then departed with a cheerful wave of his walking stick.

Exercising true Texas grit, Clementine endured the torture of the tightest corset she'd ever been imprisoned within, and two hours of boring fittings. During that time, her attempts to befriend Adelaide failed. The dressmaker remained intensely focused on her work, and her two young assistants just smiled and lowered their eyes. But at one point when the girls left the room and Clementine was alone, she overheard their smothered giggles. Unaware that she could hear their whispers, they poked fun at her accent. The ridicule stung. Much to her chagrin, she found herself blinking back tears. No one in Texas had ever laughed at her for saying "Howdy, how are y'all doing today?"

It was the friendly thing to do.

She felt relieved beyond words when Jonathan at last returned for her. Within minutes of being in her father-in-law's company, her spirits revived. His wit and charm proved a balm to her wounded pride. She supposed the ability to bewitch women ran in the Noble family.

After ordering her gowns delivered when ready, he ushered Clementine from the shop. "Just wait until Annapolis society sees you dressed in Adelaide's best. You'll do my son proud."

She attempted to smile but only managed a quiver of her lips. If the attitude of the shop girls was any indication, instead of making her husband proud, Clementine would be the laughingstock of the entire town. Unless she made the rude young women eat their words. Unless she turned the town on its ear. And that, she decided then and there, was exactly what she must do. Clementine Calhoun Noble, femme fatale.

"Ah shall do mah best to make Rand proud," she replied, inching her chin a notch higher.

"That's my girl," Jonathan said, giving her a conspiratorial wink and a smile.

On their return home from the dressmaker's shop, Clementine could not help but notice that her father-in-law could still turn the ladies' heads. He stood as straight and tall as Rand. But his blue eyes were darker, the color of dark denim, and the dash of silver at his temples lent him a decidedly distinguished appearance.

Several older women went out of their way to approach him. To a one, the ladies were cordial when introduced to Clementine, who merely dipped her head in greeting rather than risk further ridicule by speaking. Jonathan's elderly admirers swiftly and eagerly turned their attention on him. The women behaved like schoolgirls, lingering in the sun, twirling their parasols, chatting as if they had nothing else to do.

Rachel Wilson was the last flirtatious female Clementine and Jonathan encountered. The formidable-appearing widow immediately issued a coy invitation to him: "Perhaps you can stop by later?"

Jonathan tipped his hat and smiled warmly. "Why, thank you for the invitation, my dear. I'll do my best."

The woman twittered. Clementine had never heard a grown woman twitter. Her attractive father-in-law must have sensed her astonishment, because he swiftly and smoothly bid Mrs. Wilson a good day.

"You sure do have a bevy of admirers," Clementine said when they were well out of earshot.

"A bevy?"

"That's like a flock of quail," she explained. But her confidence faltered as she added, "In Texas we use a bevy to mean a flock of . . . of anything. Could be birds or ladies."

"Ah, the ladies! They do seem to flock my way." The same twinkle she'd seen in Rand's eyes lighted his father's.

"Do you have a favorite?"

"My dear! How could I ever choose but one from among the many beautiful birds!"

Jonathan Noble was more the rogue than her husband. But he was a loveable rogue, and Clementine laughed freely for the first time since she'd arrived in Annapolis.

Before reaching home she learned he'd retired four years ago and moved into a red-brick mansion on Maryland Street just five houses down from his son's home. He pointed out the stately, ivy-covered dwelling as they passed.

Her new world proved completely foreign to Clementine. She might as well be in Constantinople. The narrow, tree-lined avenue where she and Jonathan walked whispered of wealth and serenity. She had never thought to live in a neighborhood surrounded by such luxury. But she would trade it all to be at home in Texas.

"Oh!" Clementine stopped short. A three-dollar gold piece gleamed on the cobblestones directly in front of her. She stooped down and quickly picked it up. She would add it to her little red velvet pouch. A girl never knew when she might need getaway funds.

"Finding a gold piece means you shall have good luck," Jonathan noted. "But you need not worry about money. I am happy to report that the Nobles are quite well off."

Clementine didn't marry Rand for his money. She'd been happy without it. She'd married him to honor her father's pledge.

Her intrepid father-in-law walked her home but made no move to come into the house. He paused at the bottom of the porch steps. For the first time, his expression became solemn. The lines of age etching his sun-leathered face deepened.

"If there's ever anything you should need or desire, come to me. You are the daughter of my best friend, and now you are my daughter too."

Clementine's heart swelled with gratitude. Jonathan's kindness meant more to her than he would ever know. Smiling, she kissed him softly on the cheek and bid him good-day.

Rand looked up from the report on his desk. The words had begun to blur. Dusk had dissolved into night. It had been a taxing day at the hospital. A measles epidemic was taking its toll on students and faculty alike. When no one waited for him at home, long hours at the hospital had been of no concern. The academy hospital was his second home. Now, he wondered if Clementine waited for him.

A little more than ten years before, Rear Admiral David Dixon Porter ordered the huge dovecote Victorian hospital constructed on Strawberry Hill, sixty-seven acres of newly acquired property overlooking the Severn. Often referred to as Porter's Folly, the hospital could only be reached by crossing the Fitch Footbridge. From its opening day, the medical facility, located next to the Naval Academy Cemetery, had been the object of black humor.

Rand understood how ominous his workplace appeared and did his best to meet the derisive mocking head-on. In time, he hoped to overcome the jests with a reputation for superior medical care.

Rand served as chief surgeon at the request of Rear Admiral John Rodgers. The illustrious superintendent was about to be replaced by Commodore Foxhall Parker, a rather sickly older man. The change in superintendents did not signal a change in Rand's status, although there were times when he longed for a more adventurous assignment.

The report he struggled over had to do with one poor fourth classman, Andrew Withers. As part of a hazing prank, the freshman had been forced to drink ink. Although a hazing law had been implemented four years ago making hazing a federal offense, the midshipmen seemed to regard the law as a further challenge to their mischief. They accepted it as one more obstacle to overcome. Hazing continued much as it had when he had been a midshipman. Directly following the incident with the ink, Andrew had stayed in the hospital for several days. Now, months later, his parents had demanded a written report.

They insisted the ink drink had resulted in a weakened constitution that would plague their son for the rest of his life. They demanded financial restitution from the academy.

When Rand had been a midshipman, parents' complaints about hazing were duly noted and mostly ignored. He remembered with a shudder, and a smile, being pitched into the icy Severn as part of his initiation. He'd caught a chill so severe he took to his bed for days. But he'd never complained to his father, nor to the commandant of midshipmen.

He pushed aside the Withers' report. As yet, he hadn't had the opportunity to consummate his marriage with Clementine. When he hadn't been sleeping in the hospital, he slept in the guest quarters across from the master bedchamber.

The more he thought about the tall redheaded virgin waiting for him, the more he ached to claim her. He strode from his office with one mission in mind: the seduction of Clementine. But when he reached home, Clementine was nowhere to be found. Rand searched upstairs and down without success. When questioned as to his wife's whereabouts, Millie, his housekeeper, reported seeing Mrs. Noble step out to the back garden.

Encouraged by Clementine's apparent interest in gardening, a feminine pursuit, Rand quickened his steps.

He paused on the back veranda, surveying the profusion of weeds and wildflowers. A full moon shed its golden light upon the spacious but neglected garden. He saw no sign of Clementine. He was about to turn back into the house when he caught sight of smoke. Small puffs of white smoke drifted from the side of the small gardening shed. Fearing the shed was on fire, he hurried out to investigate. And found his wife.

"Clementine!"

Clementine jumped, obviously startled. Her eyes rounded. The offending object flew from her fingers.

"What do you think you're doing?" he demanded in shock.

"Ah . . . ah rolled a—"

"Cigarette." Scowling, he accused her in dire tones, "You were smoking."

The only women he'd known to smoke were harlots.

"Ah . . . ah was."

She could hardly deny it. The fingers that had been holding the offensive stub still trembled.

He couldn't quite believe it, but the evidence lay at his feet. A cigarette. He glanced at the glowing ash before returning his gaze to Clementine's pale, stricken face. "You cannot smoke. People will talk."

"But ah've been smokin' since Junior first taught me to roll the papers for him."

"You roll your own?"

"Ah do. And ah roll a mighty fine smoke."

While Rand digested this astounding information, she angled her chin to what he recognized as a contentious position.

He softened his tone, "As a favor to me—"

"Ah'll bet that you smoke cigars with your pa all the time," she interrupted.

"That's different." He paused. She'd raised another startling thought. "You bet? Does that mean you gamble too?"

"No. But how is it different, you and your pa smoking cigars and me an occasional cigarette?"

It was time to turn on the charm and defuse the situation. He'd sought Clementine out for a reason, and it wasn't to argue. He smiled as he explained quietly. "It's different because we are men and you're a woman."

A woman whose cheeks glowed like a polished apple. Her lips, pink and parted, begged to be caressed by his. But she regarded him as if he spoke in tongues.

"If word gets around that you puff out behind the shed," he added, "the town gossips will cast you as a wicked woman."

"Ah don't care. Ah need to relax. Ah need to smoke."

He stepped closer, thinking to put his arm around his unconventional wife and guide her into the house. "Why do you feel the need to relax?"

"Ah'm as wrathy as a hen in a hornet's nest. Ah don't belong here. Ah don't fit in."

"You belong. It's just a matter of time," he soothed.

Gazing into her wide, gem green eyes, it suddenly hit him. He'd done nothing to make Clementine's transition from West to East any easier. An ordinary woman wouldn't take the risk or make the sacrifice Clementine had when she'd left her home and all that she knew to marry a stranger. She'd done an extraordinary thing. She possessed uncommon pluck.

Struck by compassion for his brave wife and remorse for his selfishness, Rand's heart constricted. He was a better man than he'd shown himself to be.

"Ah don't even know how to dance," Clementine lamented. "All ah know is square dancing."

"I'll teach you to dance," he promised, wrapping an arm around her shoulder.

Clementine gazed up at him. Her light, innocent eyes could hypnotize a careless man. "You will?"

"We'll have the first lesson tonight."

Heartened by the fact that she did not object to his arm around her, Rand wondered if a dance lesson might lead to a lesson in making love.

"Ah'll be forever in your debt."

"It shall be my privilege."

They entered the house by way of the kitchen. "I assume you've already explored this room."

"Ah had to," she declared. "Ah get hunger pangs between meals. Ah'm especially partial to Saratoga chips. Never imagined they could fix potatoes so good. We don't have chips back in Oddon."

He laughed. A deep belly laugh. Clementine's straight talk amused him. He would always know what was on her mind.

"Eat all the chips you want, darlin'."

"Ah'll be havin' them for breakfast," she declared with a grin.

"Has Millie given you a proper tour of the house?"

"No. She's sufferin' from the arthritis today. She has a hard time getting around. Is there nothin' you can do to doctor her up?"

"Not much. I'm afraid she may have to retire from keeping house soon. Naturally, I'll see that she has a comfortable pension."

"Who's going to take her place?"

"That will be up to you. Whomever you wish to hire."

Clementine's eyes darkened. Tight little wayward curls framed her frown.

"But you don't have to worry yet," Rand hastened to add. "I don't wish to retire Millie. She's been part of my life for many years. Before becoming my housekeeper, she was my nanny. I suspect that she's not quite ready for the rocking chair yet."

Clementine gave a knowing wag of her head, knocking more springy curls free. "Even an old mare doesn't like being forced out to pasture."

"I suppose not." Rand smiled in spite of himself. His wife possessed an interesting perspective on life. He was more eager than ever to make love to her. "Let me give you the official tour," he suggested.

A tour that would end in the master bedchamber. A lesson in dance he intended to transform into a passionate dance of another kind.

But Clementine protested, "Ah can find mah way around. If ah can't, ah'll ask. Don't you worry. There isn't a shy bone in this gal's body."

"I didn't suppose so."

"Ah would like to see your office."

He took her hand, small, warm and . . . calloused. Unlike the delicate female hands he was used to holding, hers was leathered like a man's hand. The not-so-subtle reminder of where Clementine came from and why might have unsettled someone with less experience with the fairer sex. Rand took her rancher's hand in stride. In time the callouses would subside.

He pulled her forward through the hall.

"Does every room have a fireplace?" she asked.

"Naturally. Didn't your ranch house?"

"Not by a long hair."

Rand opened the door to his office. The gaslights remained on throughout the night, inviting anyone who might need a doctor to stop. He took pride in the home office he'd outfitted almost as well as his hospital office. In addition to his desk, a curio cabinet containing medical instruments, ointments and bandages commanded prominent space. A human skeleton dangled from its hook behind his winged desk chair.

Clementine's gaze locked on the stark white bones.

"It's not real," he lied. "Only a replica of the human skeletal frame."

She shifted her attention to the high metal table fit out with fresh sheets. "Do you operate here?"

"When it's necessary. I've saved a few lives."

"You're a right admirable man." Her eyes shone with admiration as she looked up at him.

His wife was ripe for seduction! He could feel it.

He squeezed her hand. "Let's take a look upstairs."

As Rand climbed the steps, he whistled cheerfully. The extemporaneous tune echoed in the stairwell along with the thud of his boots. Wall sconces shed the dim yellow illumination of gaslight, and the corridor smelled of lemon polish and cinnamon potpourri.

He started down the hall toward the back. "The stairs leading to the attic are this way."

"Wait!" Holding her ground, Clementine jerked her hand from his. Inclining her head toward the heavy mahogany door he'd ignored, she asked, "What's in this chamber?"

He regarded the door for only a moment. "Nothing. It's locked," he said quietly.

"Nothing?" she repeated.

"Now back here," he continued, resuming his normal spirited tone, "we come to the largest room of all, the master bedchamber."

Clementine knew the bedchamber well. He had no reason to point it out. She'd spent many hours inside with the door locked against intrusion. No one saw her tears or knew how she struggled with homesickness.

Rand stood by the open bedchamber door. He aimed a lopsided I'm-gonna-get-you grin straight at her and extended his arm in invitation.

Her feet froze to the floor. Invitation to what? Clementine's stomach felt as prickly as if she'd swallowed a cactus. "Ah have another question."

"What's that?" The smile he turned on her might have knocked a woman prone to the vapors senseless, but Clementine was made of sturdier stuff, and she recognized his crooked grin as the humoring kind.

"Why is every room in the house purple?"

The twinkle evaporated from Rand's eyes. "Ellie's favorite color was purple."

"Oh." Clementine had heard Jonathan Noble use the word lovely many times and instinctively understood this was the time to put the word to good use. "Purple is a . . . lovely color."

"Ellie had excellent taste," Rand offered without inflection, without a smile.

The crackling energy that seemed constantly to emanate from her tall, good-looking husband had quite suddenly vanished. For the first time it occurred to her that Rand might still be in love with the remarkable Ellie.

Clementine usually spoke her mind in a forthright manner, but in this instance something held her back. It was a question she could not ask, for she feared an honest answer.

Rand broke the thick silence. "If you don't mind, I believe I'll retire for the night. I've been working hard these last few days, with little sleep."

"Ah understand." But she didn't. She did not understand his abrupt change of mood or the gulf of tension that yawned between them. Worse, she could think of no words to form a bridge across the disturbing space.

In the quiet, silent hall, Clementine's pulse kicked in all suddenlike. It raced, chased at a breathless pace by a new fear. Though she might not have been included in the tour, Ellie still dwelled in this house, in these rooms. In the past, Clementine had not competed successfully with mortals to win the heart of a man. How in the world could she hope to compete with the ghost of Ellie Tidwell?

# *Four*

Once again Clementine's curiosity prevailed. Throwing caution to the wind, she woke the next morning determined to discover what lay behind the door Rand had dismissed. When she'd asked what was in the chamber, he'd said, "Nothing."

She might have been raised in the West, but she knew what "nothing" meant. Nothings concealed secrets.

None of the keys she coaxed from Millie opened the door to the mysterious room. Unwilling to concede defeat, she returned to the kitchen. Realizing she would need some sort of tool, Clementine poked about in cupboards and drawers under the old housekeeper's disapproving eye. She'd just discovered an ice pick when the front door knocker sounded. Bidding the arthritic Millie to stay seated, Clementine hurried to open the door, hiding the ice pick behind her back in the folds of her skirt.

Jonathan Noble greeted her with a disapproving frown. "Answering your own door? It isn't done, my dear."

"Ah can't answer the door?" she asked, incredulous. Learning all the silly rules of Annapolis society seemed nigh impossible, especially when the logic of them escaped her. "Back where ah come from, every able-bodied woman answers the door."

"Commendable, but you're not in Texas now," Jonathan reminded her gently.

And didn't she know it. Homesickness pricked at her heart like a rusty nail and settled deep in her bones.

"The exception would be if Millie was ill," Jonathan amended.

Clementine pounced on the acceptable excuse. "Her bones is creakin'."

He laughed. "They *are* creaking."

"From the arthritis."

"Well, never mind. It's much too nice a day to be shut in. Would you like to walk with me? I thought to stop by the sweet shop before I pay a call on Mrs. Hawthorne. Laverne is ill, and she's quite partial to Schrafft's peppermint stick candy."

"You are a very kind man." She said what she thought.

"A wise man makes it his business to see that women have what makes them happy."

"And clever," Clementine added, rethinking. Clearly, her father-in-law's thoughtfulness strengthened his standing with the ladies.

Jonathan slanted a wicked wink her way.

She felt a momentary twinge of guilt for chuckling. "Ah would be honored to walk with you. Fresh air always invigorates me."

But it was the promise of candy that persuaded her to accompany Jonathan Noble. The only candy she'd ever eaten was fudge that she'd made herself. And she'd enjoyed the chocolate mightily. Peppermint sticks held new promise.

Jonathan motioned with his walking stick. "Come along, then."

"Let me get mah parasol." On the chance that the sun made her freckles darker, as she'd read in *Harper's Bazaar* that morning, she intended to shield her face. Clementine wasn't certain where the magazine had come from. She'd discovered it in the drawing room and found it most helpful.

As she dashed up the stairs, she heard Jonathan call behind her, "Walk, my dear. A lady never runs."

After depositing the ice pick in the satchel along with her other prized possessions, Clementine grabbed her parasol.

Within minutes she and Jonathan strolled down the street at a leisurely pace. Clementine knew that today, wearing her walking costume, she appeared as stylish and sophisticated as any Annapolis silk-stocking. But appearances were deceiving, inside she felt as nervous as a tenderfoot masquerading as a trail driver. Someone was bound to find her out.

"If you would like to visit any of the shops that we pass, just stop me," Jonathan said when they reached Main Street.

Clementine's gaze flitted from window to window as they passed the shops. She also surveyed the cobblestones in the path ahead in case she might stumble upon another three-dollar gold piece. She'd always been lucky that way, finding money. She found mostly pennies, but after all, she'd been taught that a penny saved was a penny earned.

A block from Green Street, she came up short. But it wasn't a penny or a three-dollar coin that caused her to gasp aloud. A Chinese red-velvet chaise lounge sat in the window of Dixon's Dry Goods Emporium. Clementine ogled the most beautiful piece of furniture she'd ever seen.

"Is it the chaise that has caught your eye?" Jonathan asked after a moment.

"Yes." The sweeping piece of rosewood furniture had more than caught her eye. She'd fallen in love with its brilliant color and graceful lines. The intricately carved feet could have been crafted for a queen.

"Shall we go in and make inquiries?"

"Could we?"

The price was very dear, but Jonathan insisted his son could afford the riveting piece of furniture and ordered the crimson chaise delivered.

"Ah hope Rand won't be angry with me," she said as they left the shop.

Spending huge sums and provoking her husband concerned Clementine. If for any reason Rand decided to annul the marriage, her pa would be rolling over in his grave. He'd arranged this marriage for her with the best intentions. She would never do anything to disgrace Pa—not to mention that she'd be as homeless as a poker chip. She hadn't saved enough money to live independently. Yet.

"Rand won't be angry," Jonathan assured her. "Besides being a wealthy man, my son is extremely good-natured. And I shall tell him, as well, that I thought the article an excellent purchase and insisted that you buy the chaise."

At least she had a champion in her father-in-law. Without him she would be lost.

They came to the sweet shop next. Clementine's mouth watered as she viewed a tray of sticky buns in the window. But Jonathan studied, with an increasingly dire frown, a simple sign posted on the door. *Ruby LaRue, Medium. Appointments taken through August.*

Pinch-lipped, he shook his head in disdain. "Shameful. Just shameful how these charlatans take advantage of others."

Although Clementine had never visited a medium, she'd heard that they contacted the spirits and very often could see into the future.

"How do they take advantage?" she asked. A bud of an idea had begun to form in her mind.

"With their cruel lies. Believe me, Clementine, no one is able to communicate with the dead or predict the future. These mediums prey on innocent minds."

But Clementine believed in destiny. As her mother had before her, she believed practitioners were born with a gift. *The* gift. But believing so meant she must possess the kind of innocent mind Jonathan pitied.

"Are you certain that everything a medium has to say is hogwash?" she asked, giving him a chance to recant.

"I am," he replied grimly. "And I will see this woman run out of town."

A tinkling bell over the door gave notice when Clementine marched into the sweet shop behind her enraged father-in-law. He addressed the graying proprietress with unusual curtness. "Good morning, Lucy."

Lucy possessed an infectious smile, which she turned on Clementine as well as Jonathan.

"'Morning," she said, wiping her hands on the large white apron that protected her cotton dress.

Clementine attributed Lucy's plump, pear-shaped figure to sampling her wares, as every baker and candy maker must. A hazard, she supposed, of the business. A hazard she envied. "What is the meaning of the notice in your window?" Jonathan demanded.

Lucy blinked her dark eyes in a wary, nervous manner. "I don't understand."

"Why is a medium practicing her deception on your premises?"

The folds of Lucy's doughy face fell into a frown. "Ruby rents a room above the shop. I need the rent money, Jonathan. What she does is none of my concern." And none of yours, her expression seemed to say.

With an imperious impatience that Clementine had not witnessed before, Jonathan rapped his gold-handled walking stick on the floor. "I wish to speak to this woman immediately."

"Ruby left early this morning. Said she wouldn't be back until late this afternoon."

"Then I shall return late this afternoon." He turned sharply on his heel.

Clementine snatched his coat sleeve. "Did you forget the peppermint sticks?"

"Ah, yes." He raised a hand and pressed his forehead. "Thank you for reminding me, my dear. I'm afraid I became distracted." When he turned back to the sweet-shop owner, he did so with a smile. "Lucy, a pound of peppermint sticks for my daughter-in-law and another pound for Mrs. Hawthorne."

A few minutes later they bid Lucy good-day and were on their way to Laverne Hawthorne's. Clementine clutched a paper bag with peppermint sticks, but her thoughts weren't on the candy.

She must take care of her business with the medium before Jonathan made good on his threat to run Ruby LaRue out of town. As soon as she read the notice, Clementine decided to make an appointment. The opportunity to speak with Ellie Tidwell through the medium might be a once-in-a-lifetime opportunity.

She and Ellie could not live in the same house. That much was clear to her. By whatever means necessary, Clementine had resolved to remove the ghost that stood between her and Rand. Come what may, she must attempt to make this marriage her pa arranged a successful one. She'd experienced loss once, and once was enough.

The old, painful memories took hold of her as she walked. Jonathan appeared lost in his own thoughts—most likely of burning Ruby LaRue at the stake.

For years Clementine had dreamed of marrying Jake Edison. The only son of the neighboring ranchers, Jake was a tall dark-haired man with a square jaw and a muscular chest. He could ride a bucking bull to the finish and tame a maverick horse with just one whisper.

She'd loved Jake, and what he could do, from the moment she first set eyes on him. From the time she was sixteen years old, she burned like a brushfire whenever he was near. Clementine knew it was love because while she burned she'd stammer and her hands would go clammy and cold. Before long she gave up singing "Buffalo Gals" and started writing songs of love that she sang while strummin' on her banjo.

Jake walked a bit bow-legged, but he was a man's man and just one year older than Clementine. She was convinced they would make a fine match. Her constant dream through the years was that one day Jake and she would combine their ranches into one giant spread. Whenever she ran into him in town at the supply store or at church, she made sure to inform him of her latest adventures. Clementine regaled him with stories about the steer she'd wrestled, the rustler she'd shot, the horse she'd shod. No other woman in Oddon could boast of such accomplishments. But in the end it had done her no good.

Clementine's heart all but shattered, along with every hope of happiness, the day she got wind that Jake had up and married Sue Ann Breeder. The lily-livered daughter of the sheriff didn't know anything about anything exceptin' how to sew britches and bake cakes. Clementine had lost the only man she'd ever loved to a blond piece of fluff.

She felt a staying hand on her arm.

"We've arrived at Laverne's," Jonathan said. "Our stay will be brief."

Tamping back the memories that still managed to make her heart howl with pain and her blood run hot with anger, Clementine nodded, lifted her chin and climbed the steps with Jonathan.

Rand returned home early to discover that his wife had gone off with his father once again. He found it slightly irritating that the old man spent more time with Clementine than he. At this rate the marriage would never be consummated. His plan to seduce his recalcitrant wife had ended abruptly last night with the mention of Ellie.

He'd led Clementine on, fully intending to make her his. She must have known it, expected it. Instead, a cold wave of guilt rolled over him at the mention of Ellie. All of a sudden it hadn't seemed right to make love to another woman with Ellie's face dancing before him.

When Rand turned away from Clementine, she must have felt slighted. In seconds, he'd ruined his chances of making love to her. As a result, he'd struggled with an edgy, out-of-sorts feeling all day. Knowing he wouldn't feel right again until he made up his neglect to his fiery-haired bride, he left the hospital before his usual time.

Still, as he watched for Clementine from the front window, he wondered if he could, if he would, ever forget Ellie.

His father and wife returned as the sun set. Rand peered between the lace curtains to see Clementine laughing up at something his father had just said. He supposed it was something droll and amusing. His father managed to be droll and amusing regularly.

Rand opened the door just as they reached the front steps.

"Welcome home."

"Rand!" Clementine's eyes sparkled with delight.

"Good evening, son. I didn't think you would mind if I took your charming wife along with me to pay a call on Mrs. Hawthorne. She's recovering from the croup, you know."

"Yes. I know." He also knew that his father had recently ended a liaison with the widow Hawthorne. In all probability, the sly old fellow had taken Clementine on the visit to act as a buffer. He was not above such machinations. "Would you like to come in, Father?"

"I should be running along home. Our visit lasted much longer than intended."

"Mrs. Hawthorne insisted we stay for luncheon," Clementine said as she passed by Rand into the foyer. The lively scents of chamomile and peppermint drifted in her wake.

"And then Laverne urged several games of checkers upon us," his father added. He rolled his eyes, signaling his hapless position. "We were quite unable to leave as quickly as I'd wished."

"Do you know Laverne thought a nighthawk was a bird?" Clementine asked, and then burst into laughter.

Her laughter echoed in the high-ceilinged drawing room. A merry sleigh-bell sound that warmed Rand and caught him off guard. He hadn't heard her laugh before. "It isn't?" he asked.

"Mercy, no! A nighthawk is a wrangler," she explained. "He wrangles saddle horses at night. Mrs. Hawthorne didn't know a woman could use a lasso either."

"But let me guess," Rand said, unable to prevent a smile. "You set her straight on that account."

"Ah sure did."

"Do you lasso?"

"Would you like to see me?"

Rand held up a hand. "I believe you."

Her eyes rounded with excitement. "Ah brought a lasso in mah satchel."

"Laverne was quite taken with your wife," Jonathan put in quickly, deferring a demonstration of Clementine's prowess with rope.

Rand had no doubt that his Texas bride had made a profound impression on the widow Hawthorne. More than likely, Clementine had flabbergasted the strictly upper-crust Laverne. He could almost imagine Mrs. Hawthorne's expression of astonishment. "I'm certain Laverne has never met anyone quite like Clementine."

"That's exactly what she said." Clementine grinned, apparently pleased that she'd left an enduring impression. Her light, apple green eyes shone with satisfaction.

Momentarily lost in the misty pools of her eyes, Rand forced his gaze away, to his father. "Fortunately, you were able to slip away in good time for an engagement this evening."

"For this evening?" Jonathan questioned.

"Yes. It's a rather impromptu invitation which includes you, Father."

"Is that so?" A spark of interest instantly ignited in his father's eyes.

"Sarah sent a note by way of a messenger this afternoon."

Clementine lifted a questioning gaze to Rand.

Jonathan's dark brows gathered to the bridge of his nose. He blinked as if he might not have heard Rand correctly. When he opened his eyes, any previous interest in the evening engagement had disappeared. "I see," he said, making toward the door. "I beg you to extend my thanks, but I'm afraid—"

"Please come with us," Clementine urged.

His bride's reliance on his father once again proved annoying to Rand.

Jonathan turned. After regarding Clementine momentarily, he wavered. "What time are we expected?"

"Dinner is at eight."

"Very well. I shall be there." With a tip of his hat and a tap of his walking stick, Jonathan departed.

Rand took Clementine's hands in his. He looked directly into her eyes, eyes no longer shining. "Tonight you shall be formally introduced to a small segment of Annapolis society."

She pulled away, moving toward the window. "Ah don't know if ah'm ready."

"There's nothing to worry about or be ready for. You just came from a successful visit with Laverne Hawthorne. Tonight will be much the same. We're simply visiting with Sarah for a quiet evening of dinner and cards."

When she heard the word "cards," Clementine stopped, stood straighter. "Do y'all play draw poker?"

The ramifications of her question weren't lost on Rand. He groaned inwardly. His wife played poker. But he smiled gamely. "In mixed company we play whist."

She folded her arms across her chest. "Ah don't. Ah don't know how to play whist."

Her breasts rose and fell in agitated rhythm, breasts he'd never seen, never touched. Tonight. This would be the night when he would touch and love every Western inch of her.

"I'm certain that you'll pick up the game quickly," he assured her.

Rand realized that he might regret accepting Sarah's invitation, but he'd done so knowing that he could not avoid the inevitable for long. Weeks before the event, he'd told Ellie's sister, Sarah, that he planned to marry. And he'd told her why—to have a son. He'd explained that his heart would always belong to Ellie, but he desperately wanted, and needed, a son to carry on the family name.

Apparently, Sarah had grown impatient waiting to meet Rand's new wife. She'd taken matters into her own hands by inviting the Nobles and several other friends for an evening of cards. He had thought to decline but in the end came to the conclusion that a refusal would only delay matters and might make an uncomfortable situation even more so.

"Ah've been told ah'm quick at cards," Clementine allowed in her soft Texas drawl. Her arms relaxed; her breathing slowed to normal. "But who is Sarah?"

"Sarah Tidwell. She's Ellie's sister."

Clementine possessed a fair complexion to begin with, but what little color she had drained from her face, leaving it as white as pristine winter snow. The freckles that played across the bridge of her nose darkened in contrast.

Rand swallowed hard, bracing himself for whatever storm might be brewing within her. But to his surprise, there was no storm. No bluntly stated rejection.

"Ah have a . . . a fierce headache. Ah was planning on goin' straight to bed as soon as your father left." She started toward the door. "But don't let that worry you. Ah always recover from these things. You go on without me and . . . and have a good time."

With just a few steps, he cut her off, blocking the doorway with his body. "You must accompany me, Clementine," he stated softly. "You're my wife."

"But ah'm in pain," she cried, flinging her arms in the air. "Mortal pain!"

He had to give her credit. She was a fine actress. He swallowed a chuckle in order to reply as seriously as possible. "You didn't appear to be in pain a few moments ago."

"Ah was attempting to be brave. Ah didn't want your pity."

"I could never pity you."

She chewed on her plush bottom lip. Her lips beckoned him to kiss away the worry hovering there. Clearly, she was working on another excuse.

Rand knew he was asking a lot of her. If he were in Clementine's place, he might feign sudden insanity. Convinced he must offer her something in return, he went out on a limb. "If you will just accompany me for a few hours, I'll . . . I'll see that you have anything you want."

She bit down on her lip. Her narrow, arched,

auburn brows dove downward. "You can't give me what ah want."

"How do you know?"

"Because ah want to go back to Texas."

"Whoa! Yes!" Rand experienced true elation and relief. He could provide her request. "Yes, I can. We'll have a . . . Texas honeymoon. I should have thought of that before. We'll visit your ranch, your brother and anywhere else you care to go."

"Ah don't want to just visit Texas—"

"Where else would you like to go? Paris? London? New York?"

She shook her head. Her defiant copper curls bounced on her shoulders.

"You're not going to be unreasonable, are you?" he asked cautiously.

Again she shook her head. But he already knew how stubborn she could be. He tried again, using his most persuasive tone. "I understand that meeting Sarah may be uncomfortable for you. I'm attempting to make it up to you, to give you something nice, something you'd like in return."

Clementine lowered her eyes. "Feels like ah'm bein' bribed."

Rather than deny her feeling, which he couldn't do in all good conscience, he pressed on. "Sarah lives in this town. You're bound to meet her someday, and perhaps the circumstances won't be as pleasant. At least tonight you'll have my father and me to support you—if you should need support. Sarah would not dare to do or say anything untoward in our company."

"She will not like me."

"She cannot dislike you."

"Ah'm taking her sister's place," she insisted. And

in a voice softer still, added, "And no one can take Ellie's place."

Clementine's quiet assertion shook Rand. A bullet to his heart couldn't have surprised him more. Her raw vulnerability sliced straight to his core. "You are my wife now," he said at last, enunciating each word slowly and firmly. "I vowed to support and protect you in every way. And I shall."

"My wedding band, the one that doesn't fit. Was it . . . was it Ellie's?"

"No, oh no." Rand ached for his Texas bride, for not knowing him well enough to believe for one minute that he would be so callous. "Your ring is an heirloom. It belonged to my mother."

He rested his hands lightly on Clementine's shoulders. She raised her head. Her eyes, clear as liquid jade, innocent and anxious, met his. Overwhelmed by the need to comfort her, Rand brought his lips down, tenderly brushing hers.

The spark jarred him. A spark kindled by the barest of touches. Unlike the teasing kiss he'd given her at the end of their wedding ceremony, this kiss triggered an unexpected sensation. The instant their lips met, a rush of sweet heat shot through Rand.

Unnerved, he lifted his head and set his wife back from him.

She placed her fingertips over her lips as if protecting them from another kiss. Her fingers trembled. "Very well. Ah shall accompany you to Sarah Tidwell's."

The bell on the sweet-shop door tinkled as Jonathan entered. The heavy sugary fragrance enveloped him. He had just time enough to give the charlatan medium a piece of his mind before making ready for this evening's engagement at Sarah Tidwell's. It was an engagement he would rather miss. If it weren't for Clementine, he would have held steadfast to his refusal. He'd vowed to watch over his best friend's daughter, and he would honor his vow.

"Lucy!" he called.

The sweet-shop owner swiped flour from her cheek as she bustled through the beaded curtain that separated the shop from the kitchen.

"I've returned to see Ruby LaRue," he announced.

"She's not here. I told her that you wanted to see her, Jonathan, but she said she had an important matter to attend to."

"My matter is important." More important than any matter a medium might have, he steamed silently.

"I'm sure it is. Ruby said that you can have an appointment with her first thing in the morning."

"I shall return."

When he did, he would personally escort Ruby LaRue out of town.

# *Five*

Determined to make a favorable impression on Ellie's sister, Sarah Tidwell, Clementine took pains dressing for dinner. At the end of an hour, she studied her reflection in the looking glass and decided that she looked as presentable as possible, considering that her corset made breathing perilous and her beryl blue gown featured a small bustle. The bustle's padding presented a challenge to sit comfortably to any woman who'd known a saddle. The evening ahead would entail a great deal of shifting of skirts and derriere for Clementine.

As always, her hair provided the greatest problem. Gone were the days when she could just slap a ten-gallon hat atop her head and hide the mess. Tonight, she'd gathered the springy cinnamon locks to the crown of her head and fastened the mass with long blue strands of grosgrain ribbon. Attempting to subdue the restless curls at her temples, she'd achieved a temporary solution by dousing them down with chamomile.

Rand's tender kiss had persuaded her to attend what promised to be a difficult dinner party. Pleasing him became a priority with that single kiss. Just the memory of his fleeting touch rekindled an odd but pleasant tingling sensation that danced upon her lips like the fizz of champagne. Unlike her devilish husband's bruising, tongue-plunging wedding kiss, this kiss had settled on her mouth like a soft sprinkling of magic dust.

Her heart gave an agitated wiggle. The tall, compelling surgeon was beginning to get under her skin. She liked him much too much. For Rand loved another. He loved a ghost, the ghost of his first wife. He'd not denied it when she said that no one could take Ellie's place. He'd not known how her heart pinched up in pain.

A rap on the door brought her musing to an end.

"Are you ready?" Rand asked.

No matter how she looked or what she said, Clementine understood that she would never win the approval of Ellie's sister, Sarah. Heaving a sigh of resignation, she headed for the door and the husband who waited for her on the opposite side.

"As ready as ah'll ever be."

Jonathan hired a carriage for the ride to Sarah Tidwell's home. While he and Rand discussed the deplorable state of the navy's fleet, Clementine allowed her mind to wander. She clutched the seahorse her pa had made for her in the palm of her hand. Tonight she required all the luck the tiny sea creature could bring. Whenever she felt alone and uncertain, holding the seahorse comforted her. The small figurine held memories of the happiest Christmas she'd ever known.

Pa had come home from the sea. He'd shipped into Galveston and brought apples for Junior and Ma and her. Christmas Eve, he held Clementine in his lap by the fireplace. He smelled of salt and bay rum, and she remembered thinking that he smelled better than a field of bluebonnets. Her robust pa was the only man in her life who had loved her unconditionally, who had loved her at all. That night, with his arms about her, he'd patiently taught her how to tie a slipknot. Each time she recalled his round, laughing face, her heart swelled with love and loss.

Clementine cherished her seahorse. It served to remind her of that holiday when the small ranch house overflowed with love and laughter. The gift her father had crafted allowed her to celebrate Christmas in her heart anytime.

When the carriage pulled to a stop, Clementine tucked her seahorse into her reticule for safekeeping. She would keep him close tonight.

Sarah Tidwell stood in the foyer of her brownstone home greeting her guests as they arrived. She had invited another couple, Lieutenant Steven Markham and his wife, Liz. Steven, a seamanship instructor, and Rand were fast friends.

As she waited to be introduced, Clementine felt as if she'd slipped her neck into a noose. While she waited, the noose slowly tightened. Forcing a smile, she held her breath.

And then the deed was done.

Rand introduced her to Sarah Tidwell. The thin, older woman offered a limp hand while her cold gaze swept Clementine from head to toe.

"Howdy." Clementine's muscles ached from smiling as she pumped Sarah's hand. "Pleased to meet you, ma'am."

Tipping her head, Sarah withdrew her hand. "Welcome to Annapolis." Her frosty tone held no welcome.

"Ah do appreciate that, ma'am." Clementine

bobbed her head nervously. "You're mighty kind to have me."

*Dang.* She felt like a fool. The truth was that she would rather be poked with a hot branding iron than be here, confronting Ellie Tidwell's spinster sister.

Clementine's height gave her some advantage. She stood two hands higher than Sarah, a petite woman with dark hair, dark eyes and a mottled turkey neck.

Sarah gave her a tight-lipped, condescending smile. "Congratulations," she said, "on capturing the most eligible man in town—since the death of my dear sister."

Sarah Tidwell wished her dead. She could feel it. If looks could kill, Clementine would be writhing on the floor.

"Rand is a good man," she replied quietly, mustering up as much dignity as she owned.

Jonathan, who must have sensed trouble, stepped between them, smoothly offering an arm to Sarah and escorting their hostess into her drawing room. "Sarah, did you know there is a seeress in town?" he asked.

Clementine didn't hear Sarah's reply, for Rand came up behind her. He gently turned her about to face him. His smile was warm and wide enough to melt the heart of every woman in Annapolis. "There, that wasn't so bad, was it?"

Bad being a relative condition, Clementine was ready to leave before bad became worse. She considered feigning a swoon in the hope that Rand would carry her home. But she knew the doctor in him would not be fooled. There was no recourse but to endure the evening and resign herself to the fact that Sarah Tidwell would do everything and anything she could to discredit Clementine.

Spindly antique furniture that looked as if it might break if you sat down too hard crowded the small rooms. Dominant shades of olive green and walnut brown robbed the house of any light or cheer. The somber home matched the make-up of its owner.

The next test of Clementine's patience came at dinner. She'd never seen so many instruments set to eat one meal.

"Is your salad fork missing, Clementine?" Sarah asked.

"Oh, no, everything is right where it should be. Ah just prefer a bigger utensil. Bird bites won't do for me. Ah possess a hearty appetite. It comes with the territory out West. We use shovels rather than spoons."

Steven Markham laughed. "That doesn't surprise me. I've heard you do everything in a big way out in Texas."

His wife, Liz, leaned forward. "Did you really live on a ranch?"

"Ah sure did."

"What do women do on the western ranches?" Sarah asked in a tone of utter disinterest.

"What most women do anywhere: tend to the house and meals and such. But bein' there was just mah brother and me for the past few years, ah did a lot more."

Rand signaled to her with a discreet waggle of his finger. She thought he might have wanted her to stop talking, but she couldn't be sure. Unwilling to risk trouble by appearing rude to Sarah by not answering her question, Clementine instead ignored Rand and warmed to her story.

"Ah rode the range and herded our cattle. Once ah had to take on a cattle rustler. Couldn't believe the varmint was fixin' to steal our best herd in broad daylight."

"You took on a cattle rustler?" Obviously shocked, Liz Markham splayed a hand over her heart. "What does that mean?"

"Ah shot him. Ah was on a bluff overlookin' the spot where he rode. He was the biggest, meanest man ah ever did see. He sat like a giant in the saddle, face covered with whiskers. That rustler looked as wooly as a grizzly bear. He could squash me with his thumb. But he didn't see me, or maybe thinkin' that ah was only a woman and didn't pose any threat." Clementine paused for a breath. All eyes were upon her, spellbound. "So's ah showed him. Ah took out mah Winchester and let that big old bear of a rustler have it. Blew his Stetson right off his head and sent him scurryin'!"

Sarah's hands flew to cover her ears. "Dear heaven!"

"This might not be dinner conversation, Clementine," Rand admonished her beneath his breath.

"I am fascinated," Liz exclaimed. "The rustler must have been surprised to discover a woman brave enough to do what you did."

"Ah just did what any rancher would do. Saved the cattle, which was the most important thing."

"I've never met anyone quite like you," Steven remarked.

Clementine wasn't sure Rand's colleague meant his statement to be a compliment or not. She decided to accept it as one, however, and felt the heat of a blush warming her cheeks. "Ah'm nothin' special. Women can do most things. But not if they listen to men telling them that they can't."

Liz inclined her head. She nodded as if she'd just made an important discovery. "You're right. I've never

thought of it that way before. Too many women believe whatever men tell them."

Clementine felt a small swell of pride that this city
woman had vindicated her western ways. But as she
glanced around the table, her confidence gave way.

Sarah's eyes narrowed on Clementine as if the stern
hostess had just discovered a viper at her table. Rand
concentrated on his plate, pushing potatoes from one
spot to another. But Jonathan smiled, and his encouraging smile reassured her—temporarily.

When the group adjourned to the drawing room,
Clementine met her next test.

"Liz, would you be so kind as to recite a poem?"
Sarah asked as she made her way to the piano.

"Of course, Sarah. It would be my pleasure."

Ellie's older sister responded with a gracious dip
of her head and slipped to the stool behind a large,
gleaming grand piano. "And I shall play Beethoven."

Clementine's insides stung. She'd been singled out
again. Sarah had let her know she didn't fit in here.
There didn't seem to be anywhere she fit. On the
chance the mean-spirited spinster might see the anguish reflected in her eyes, Clementine lowered her
gaze, stared at the hem of her skirt.

Rand came to the rescue. "Would you like to con-
tribute to the evening's entertainment, Clementine?"

Taken by surprise, she cast her husband a grateful
smile but shrugged her shoulders. "If ah had known
we were going to entertain, ah would have brought
my banjo."

Steven broke out in a broad grin. "You play a banjo?
That's a darn sight more interesting than listening to
a poem. Not that you don't recite better than anyone,
Liz," he added hastily to his wife.

"That's something ah could never do. Ah could

never recite," Clementine offered in a further attempt to save Liz's feelings.

Liz flashed a rueful smile. And Clementine knew she'd gained a friend in one brief moment of unspoken understanding between women.

"Ah'll sing," she volunteered quickly. "Sarah, do you know how to play that new ditty, 'Home on The Range'?"

"No," Sarah responded sharply. "Perhaps you can entertain next time."

Clementine's father-in-law stepped in. Her own pa could not have stood up for her better. "Clementine doesn't need a piano accompaniment. She sings like a nightingale."

A nightingale! Mercy! Now how would she prove him right?

Standing by the piano, Clementine took a deep breath and, focusing on the crystal chandelier in the center of the room, sang as sweetly as she knew how. The homesickness she held in her heart flowed into the lyrics and music. By the time she finished, Liz and Jonathan Noble were misty eyed.

She earned a round of applause, even from a begrudging Sarah Tidwell. Clementine smiled, curtsied and threw kisses with both hands as if she were a great actress upon a theater stage.

Thanks to her seahorse, she would survive the drawing room, just as she had the desert.


Rand thought the evening would never end. He was never as happy to be back at home.

"I'm walking from here," his father said as he alighted from the carriage he'd just discharged. "The night air is invigorating. Almost as invigorating as you were tonight, Clementine. You breathed fresh charm into an evening that otherwise would have proved deadly indeed."

"If only everyone felt like you do." She kissed him lightly on the cheek and whispered something in his ear that Rand could not hear.

The old man replied with a grin. "I'll call on you tomorrow afternoon to see if I can be of service."

"After tonight, I'm convinced Clementine can take care of any matter by herself," Rand said. "You don't have to spoil her, Father."

"What else does an old retired sea dog have to do? Until tomorrow." With a wave of his walking stick, he ambled his way down the street toward his home.

Rand steered his wife up the steps and into the house.

"What makes you think ah can take care of any matter?" she asked.

"Those lies you told." He grinned. Her story had been the best of the evening. "A rustler bigger and meaner than a grizzly bear?"

"It's true."

"As true as anything told by Mark Twain."

"Perhaps it was a bit of a tall tale."

"Complete fabrication," he amended.

"Exaggeration."

"I give up." Laughing, Rand threw up his hands.

She smiled. A smile as pretty as any he'd seen. And he felt a softening inside, near his heart. This wife who played the banjo, scared off rustlers, rolled her own cigarettes and sang like a nightingale amazed him. The emotion she displayed while singing her song had tugged at his heartstrings, something Rand did his best to conceal. Clementine was full of surprises.

And she was his.

Dressed in a blue silk gown adorned with lace and flounces, she looked no different than any other well-born woman. She could easily pass for a lady of Annapolis—until she spoke. But then, he admitted to himself, her Texas drawl had enchanted her audience tonight.

His gaze drifted to the high, stiff lace collar of her gown. His fingers ached to unbutton the dainty row of mother-of-pearl buttons and set her free. Free. The thought of liberating Clementine from the restrictions of her dress gave wings to Rand's imagination. Beneath Clementine's tight, form-fitting bodice he envisioned a perfect body, pure and untouched.

Beneath what the eye could readily see, whatever rough edges his bride possessed gave way to smooth velvet skin and lush round curves. Her full, firm breasts would shimmer like rich cream and feel like satin to his fingertips. Delicate nipples of pink and gold would pebble at the touch of his lips. And at the first hint of her arousal, Rand would slide his hand down to stroke her thighs. First one, and then the other. Feathering slowly up, slowly down. And all the while he would whisper in her ear, describing how she excited him, what touching her did to him.

His imagination served him well, too well. The ache that had warmed his loins, burned. Fiercely. He wanted her. He wanted Clementine now.

She gazed up at him with an air of innocence that served to temper his lust. Deep within the irises of her light green eyes he detected flecks of gold gleaming like buried treasure.

"Is there something wrong?"

"No, Clementine, nothing at all."

He found the fresh scent of chamomile clinging to

her hair more intoxicating than expensive French perfume. Perhaps, he speculated, because the fragrance was as much a part of the funny, freckled, adorable face before him as light was to a firefly. Although he couldn't explain it, Rand was inordinately captivated by the sheen on the tip of his wife's nose. He might dust the shiny spot with powder. Or kiss it. He preferred the latter solution.

A tight, rusty red ringlet fell to her forehead. The wayward curl demanded immediate attention. Using the tip of a finger, Rand gently pushed it back.

"Is there a prize for enduring an evening with Sarah Tidwell?" she asked with a grin.

She was hinting. A prize. God forgive him his arrogance, but her meaning was clear: Clementine wanted him. Hallelujah! He'd known it wouldn't take long before she came around. When he'd been a single man, his way with the ladies became legend. Why would his wife be the only woman in Annapolis immune to his charms?

Rand nodded slowly, smiled. "You shall have a grand prize."

"Wonderful!" Beaming with pleasure, she clasped her hands together beneath her chin. "Ah should like to have a dance lesson."

Rand wasn't quite certain that he'd heard her correctly. He had been so confident that she had been thinking along the same lines as he. "A dance lesson?"

She grasped his hand and pulled him into the reception room. One gaslight shone, and a soft spring breeze parted the lace curtains. "You promised. Ah'd like to learn the waltz."

"The waltz?" He'd planned to lead her in an altogether different type of dance. A dance where their feet would never touch the floor. But a waltz would take him where he wanted to go. The lesson would only be a minor delay.

Sweeping Clementine into his arms, Rand held her to his chest. She pushed back.

"Ah believe the man holds the woman at arm's length."

He dipped his head in apology. "Begging your pardon. I must have been thinking of some other dance."

The small copper curl he'd put in its place had sprung back in defiance to dangle upon her forehead. Her lips parted in a tenuous smile, lips that he had tasted briefly. Before the night was over, he vowed to taste her delicious lips again. Very soon now, his wife would become his in more than name.

"The waltz is a one-two-three count," he began.

She tilted her head. "Did you hear something?"

"No." He was determined to have his way with her—within the hour.

"Listen," she insisted.

Rand listened. The door knocker. He sighed in frustration. "Someone's at the door."

"Aren't you going to answer?" she asked when he didn't make a move. "It might be an emergency."

At this time of night, he could be certain of it.

She pulled out of his grip and started from the room.

"No," he protested. "Wait. I'll get it."

He reached the door before Clementine. "There might be bleeding involved," he warned.

She turned her back.

But the young man who stood in the door had come as a messenger. "Superintendent Rodgers requires your attendance, sir."

The superintendent of the Naval Academy had sent for him. Superintendent Rodgers, the only person in

Annapolis that Rand could not deny. He clenched his jaw. "I'll get my bag."

As he turned, he rested a hand on the nape of Clementine's neck and spoke softly into her ear. His words had nothing to do with what he earlier had imagined saying. Instead, he apologized. "I regret this more than I can say. I should have warned you about the life of a doctor's wife."

"Ah understand."

Her earnest smile of support caused Rand's heart to somersault like a schoolboy's. "Don't wait up for me," he said.

Within minutes he was on his way. He strode from the house with a purposeful step, his bearing that of a man who honored his obligations and never shirked his duty.

Clementine stood alone in the foyer. Up until this point, she thought the evening had gone well, better than she'd expected. But to have a promising interlude with Rand end so abruptly was cruel, downright cruel. The hope she'd held moments ago slid from her heart.

As she started up the stairs, she thought she heard laughter. She paused on the carpeted step. The laughter of Ellie Tidwell Noble echoed through the halls.

Early the following morning, as soon as the Main Street shops opened, Jonathan Noble entered Lucy's sweet shop, sounding the bell in a mad jangle. He tipped his hat to Lucy and without further discussion climbed the narrow stairs leading to the rooms above the shop.

Righteousness surged through him thicker than blood. He rapped the gold-tipped handle of his walking stick sharply on the charlatan medium's door. No one answered. Tapping his toe in agitation, he used his fist to pound.

Just as he was about to call out, the door opened.

The woman with raven hair, golden eyes and a dimple in her chin did not look like the gypsy woman swathed in gold bangles that Jonathan had expected to see. For a heartbeat in time he had been caught off-guard.

"Yes?"

He recovered. "Ruby LaRue, I presume?" he asked, removing his top hat.

"I am. Won't you come in, sir?" She did not smile or fawn over him, as he was used to women doing. The skirt of her fashionable, forest green silk dress swished as she stepped aside.

The small, close room had just enough space for two chairs and a round table that had been covered with a paisley scarf dripping indigo fringe. What looked like a cot had been disguised as a lounge, piled with thick, faded pillows. A yellowed muslin curtain covered the single window.

The attractive medium gestured to one of the hard wooden chairs. "Please, have a seat."

Jonathan stood even straighter. "That won't be necessary. What I've come to say won't take long."

She raised both angled, dark brows. One corner of her scarlet red mouth hitched up. Scarlet, the hussy! If he wasn't mistaken, she regarded him with what appeared to be amusement.

The amber-eyed charlatan's attitude only served to increase his ire, his outrage. Who did she think she was?

For one thing, Ruby LaRue wasn't at all what Jonathan had expected. Tiny lines upon lustrous olive skin marked her as an older woman, somewhere in her forties, he gauged.

"I can bring up tea from the sweet shop if you would like," she said.

"No, thank you."

"With sugar." She emphasized the word "sugar," insinuating that he needed the sweetening.

"No, *thank you.*"

"Do you wish to contact someone on the other side? Or do you simply wish to know what the future holds?"

"I know what the future holds, madam," he replied tersely. He would give her no quarter. Miss LaRue did not deserve the type of attention he gave respectful women. She must understand at once that her beauty could not distract or deter him from his mission. "Let me introduce myself. I am Jonathan Noble, retired surgeon from the United States Navy."

She dipped her head politely. "A pleasure to meet you, Dr. Noble. If you do not care to use my services, what brings you here?"

"I wish you to leave Annapolis immediately."

Her eyes widened. Her tone dripped with disbelief. "You want me to leave town?"

"Yes. By the end of the day."

"May I ask what brings on your request? Have I done something to offend you?"

"You offend me each time you claim to some poor innocent soul that you have contacted the dead."

"Have you heard me do this?"

"No. I do not need to. I know what mediums do."

"Are you also aware that the spiritualists' movement has been widely recognized and accepted for the past thirty years?"

"Not by me, madam."

"Some of us, sir, have a gift. Mediums have been known to help those who come to them."

"Help," he muttered. "You rob them blind."

Ruby LaRue balled her hands upon her hips. Generous hips, he noticed. "I think you should leave now," she said.

"Not until I have your word that you will pack up and take your traveling show to another town."

"Dr. Noble, I will not leave. I've broken no laws, and I do not intend to break any."

"You sell a false bill of goods. That's robbery, and that is against the law."

"And *that* is merely your opinion," she hissed. Her golden eyes, flashing angrily, locked on his. "For the record, sir, I charge a fair amount to my clients in return for what I give to them."

"You can hoodwink a few poor souls, but you can't hoodwink me," he snapped.

"I should not try! But hear me well. I shall stay in Annapolis until my business is done."

"You are a . . . a scandalous woman!"

"And you are a judgmental man." She opened the door.

"I'll be back," he warned. "If there is no legal way to make you go, I shall harass you until you leave."

"If you do, I shall have you thrown in jail."

"I am a doctor and a respectable citizen of this fair city."

"Truly? You had me fooled. Based upon your behavior in my place of business, I would not have attached the word 'respectable' to you."

"No one talks to me like . . . like this. You're an evil influence. A wicked woman."

"And you are an old curmudgeon!"

For a long, horrible moment, Jonathan was rendered speechless. His heart pounded with fury as he glared at the medium who dared defy him. No woman ever defied Jonathan Noble. "I shall prove you a fraud if it's the last thing I do," he vowed. "Good day, Ruby LaRue!"

Jonathan slammed his hat atop his head, turned on his heel and marched down the stairs.

His blood boiled. Rage consumed him. A myriad of thoughts chased through his mind. Throttling the beautiful Ruby LaRue was one he particularly favored. He could almost feel his hands around her elegant, swanlike throat. Absorbed in murderous thoughts, he saw red and nothing else. Until he ran straight into Clementine, almost knocking his daughter-in-law over.

"Dr. Noble! Ah am so sorry. Ah thought you saw me coming," she said, straightening her hat, which had been knocked askew.

"I was distracted, my dear, terribly distracted. I beg your forgiveness."

"Why, ah'm downright glad to have run into you."

"Really? I must confess I'm surprised to see you here."

She gave him a dazzling smile. "Ah've come for more peppermint candy."

"Very well, then," he said, pleased that she had enjoyed his choice in sweets. "After you've made your purchase, I shall be happy to escort you home."

# *Six*

Rand passed through the academy gates on his way home just after dark. He hadn't yet shared his news with Clementine. When he returned home from Superintendent Rodger's home last night, she had already retired.

But she would not go to bed without him this evening, dammit!

If they did not consummate their marriage tonight, it would be months before the opportunity would arise again. He had no intention of waiting any longer.

A concern he dared not share with anyone weighed heavily on his mind. With Clementine's cooperation, his predicament might be cleared up before summer's end.

Rand had been married to Ellie Tidwell for almost a year before she fell ill. He and his delicate wife took advantage of every opportunity in their effort to start a family. Although Ellie did not evidence any desire or fondness for making love, she echoed his wish to have children. But she never became pregnant. When she first showed symptoms of consumption, all thoughts of having children were abandoned.

To Rand's knowledge, no woman he'd been with in his bachelor days had ever become pregnant either.

Uninvited doubts crept into his mind. The niggling concern continued to grow, taunting him. In quiet moments, he questioned his manhood. The need to prove his virility and erase the undermining fears gnawing at him were important factors in the decision to marry Clementine. As much as he wished to appease his father by honoring the ancient arrangement, Rand regarded this marriage as a way to quickly prove his prowess and set his mind at rest.

He'd accomplished neither.

Arriving home in record time, he strode into the foyer with staunch determination. Depositing his black surgeon's case, which had been his father's before him, and his uniform cap on the marble-topped table, he met with Millie and then called for his wife. "Clementine, I'm home!"

Almost as if she'd been waiting for him, she dashed from the drawing room, a vision in sage green silk. A radiant smile curved her pink lips and genuine pleasure shone in her eyes. Her seeming delight to see him gave his heart an unexpected jolt.

"You're home early," she declared.

His father emerged from the drawing room to stand behind her.

Damn. Ever since Clementine had arrived, his father had practically lived with them. The old man might as well install his butler in Rand's home.

"Hello, Father. I didn't expect to see you, but I'm glad you're here," he added hastily. Before Jonathan could reply, Rand turned to the unconventional but beaming female at his side. "Would you ask Millie to bring champagne into the drawing room?"

"Are we celebrating?" she asked.

"Yes." He grinned, barely able to contain his excitement.

"Is this a private celebration?" Jonathan asked.

"Not at all."

His father followed him into the drawing room, the room now referred to as the parlor. The chamber's dark colors and large overstuffed furnishings were completely at odds with Rand's cheerful mood this evening. But the curtains had been parted, and the breeze brought with it the fragrant perfume of the lilac bushes surrounding the house.

Rand noticed a grammar textbook lying on the settee. His father grabbed the book before he could question its presence. Immediately, the old man diverted him, quizzing Rand about the medical definition of madness.

"Do you think a person who purports to speak with the dead is in truth mad?"

"Mad, meaning insane and a threat to society?" Rand asked warily, fearing his father might be speaking about himself. At his age, Jonathan might be displaying signs of dementia.

"Yes. A definite threat."

"Have you met someone who speaks to the dead?"

"Yes. And surely she belongs in a sanatorium."

"She?" Clementine repeated, casting a crinkled frown Jonathan's way. "You wouldn't be referring to—"

His father held up a hand to stop her. "If you please, do not mention that woman's name in my presence."

Rand had no idea what or who the two were talking about.

When Millie shuffled into the purple parlor, effectively silencing both his father and wife, he let out a sigh.

After pouring and distributing the bubbling champagne, Rand raised his glass. "To the success of the eighteen hundred and seventy-eight United States Naval Academy summer cruise."

His wife and father, sitting side by side on the plum-colored settee, simply stared at him.

"You wonder why we are toasting the summer cruise?" he asked, and grinned. "Because I've been assigned as the cruise surgeon. I leave tomorrow."

Clementine's mouth formed a wide "Oh" before she jumped up from the settee. "Tomorrow!"

"Yes. Tomorrow. My hospital assistant, Dr. David Smith, will step up to replace me while I'm gone."

His father frowned. "Isn't this sudden—and rather unusual?"

"The superintendent had no choice," Rand explained. "The surgeon scheduled for the cruise met an untimely end yesterday. He was on his way to the academy when highway robbers accosted him near Baltimore."

Jonathan shook his head. "Each day the world becomes a more dangerous place."

"Indeed." Rand glanced over at Clementine, who continued to stare at him with wide, darkened eyes, as if he'd grown another head.

Unwilling to offend either his wife or father by displaying the excitement he felt, Rand suppressed his feelings in favor of further serious explanation.

"I dislike leaving you, especially on short notice. But I must obey orders. May I count on you to watch over Clementine, Father?"

"Naturally." Jonathan's dark blue eyes flashed with annoyance. "But does the superintendent understand you are newly wed?"

"Yes. He seems to believe that Clementine and I will have a lifetime together to make up this time. But since Rodgers is being replaced himself in a few days, he didn't think it right to leave the new superintendent, Commodore Parker, with a stalled cruise and a medical position to fill."

"But why not send Smith, your assistant?" Jonathan snapped.

Rand had prepared for distress, argument and resistance. However, he'd expected the angst to come from his bride. Clementine remained statue-still. He couldn't decipher the glazed look in her eye or determine with absolute certainty if she were still breathing.

He answered his father's question. "The superintendent decided against sending Smith because only the new fourth class will be here during the summer. I've trained David well enough. Rodgers and I are confident he can handle thirty or so healthy young plebes."

"How long will you be gone?" Clementine asked quietly.

"Just three months."

Both of her gently arched eyebrows shot up. "Three months is a long time."

"Originally, I joined the navy to be at sea. I love the sea just as my father does."

Jonathan responded with a fierce scowl.

"We'll be traveling along the eastern coast of the United States and into the Caribbean."

Clementine chewed on her bottom lip.

Caught up in his own excitement over the assignment, Rand had forgotten completely that Clementine's father had died during a foreign engagement. Her stricken expression reminded him and brought him up short. "And you needn't worry. The summer cruise is an extremely safe, purely educational voyage."

"The British are at war with Afghanistan," Jonathan grumbled. "The Russians have invaded Turkey, Rumania, Bulgaria and who knows where else. The world is a hotbed. Are you certain there is no possibility this cruise will turn into something more?"

"Dang," Clementine breathed. Her already fair complexion drained to a dead white shade.

"None," Rand replied emphatically. "We don't take green midshipmen into battle."

Plainly unsettled, but showing signs of life and breathing again, his red-haired bride sank down into the settee. Her light green eyes had darkened to the deepest jade.

"I'm taking the third-class engineering summer cruise," Rand announced, anxious to put his wife's and father's minds at ease. "We'll be traveling in a small steamer, the *Manitou,* visiting navy yards and shipbuilders. There's nothing dangerous in this voyage."

"And ah thought there was enough adventure in just bein' a doctor."

Rand sat on his heels in front of her, just a bit lower than eye level. He wanted her to be able to read his eyes, to see his sincerity and understand the truth of what he was saying. "I was a navy officer before I became a surgeon. But you needn't be frightened for me, Clementine. The navy would never knowingly put its future officers in harm's way. And if we found ourselves in bad straits, let me assure you that I can take care of myself. While a student, I excelled in marksmanship."

With a blink of her eyes, her vivacity appeared restored. "Ah could lend you mah derringer."

He reared back. "You have a derringer?"

"In mah satchel." She started to rise. "Ah'll get it."

"No." He laid a staying hand on her arm. She'd bragged about her ability with a Winchester. Rand had good reason to fear her expertise extended to the derringer. In the future he would think twice about angering Clementine in any way. "No, that won't be necessary. The navy supplies our weapons."

Further discussion of the cruise came to an abrupt end when Millie announced dinner. Rand could not have felt more relieved. "Would you like to join us, Father?"

The old man grinned and gave him a hearty slap on the back. "Thank you, Son. As it happens, I have no plans for this evening. I'd be pleased to have dinner with you and Clementine."

Rand had been afraid that would be the case. If his father would just marry one of the many widows always at his heels, he would not be lonely. Jonathan had been at loose ends since his retirement but was too proud ever to admit that his life was anything less than perfect.

Millie served fresh chilled oysters from the bay and her curry of lamb a l'Indienne specialty. Rand and Jonathan downed a good bit of wine in an effort to bank the fires from the curry. Clementine sipped water and avoided looking at the plate of slimy Maryland oysters.

Her thoughts focused on how best to excuse herself and flee to the garden, where she could roll a cigarette—or two. The topics of her husband and father-in-law's dinner conversation included war, midshipmen on their first cruise and essential medical supplies to carry aboard ship. The discussion did not serve to ease her troubled heart or make her less nervous.

By the time the meal ended and Jonathan took his

leave, Clementine's stomach churned as if she had eaten something spoiled, when in fact she had barely touched her meal. If she'd had any appetite at all, she would have preferred a Texas steak. And she desperately longed for a cigarette. She'd discovered that smoking calmed the nerves early on, when her brother, Junior, irritated her. The notion that women should not smoke was downright silly. Tonight, however, she had no choice in the matter.

Rand's excitement could not have burned any brighter if he were afire. The promise of adventure lured him away. While she shouldn't have been surprised—after all, he hadn't married her for love—the realization sucked the hope from her. She desperately wanted him to stay so that they could get to know each other, maybe even fall in love. But a good officer obeyed orders no matter what his situation might be. Rand was a good officer, and she felt lower than a lasso draggin' in the dirt.

At her whistling husband's insistence, Clementine followed him into his office. Perching on the leather chair used by patients, she silently marveled at the man while he packed his personal medical instruments. He exuded the rugged virility of a pirate who knew a great treasure awaited him. He'd been galvanized; he was alive with an eagerness she'd not witnessed before.

Watching him, memorizing the angles of his face and the strong set of his jaw, she knew without doubt that his riveting, broad-shouldered figure would command attention in a room filled with extraordinary males. He'd been trained to save lives and as a leader of men.

The man she'd married put Jake Edison to shame.

Jake, the cowpoke Clementine had fancied herself in love with not so long ago.

Rand worked hurriedly, every so often sliding his fingers through his dark brown hair. He'd made himself comfortable, long ago removing his uniform jacket and unbuttoning his shirt collar. He'd rolled the shirtsleeves up to his elbows, revealing sun-darkened muscular forearms.

"Can ah help?" she asked.

He flashed a knee-knocking grin. "You're helping by keeping me company."

"What do you keep in your case?"

"This is my pocket instrument case." He opened the leather case to show her. "Scalpel, scissors, probes. I'll also be carrying my own hand soap and suture needles. No surgeon worth his salt would leave home without his own pocket case."

Clementine nodded numbly.

"And my stethoscope goes into the bag." Smiling proudly, he held the instrument out for her to admire. "This is one of the newest, made by Caswell with ivory earpieces, silk-wrapped rubber tubing, silver tubes and an ebonized wood bell."

"It's mighty fine, Rand." But not as fine as the man who held the stethoscope.

His pearly, near-constant grin caused her heart to bounce against the walls of her chest like some caged wild critter.

Dear heaven, she longed with all her heart to be the cause of his excitement. Rand's raw, bone-deep masculinity swirled around her like the untamed wind. If only she could reach out and ride its dizzying, pulse-pounding current. But all Clementine could do was watch silently as he prepared to leave her. Too many times in the past she'd watched her pa preparing to return to the sea. Each time he left, he took a piece of her heart, until she felt as hollow as the shells he brought home for her. She wondered if she would feel the same when Rand said good-bye.

"I'm finished here," Rand said. "But I'll need to pack a few clothes and perhaps that picture I have of you in the hairy chaps."

Embarrassed, Clementine lowered her eyes. "They were mah favorites," she said softly.

Rand's big, rolling laugh filled the room. "And that is my favorite image of you," he said, ruffling the top of her head, setting free a clump of little curls.

Pinning the tight locks back, Clementine followed Rand to the master bedchamber. She silently observed as he removed a leather duffel from atop the rosewood armoire and threw it onto the bed.

The Chinese red chaise lounge had not yet been delivered. Nothing saved the dark room from its eggplant gloom. It might only have been her imagination, but tonight the gaslights seemed to cast an ominous glow.

The light in Rand's eyes was brighter. Everything about him seemed intensified: his constant smile, his calm explanation of a surgeon's life aboard ship. Clementine listened from a dim corner. There was nothing she could do to stop him from leaving. Her husband would not be courting her anytime soon. Neither would she have the opportunity to win his heart.

However, she *would* have ample opportunity to pry open the door of the mysterious locked room. And she would be able to engage the medium to rid Ellie's ghost from the house. Her studies with Jonathan would go undetected. But these things were a poor trade for the company of Rand, which she'd just begun to enjoy. The things she might do offered little consolation.

Midway through his packing, Rand stopped and fumbled in his trouser pockets. He pulled out a roll of bills and pressed it into her hands.

"This is for you. In case of any household emergencies that might occur while I'm away. I wouldn't want you to be short of funds."

He turned back to his task while Clementine counted the bills. "This is too much money. Ah won't be needing even a penny of it. Ah'm a frugal soul."

"Keep it just in case. Put it somewhere safe."

"Ah have a place." She dropped to her knees and pulled out her satchel from beneath the bed. If she couldn't trust Rand, whom could she trust? She felt him watching in puzzled silence as she stashed the bills into the red velvet pouch for safekeeping.

He helped her to stand. Her husband—tall, splendid, and smiling at Clementine as if he genuinely liked her—despite having had to marry her. In the silence, her heart hopped like a hare being chased by a ranch hound. But then reason returned. Rand, magnificent in every way, smiled because he could not wait to leave her—for a ship.

"Done." He swung his duffel bag from the bed.

The bed they'd never shared.

His gaze lingered on the bed. As did Clementine's.

She could hear the ticking of the grandfather clock in the corridor.

He dropped the duffel.

The time had come.

She knew then that he would take her into the bed and consummate their marriage. Clementine would be his wife without knowing her husband the way she'd wished. But she could not refuse. Rand was going away, and though he'd spent most of the evening calming her fears, danger always lurked at sea. She'd heard her pa talk of storms and shoals and unseen enemies. Whales and sharks and foreign folks waited for sailors.

The man she'd vowed to honor and obey moved closer to her. He framed Clementine's face tenderly between his hands. Her heart beat so swiftly she feared it would shatter. His eyes, bluer than the bluest sky, settled on hers.

"What is the one thing you want most in the world, Clementine?"

Before tonight, and this moment, she knew. Now, she wasn't certain at all. "Ah . . . ah don't know."

"Don't be afraid to tell me."

"Ah want to go home, back to Texas."

Ever since she'd arrived in Annapolis, returning home was all that she had wanted. So that's what she told him. But new feelings—uncommon, strange feelings—stirred within her now. She thought what she really wanted most in the world was for Rand to return to her soon and safely. But she wouldn't say it and risk making a fool of herself, not over a man who'd been forced to marry her.

Rand nodded; his gaze never wavered. "The one thing that I want most in the world is a son. If you give me a son, I'll see that you have a home of your own in Texas. Your own ranch, where you can go as often as you like."

*Her own ranch!*

A son. She hadn't thought about having children, but suddenly the idea of showing her boy how to rope a calf and ride a horse was downright appealin'. A handsome son who resembled his pa would suit Clementine just fine. Rand could teach him how to sail—as long as he didn't venture any farther than the bay.

"Ah'll . . . ah'll do mah best." She wasn't loco enough to believe that she could guarantee a son.

His blue-eyed gaze remained locked on hers, and his lips gave way to form a slow, seductive smile. An intangible, delicious heat settled between them.

The time had come. Again.

Rand lowered his head and closed his eyes. Clementine could feel his warm breath on her cheek. She could hear . . . screaming and pounding from below.

With a groan, Rand jerked his head back. Lifting Clementine aside as if she weighed no more than his medical bag, he made for the door and sprinted downstairs. She dashed after him, close on his heels. The doctoring always came first. And at the moment, she didn't know if she felt relieved or not.

Somehow Millie had made it to the door first. Jonathan's butler, Alvah, stood on the stoop shouting and flailing his arms. "The doctor is dying! Dr. Noble is dying!"

Rand did not stop to bid Clementine good-bye. He ran.

She gave chase.

Jonathan Noble had been her pa's best friend. He had been kind and had taken care of her since she'd come to town. She had only one little secret from her father-in-law. When she bumped into him in the sweet shop, she'd been on her way to see Ruby LaRue. And she didn't want him to know. Neither did she want the dear old rake to die.

Clementine would do anything to help her husband save his father. She only hoped there was no blood involved.

\* \* \*

Rand couldn't believe it had happened again. Another interruption, just as he was finally about to make Clementine his.

At two o'clock in the morning, he finally left his father's bedside. Jonathan's old stethoscope dangled around his neck, and Rand's shirt hung limply from his shoulders. He had to report aboard ship in three hours. He was dog-tired, and his wife had fallen asleep downstairs.

She lay curled up in a ball on the sofa in his father's drawing room. He squatted down to wake her. Rand hadn't required her help, but he appreciated her support. No one had ever accompanied him on a sick call before.

In sleep, her dark auburn lashes curled softly against rosy cheeks. Her lips were parted slightly, moist and inviting.

Oh, how he wanted to wake Clementine and make passionate love to her. If only he had the strength. When he made her his, he would need all his energy. He meant to take her slowly and with utmost sensitivity.

Stroking her arm gently, Rand whispered in her ear. "Come, Clementine. It's time to go home."

Her lashes fluttered.

"Time to leave, darlin'."

She rubbed her eyes with her fists like a child. "What happened? Is . . . Jonathan all right?"

"Yes. He experienced either a heart attack or a very excruciating attack of indigestion. I can't be certain yet."

"When will you know?"

"I'm afraid not until I return from the cruise. He insists that I go."

"He should stay with me while you're away," she murmured, appearing dazed and half-asleep. "Ah can look after him."

This wild woman of the West possessed a kind and generous heart. Rand smiled, thankful his bride had a caring nature. "That's an excellent idea," he said. "I'll feel much better knowing that there's someone other than servants around in case he should have another attack."

"Ah'll be happy . . ." Her voice trailed off. Her eyes fluttered closed.

"Clementine?"

She'd fallen asleep again. He hadn't the heart to wake her. Gathering her into his arms, where she fit very nicely indeed, Rand carried her the short way home. The summer night had cooled and the fragrant mixture of summer roses and lilacs perfumed the air.

Much closer at hand, he inhaled the fading fragrance of Clementine's chamomile, felt the soft silk of her dress beneath his palms. Despite his wife's hearty appetite, she weighed no more than an angel. She snuggled against his chest, and his heart constricted. Had Clementine managed what no other woman had done since Ellie died? Had she touched his heart?

When he reached home, Rand took the utmost care not to wake her. He settled the sleeping beauty into their bed and covered her with the light sheet. He would be rising early and hadn't the heart to wake her at dawn after she had stayed by his side for most of the long night.

Rand gazed down at his sweet, strange wife for one

last look. He didn't always appreciate her beauty. And he feared he had underestimated her, thrown off by her blunt, opinionated way of expressing herself and her twangy Texas drawl.

Leaving Clementine was not as easy as he had expected it to be. He leaned down and gently kissed her forehead, warm and porcelain-smooth.

"Goodnight, darlin'. The next time we meet, you will not escape from me so easily."

# *Seven*

Clementine ran to City Dock. Gasping for breath, she arrived just in time to see the summer-cruise steamer *Manitou* slowly pull out from the academy pier. She'd hoped for one last word with her charismatic husband, one last look. But that was not to be.

In the gray early morning light, the small crowd of onlookers that had gathered for a final salute cheered at the departing blast from the steamship.

"Godspeed," Clementine whispered, raising her hand in farewell, a gesture Rand could not possibly see.

Clutching her ivory seahorse in the other hand, she made a wish upon the tiny Christmas gift. She wished Rand a safe journey and good fortune while he was away.

He'd slipped from the house without waking her this morning. While she appreciated his thoughtfulness, her heart felt as heavy as the *Manitou*'s anchor. She'd missed the opportunity to say good-bye and had only a hazy recollection of the previous evening's events.

She recalled that after holding her father-in-law's hand for well over an hour and offering words of comfort, Rand urged her to wait for him downstairs. She'd fallen asleep on the sofa in Jonathan's drawing room but then woke up in her own bed. Rand must have carried her home. Her chivalrous husband possessed the strength of ten ensigns.

As she watched the ship sail out of sight, a strange emptiness settled in the pit of Clementine's stomach.

"Ah'll write to you every day," she vowed beneath her breath. "Just like ah used to write Pa."

But before she sat down to write her first letter, business awaited her.

Hurrying home, she found a penny in her path. Not one to pass a penny, she picked up the coin. As soon as she reached home, Clementine pulled out the satchel and removed her velvet pouch. Curious as to how much Rand had given her for household emergencies, she paused to count the bills. One hundred dollars! With what she'd already put away, she had more than one hundred and twenty dollars—plus a penny.

The scarlet pouch contained more than enough funds to return to Texas. If only she could. Although Rand wouldn't miss her—his interest was limited to her producing a son and heir—she'd given her word that she would take care of his father.

Clementine slid the satchel back beneath the bed and started out of the room just as the front door knocker sounded.

Her guest had arrived. "I'll answer, Millie," she called.

Now that she understood how improper it was for the lady of the house to answer her own door, doing so made Clementine feel a bit of a rebel.

"Good day, Mrs. Noble."

"Good day to you, Mrs. LaRue. Come in, please."

The attractive medium smiled softly and swept into

the foyer as regal as royalty. Innate grace softened the effect of her rigid posture.

"You have a lovely home." Ruby LaRue's admiring gaze swept the high ceilings of the foyer and the intricately carved cornices.

"It is a lovely home, but frankly"—Clementine lowered her voice to confess in a confidential tone—"it's too purple for mah taste."

Her guest arched one brow and offered a slight, puzzled smile.

"Follow me, please, and you'll see what ah mean."

Clementine ushered the only spiritualist she'd ever known into the drawing room. Without Johnathan's knowledge she'd paid a brief visit to Mrs. LaRue in her room above the sweet shop. After explaining her predicament, she invited Mrs. LaRue to the house for help.

With no more than a flickering glance, the darkhaired medium bobbed her head, bouncing her thick sausage curls. The peacock feathers swooping from the side of her forest green hat looked as if they might take flight of their own accord. "I understand. The color is rather dark for a woman of your sunny disposition."

"Purple was Ellie Tidwell's favorite color."

Ruby's index finger fit perfectly in the dimple of her chin. "Does Ellie Tidwell live here?"

"No. Well, no."

"I believe that you are the lady of the house now."

"Yes. Ah suppose . . ."

"Therefore you may make any changes you feel necessary."

"But ah wouldn't feel right without Rand's approval. This is mah husband's house, and he left today for three months at sea."

"I see."

"Please sit down, Mrs. LaRue."

The medium perched on the settee, studying the room.

Clementine sat beside her. "Do you read minds?"

"I beg your pardon?"

"Do you know what ah'm thinking or what ah'm going to say before ah actually do? Because if that's the case, ah'll just be quiet and let you work. However that is that you work."

Ruby gave her a warm smile. "My ability to read minds is limited. Please talk to me."

Clementine puffed a small sigh of relief. "Well, in that case, this is where ah feel Ellie most. Her ghost roams the entire house, but she seems to like this room the most."

Ruby nodded. "Yes. I feel her here too."

Cold chills skittered down Clementine's back, causing her to shudder. "You do?"

"Most certainly."

"Ellie has no reason to be here that ah can see. A mighty big stone with two cherub angels carved from marble marks her grave in the cemetery. Why is she not residin' there?"

With a wag of her head, Ruby released her own sigh. "I'm not certain. Ellie Tidwell may have passed over, but she has never left this house."

Fearing the worst, Clementine hesitated before she asked, "Will she ever leave?"

Nodding her head, Ruby adopted a businesslike manner. "I believe she might be persuaded to go. We shall talk with her and discover why she lingers. If we know her reasons, more than likely we will be able to negotiate."

Unwilling to admit being jealous of a ghost,

Clementine nonetheless made her request. "Ellie must be gone by the time Rand returns."

"I can make no promises. I can only try."

"Can you try at once?"

Ruby's amber eyes softened with understanding. She laid a comforting hand on Clementine's arm. "First we must plan a proper seance."

"Seance?" Without truly understanding the meaning of the word, Clementine agreed with an enthusiastic nod. Swallowing hard, she proceeded to do something completely out of character. She did not ask the cost of a seance. Ridding the house of Ellie Tidwell's ghost was worth all the funds cached in her velvet pouch.

"Yes, a seance is my recommendation."

"Ah'm prepared to plan this instant." Instead of asking Ruby to name her fee, Clementine rang the silver bell to summon the housekeeper. She asked Millie to bring them tea and biscuits.

As soon as they were served and the wary housekeeper had closed the door behind her, Clementine wasted no time in getting down to the business at hand. "Is this the best room to hold the seance?"

"I think the drawing room shall do nicely," Ruby replied. "But I have not seen the second floor. Does Ellie frequent the chambers above too?"

"Oh, yes! Ah've even felt her presence in the master bedchamber."

Ruby tsked. "I should like to visit your bedchamber if you will allow me."

Willing to do whatever was helpful to the medium, Clementine guided Ruby upstairs.

"What a lovely, spacious home," the seeress declared. "You shall be able to raise a large family here."

"Ah . . . ah guess so. Do you have any children?"

"Yes. I have three: two boys and a girl." Once again,

Ruby's professional demeanor evaporated, lost to a loving smile. "They are my life."

"Being a medium, you must have expected them. Knew if they'd be a boy or girl and what color hair they would have and the like?"

"Let us just say that there were no surprises," she chuckled.

"Does your husband help with your boys?"

"No." She lowered her eyes for a fleeting moment. "My husband died years ago."

"Oh, ah'm sorry. Ah didn't mean to be a meddlin'—"

"Please don't fret. It's been several years now. Henry died in a carriage accident. But he lives on in my heart and through the children. I'm grateful that he left me with children."

Clementine felt a swell of admiration for the pretty medium. Supporting and caring for three children must be difficult at best. Mrs. LaRue's one small room above the sweet shop did not look large enough to accommodate three youngsters, but Clementine tempered her curiosity and did not ask about their living arrangements.

"You must be a remarkable woman, raising children by yourself. Ah don't know anything about bringin' up a young un'."

"For the most part, the rearing comes naturally. Your heart tells you what to do."

Ruby's quiet counsel and encouraging smile made Clementine feel better. Perhaps she could fulfill Rand's request. If she gave him a son, he might not think of Ellie quite as much.

She opened the door and led Ruby into the warm room. Even though the drapes had been fastened

back, the light breeze provided no relief. "This is mah
. . . our bedchamber."

"My, it *is* purple," the spiritualist commented dryly.

"A chaise lounge is being delivered today from
Dixon's Dry Goods Emporium. And it's Chinese red,"
Clementine blurted.

"Chinese red? A good start. You would do well to
brighten up the other rooms in the house. It's the
perfect time to freshen up, while your husband is at
sea."

"Ah don't know."

Ruby splayed long, elegant fingers against her hips.
"Take it from me, men know nothing of these things
and don't care a fig about them either."

"Ah . . . ah don't reckon as ah know how to spruce
up the looks of a room any. Back home in Texas the
best ah could do was nail my ma's samplers to the
wall."

Ruby's steady gaze settled on hers. "Would you like
me to help?"

"Ah don't think ah could afford—"

"Clementine, I would not charge for helping to give
your home a new appearance."

"Ah would be much obliged." Clementine grinned.
She'd gained a new friend. The connection of like
spirits felt strong and good. They were two outsiders
living in an insiders' city.

"Believe me, it will give me great pleasure," Ruby assured her. "And the less of Ellie's influence in the
house, the happier you shall be. There is no reason
for every chamber to resemble a plum. If you replace
her selections with furniture and colors that you like,
Ellie Tidwell will have even more reason to leave—for
good."

"Of course!"

Her new friend's reasoning was so sound, Clementine didn't know why she hadn't thought of it before. But then, she had. And swiftly rejected the idea as silly. Folks from Oddon, Texas, didn't know Romanesque from Renaissance or the color buff from a bronze green shade.

After returning to the drawing room, Clementine and Ruby discussed various methods to improve Rand's home with color and comfortable furnishings. Clementine learned a great deal from her new friend, who quickly felt like an old friend, oddly enough. One hour drifted into two as they chatted over tea and biscuits. Lost in plans, she was only vaguely aware of time, until close to the hour that Jonathan and his butler were due to arrive. Too close.

Begging another appointment, she regretfully brought the delightful visit with Ruby to a close.

The medium rose, head held high in her usual proud manner. "I completely lost track of time myself."

"Before you leave, ah must run upstairs for a minute."

"Don't run," Ruby cautioned with a wag of her finger.

"Ah know." Clementine sighed. "Ah must slow down and walk sedately, like a true Annapolis lady."

"Well," the medium grinned, "you might want to put a little wiggle in it."

Laughing, Clementine started up the stairs. She glanced at the grandfather clock in the entrance hallway and discovered to her horror that Jonathan would be arriving at any moment. Her father-in-law would have another attack if he found Ruby here.

The knocker sounded.

Clementine's heart skipped. She'd been too slow. Imminent disaster loomed from walking like a lady.

"I shall answer," Millie called out. "'Tis my job, after all."

Clementine hovered on the landing, hoping that by chance the chaise delivery had preceded Jonathan's arrival. No such luck.

When Millie finally appeared in the foyer, she opened the door to Jonathan. Clementine's heart sank.

Jonathan swept off his top hat with the flair of a true gallant as he strode through the doorway. "Good morning, Millie."

His butler, Alvah, followed carrying two sizable leather satchels. Alvah gave Millie a smiling but silent greeting. Her father-in-law did not appear to be sick, nor in pain. Whatever attack he'd experienced the night before seemed to have vanished. Nevertheless, well or ill, she must show Jonathan to the guest room before he discovered Ruby LaRue in the drawing room.

Clementine proved too slow once more.

Ruby made her presence known, sailing into the hall. Impervious and beautiful in her forest green walking costume, she advanced on Jonathan like a queen to a knight. "Dr. Noble. I thought I recognized your voice."

"You." He uttered the one word in a deep, accusing tone. His forehead contorted into a most forbidding frown.

Bad blood hissed between the two. Clementine could taste the tension. She dashed to stand between them as they glared at each other. "You've met," she stated cheerfully.

Ruby replied without removing her chilly gaze from

Jonathan. "Dr. Noble called on me at my place of business."

"Monkey business is what you do, madam," he snapped.

"Please," Clementine coaxed, "do not upset yourself, Jonathan." She then turned to Ruby. "Just last night my father-in-law suffered either a heart attack . . . or a debilitating case of indigestion."

"Indigestion," Ruby bristled. "Your bile is backing up, Dr. Noble."

Jonathan's chin jerked upward, along with both dark brows. "I beg your pardon."

"A judgmental man is bound to suffer from his own bile," the medium informed her outraged nemesis. "However, I might be able to help you."

"There is no one I wish to speak with on the other side!" Jonathan growled. "If that's how you intend to help me."

"I meant that I would help you understand how professional mediums like me offer assistance to their customers."

At that Jonathan turned his frown upon Clementine. "Have you been hoodwinked into becoming a customer of this woman?"

"Ruby has helped me already," Clementine confessed in a quiet tone.

When the door knocker sounded again, Clementine whirled about. The tension between Ruby and Jonathan had put her on edge. She eyed the door warily, wondering if she should welcome or decry the diversion. Having little choice, and hoping for the best, she opened the door.

"Delivery from Dixon's Dry Goods."

The best had arrived: her Chinese red chaise lounge. "Oh, yes! Come in." She opened the door wider, issuing a plea beneath her breath to the warring doctor and spiritualist. "Please be kind to each other while ah am gone. Ah'll only be a minute."

Jonathan regarded Ruby with resigned disdain. "We should move out of the way and make room for the delivery."

"Yes, we should," she agreed in a stilted tone. "Perhaps we should remove ourselves to the drawing room?"

Jonathan handed his walking stick to Alvah and followed the medium as she glided ahead of him.

Clementine watched for a moment, holding her breath, waiting for the next unkind word or an explosion. A moment ago, Ruby had been ready to leave, but with the appearance of Jonathan, she'd stayed. Curious.

The house fell silent except for the grunting deliverymen. Their sounds of distress reminded Clementine of what she had been about. "Oh, ah do apologize. Follow me."


Jonathan followed the trailing silk train of Ruby LaRue's gown into the drawing room. He noticed it was the same gown that she'd been wearing yesterday when he'd asked her to leave town.

The uppity medium sat on the settee by a table of tea and biscuits. Jonathan sat as far away as possible, in a wing chair by the fireplace.

"Would you like tea?" she asked. "I don't believe Clementine would mind if I poured."

"No, madam. No tea."

"Very well. The biscuits are delicious. I highly recommend them."

He scowled. Ruby LaRue was a fine-looking curvaceous woman with remarkable golden eyes that telegraphed a keen intellect. Only a dead man wouldn't notice the charlatan's attributes, bold, beautiful and astonishingly proud. For a woman of her ilk. But Mrs. LaRue was little better than a thief. Behaving like some high-handed lady of the manor would get her nowhere with him. Jonathan recognized her for what she was, and he wouldn't allow her to take advantage of Clementine.

"Don't think you can rob my daughter-in-law blind," he warned.

"I don't intend to do anything of the sort," she huffed. "I like Clementine, and I shall help her find peace."

"*You* shall help her find peace?" He snorted.

"Something you could use some of yourself."

"I am perfectly content."

"Do not attempt to deceive me," she argued with a dismissive flick of her wrist.

The woman was impossible.

"You are restless and bored," she told him.

She was not far from the truth.

"Do you truly think my attack last night resulted from indigestion?" he asked quietly.

"Yes."

She sounded very certain.

"Sometimes it is difficult for a doctor to doctor himself," he muttered.

The medium inclined her head and pursed her lips. Her lips were the color of Clementine's new chaise lounge, a vivid, clock-stopping red. Deciding the vixen's mouth might be dangerous territory, Jonathan tore his gaze away to fix on the dark curls that brushed her shoulders. Silver strands threaded through the fine raven mass in a most striking manner.

"What did you have to eat yesterday?" she asked.

"Millie's special curry."

"Aha!" Ruby threw up her hands. "Spicy food along with a good head of angry steam will do it every time. You were quite irritated when you visited me, Jonathan. The combination of an ill spirit and a spicy meal led to your attack."

The brazen hussy thought she knew it all!

"Have you forgotten? I am a doctor, madam."

"Heal thyself then, Doctor. Do not let unwarranted rage send you into a conniption."

Leaning back, he crossed his arms over his chest and folded one leg over the other. "If you will leave town as I requested, I shall have nothing to irritate me."

"For a wise man, you are behaving foolishly."

Jonathan reared up. "How dare you talk to me in that manner?"

"For your own good, sir."

No woman had ever given him a set down. He was beyond reproach. He enjoyed a reputation as an intelligent, well-traveled man with excellent manners and a lively wit. Widows and single women adored him. Except for this poor, deluded female. Intimidation had not run her off, had not even seemed to faze her. He had nothing left in his arsenal but charm.

"Clearly, I have misjudged you, Mrs. LaRue. That you would care about my well-being after I issued a tyrannical ultimatum is extraordinary. I beg your forgiveness."

Instead of smiling and fawning as he expected, Ruby blew out a weary sigh. "Have you had an unfortunate experience with a spiritualist in the past?"

"My intelligence forbids me to believe that you, or anyone, can talk with the dead."

"Is it truly a terrible thing, if speaking to those on the other side eases the pain of those still living?"

She confused him.

"Don't tell me dead people speak through you," he protested.

Ruby shot him a smile. "I won't. I should not like to be the cause of another attack. I expect that indigestion can be quite as painful as a heart attack."

Jonathan thought her remarks condescending, but he couldn't be certain. There was much more to this woman than the simple sign that proclaimed her a medium.

"Yes, it is painful. Quite," he said at last.

The clock in the hall sounded twelve times.

Clementine worried she'd been gone too long. Although it had only been a matter of minutes, she feared Ruby and Jonathan might have skewered each other. She hurriedly showed the deliverymen where to place the new chaise. They were also removing the old lounge, which she had donated to the church. Believing the men capable of following her instructions, she left them to their work.

On Rand's first day away, his home was in turmoil. Thankful that he would never know, Clementine rushed downstairs, determined to prevent hostilities in the drawing room. But she found no signs of war. Ruby sipped tea and Jonathan regarded the plate of biscuits with a hankering eye.

Grateful for the reprieve, she gave a little Ruby-inspired wiggle as she strode into the room. "Ah beg your pardon. Funny how everything seems to happen at once, isn't it?"

"How does your new chaise look?" Ruby asked.

"The delivery fellows are placing it now."

"Rand will like it, my dear," her father-in-law said.

"And if he does not, fear not," the seemingly fearless medium added. "He will become accustomed to your colors, your taste, your way of doing things."

Jonathan shot her a reproachful frown.

"I hope you're right, Ruby." The last thing Clementine wanted to do was displease Rand. Oddly enough, she missed him already.

Ruby rose to leave.

Jonathan, ever the gentleman, stood.

"Thank you for the tea and biscuits, and a lovely visit, Clementine. I shall see you soon," Ruby promised as she swept from the drawing room. Pausing at the door, she turned and leveled a challenge. "Dr. Noble, do take care of yourself. Let nothing upset you. We are all in this life together."

Throwing his shoulders back, Jonathan lifted his chin. "Rest assured. I can take care of myself. Madam."

Clementine breathed a sigh of relief after seeing Ruby out and Jonathan to his room. She liked them both; if only they could like each other.

Moments later, she watched the deliverymen cart out the old purple chaise. The beginnings of many changes were underway. She could feel it in her bones. On the way back to her bedchamber, she sedately climbed the stairs. A true test, for, eager to see the new Chinese red chaise installed, she would rather have scrambled upstairs.

More importantly, she could not wait to sit down and write a letter to her husband.

# Eight

*Dear Husband,*

    *Your pa appears to be fit as a fiddle. But he's agreed to stay with me for a few days to be certain his heart is beating the way it should. I suspect, by staying, Jonathan believes he is protecting me. When I am certain his heart is strong, I will show him my derringer. He should know that I can protect myself.*

    *The weather is hot and humid, just like in Texas. The heat reminds me of one day in July when my pa came home from sea duty. He dug a ditch a mile deep and a mile wide. The spring water that sprung up wasn't too clear, but Pa said it would do just fine. He added some pond water to the hole and splashed around for days getting himself cool. He said we ought to move to the oceanside, where we could have all the cooling water we wanted, but Ma flat-out refused. She was a Texas gal. And my pa would do anything to make my ma happy.*

    *But he said as how I should learn to swim. One day he tossed me in the center of his swimming hole, clothes on and all. I went under like a chunk of lead and came out sputtering water that tasted like old boot socks. Swallowed more than I liked, too! That water was so cold and sharp, it stung my skin like a swarm of bees. I made my way to the edge, but I rightly couldn't tell you how.*

   *Never mind that Pa didn't know how to give a decent swimming lesson. He was a good man. I hope you don't hold it against him and Jonathan for arranging this fix we find ourselves in. They meant well. And I'll try my best to be a good wife.*

   *Wishing you a safe journey,*

                     *Clementine Noble*

Rand grinned. "Ah, darlin'," he murmured aloud, "you've done it again."

No complaints. Instead, her letter had brought a smile to his face. But if he wasn't mistaken, a swimming hole in the middle of Texas read like another of Clementine's tall tales. The idea of Roy Calhoun digging a ditch a mile deep and a mile wide right over a cold spring amused him, however.

Rising from his narrow bunk aboard the steamer *Manitou*, a relic of the Civil War, Rand made his way across his cramped cabin. At the last minute, before leaving home, he'd stashed the only daguerreotype he owned of his bride in his black surgeon's case. At the time, he wasn't certain why he'd done it. Staring at the picture now, he realized that despite the big hat and hairy chaps she was wearing, it helped him to visualize Clementine in the act of writing the letter. He conjured plump pink lips, obstinate copper curls and sparkling green-meadow eyes. A pretty package, he thought, by most men's standards. Raising the envelope to his nose, Rand inhaled. Could he smell a trace of chamomile?

He hadn't expected Clementine to write to him. But from the start, Roy Calhoun's daughter provided one surprise after another.

The good news regarding his father's health did much to ease Rand's mind. At the time, he strongly felt that Jonathan had suffered from a particularly bad case of indigestion. But owing to his father's age, he hadn't been able to rule out a heart attack.

The practice of medicine had improved greatly since he first began to study, shortly after Ellie's death. Still, medicine remained a developing science, and there was much even the best doctors neither knew nor could explain.

He'd been at sea when Ellie's symptoms began. He applied for emergency leave and returned to Annapolis. From that moment on, Rand never left his fragile wife's side, escorting her to doctor after doctor. But none could do anything to save her. No one could cure consumption.

After Ellie's death, Rand entered medical school under the navy's auspices. He'd been a guilt-racked widower, determined to save lives, to make up for failing Ellie. And he had failed her. Just nine months after their marriage, he'd signed on for an Atlantic crossing.

The bitter, propelling truth was that, disappointed in his marriage, Rand had taken refuge in his naval career. He'd fled like a coward. Although Ellie's letters spoke endlessly of her loneliness, he'd dismissed his wife's grievances as petulance. Owing to her habit of complaining about most everything, Rand had turned a deaf ear . . . until it was too late.

Ever since, he'd lived with deep remorse. As self-imposed penance, he had vowed to keep Ellie alive in heart and mind for as long as he lived.

He hadn't counted on another woman absorbing his thoughts. Especially one who rolled cigarettes and swam in the desert.

\* \* \*

Clementine started each day with prickly fear. The thought of losing her rugged, handsome husband before she truly knew him disturbed her more than she let on.

This morning was no different. After piling her breakfast plate high with bacon, eggs, potatoes and two flaky biscuits heaped with butter and honey, she sat down at the long table and simply stared at her food. Clementine had lost her appetite.

In every way, Rand provided the very best of what money could buy. She'd never lived in such luxury. And yet, without him, she felt more a pauper than ever before.

Jonathan caught her in contemplation.

"Good morning, my dear."

She forced a smile. "Good morning."

Jonathan had not left the house since he had come to stay with her. Apparently, his attack had frightened him more than he would admit.

Summoning a discipline she'd not been aware that she possessed until now, Clementine waited patiently for her father-in-law to leave. She'd resigned herself to wait until Jonathan returned to his home before insisting Ruby conduct the promised seance. Unwilling to risk being caught in the act, she'd also put off prying open the door to the mysterious room. But if he didn't leave soon, she would be forced to bring out her derringer.

He appeared to be in a cheerful frame of mind this morning. "A penny for your thoughts," he said with a conspiratorial wink.

"Mah thoughts are not worth a penny," she said, finding it impossible not to return his smile.

"Come now!"

"Ah was simply chastising mahself for having eyes far bigger than mah stomach this morning."

"You wouldn't be worried about Rand?" he asked, filling his plate from the sideboard.

"No, not at all."

"My boy is well able to take care of himself."

"Against the forces of nature?" she countered.

Clementine knew the oceans possessed a vociferous appetite. The sea swallowed ships whole, carried good people to icy depths.

"There are no more dangers on the sea from storms than there are on land," Jonathan said, taking a seat opposite her at the table. "For most of my navy career, I was a shipboard surgeon, you know. I traveled thousands of miles over the Atlantic and Pacific oceans. In all my days at sea, I never suffered so much as a scrape."

"You were fortunate. Not everyone is so . . . lucky."

Visibly shaken, Jonathan reached over and placed a warm hand over hers. "My dear, when I heard that your father died at the Salee River in Korea, my heart broke too. Roy was a long way from home, and the skirmish was quite unexpected, but he was doing what he loved. You must always remember that."

"Pa loved the sea," she acknowledged softly.

"As does Rand. Adventure calls to certain men. They are born to it." Jonathan withdrew his hand and dug into his breakfast with his normal gusto.

Clementine hoped it was the adventure in Rand's soul that had led him to the sea and not a desire to get as far away as possible from her, his embarrassing Texas-born wife.

"Mah pa came home as much as he could," she

said, dismissing thoughts that Rand had taken the first opportunity to leave her.

"I wish I had been as good a father to my son as Roy was to you and Junior. I didn't come home often enough," Jonathan admitted with a regretful nod of his head. "I was off too frequently, leaving Rand to the care of nannies."

"He loves you. Ah see it in his eyes."

"Our relationship was strained for a time. But my boy possesses a forgiving spirit. He has never spoken of my neglect—for which I am grateful."

"You have what every man desires, a good . . . son."

Her father-in-law nodded in agreement as he sipped at his steaming coffee. "Rand and I actually became close after Ellie's death."

At the mention of Ellie's name, Clementine felt an odd, piercing pain. It was like being stuck with a sharp hatpin straight through her heart. And it was all she could do not to gasp from the sudden shock of it.

"Rand must have loved Ellie very much," she managed to say after a moment.

Jonathan busied himself adding sugar to his coffee. "Her illness was difficult for him. Rand felt helpless."

"Ah understand."

"And you, my dear, are the best thing to happen to my son in years," he declared with a cheerful change of tone.

"And you are a smooth-talkin' devil, just like your son."

Smoothing a hand over the silver hair at his temple, the old man shot her a wry smile. "Where do you think Rand learned? As they say, the apple doesn't fall far from the tree."

"And you are both full of juice," Clementine chuckled before she was struck with a serious thought. "Do you think you might remarry someday too?"

"Highly unlikely. Rand's mother, the lovely Rosalind, captured my heart when I was but a boy of eighteen. She died in childbirth before Rand cut his final baby tooth."

"Ah'm sorry."

"For my son's sake, I had thought to remarry."

"But you didn't."

"I could not decide upon just one lady to love!"

Clementine found herself laughing again. Jonathan's teasing banter, sparkling blue eyes and bemused smile were contagious. "You are incorrigible."

"But I am becoming an excellent instructor. Shall we have a grammar lesson after breakfast?"

"Ah-ah-ah have an appointment," she stammered.

The frown that deepened the crevices of his brow took the form of a question, demanding an answer.

"Ruby and ah are shopping for fabric and ordering some items from the catalogue today."

"Ruby?" He stiffened. "You are spending far too much time with that woman."

"She has a good heart, Jonathan."

"A larcenous heart."

"Mrs. LaRue supports three children. Did you know that?"

Her father-in-law's head snapped up. His eyes met hers, and then he hid his surprise behind a frown. "In that case the woman should find a respectable occupation."

Plainly there was no sense talking to him about Ruby. For some reason Mrs. LaRue brought out the judgmental worst in him. "What will you do today?" Clementine asked, changing the subject.

"Before the sun grows too warm, I shall pay a call on

my tailor. I should like to wear my new waistcoat to the Markhams' dinner."

Clementine had almost forgotten the prized invitation. In a few days' time, the Markhams would host the social event of the season. As delighted as she was to be included, she feared doing or saying something that might embarrass Rand. All of Annapolis society would attend the Fourth of July celebration, and all eyes would be on her.

"Might we have an elocution lesson after dinner?" she asked. "Ah know you're improvin' my diction. Ah'll never fit in if ah sound like ah just stepped off a train from Texas."

"My dear, it shall be my pleasure."


Jonathan felt perfectly fit as he left his son's house on the way to the tailor. After a period of time the truth became clear. He'd officially diagnosed his previous indisposition as a cruel case of indigestion rather than a heart attack. He swung his walking stick as he swaggered along beneath the sheltering canopy of oaks.

Taking leave of Clementine's company had become the rub. He had not the least desire to return to his large, empty house. He enjoyed having someone to talk with and look after. Heaven knew, his daughter-in-law did not need his protection. If any woman could take care of herself, it was Clementine.

And that one.

Jonathan came to a full stop.

Ruby LaRue sailed down the street toward him carrying a large brocade satchel at her side. Like a magnificent figurehead adorning the bow of a ship, she led with her chin. Her neck extended like that of an elegant swan rather than the dark, preying vulture that he knew her to be. The medium's icy imperiousness rankled him no end. Her round hips, flashing eyes and bold, ruby red lips enticed him beyond good sense.

"Good morning, Dr. Noble." She slowed but did not make any effort to stop.

Tipping his hat, Jonathan stepped in front of her, forcing the pretentious woman to a halt. "Mrs. LaRue."

She tilted her head, brazenly scrutinized his person from head to toe before meeting his gaze directly. "Are you out for a morning constitutional?"

"I require no constitutional."

"Your bile is better then?"

"I have not suffered indigestion in several days," he informed her. Her satchel moved.

"That is good news." She gave him a perfunctory smile. "I am happy for you, but I must be on my way."

She started around him. She was hiding something in her satchel.

Once again, he blocked her path. "Madam, I should like you to stop seeing my daughter-in-law."

Sudden fury sparked in the golden irises of Ruby's eyes. "First you had the audacity to demand that I leave town. Now you wish to sever my friendship with Clementine. Tell me, sir, what *have* I done to earn your animosity?"

"Until Clementine is established in Annapolis, her reputation must remain unblemished. She cannot be seen with a clairvoyant."

"You are too late with your warning. We have been seen together all over town. Besides, I am a medium. I have no clairvoyant powers. If I did, I would have known you would be walking on this street and avoided running into you by taking another route!"

The temerity of the woman took Jonathan's breath away.

"You fill Clementine's head with foolish ideas," he accused.

"Your daughter-in-law's thoughts are her own. She possesses an independent nature and is not influenced by others."

"You mean to tell me that she has not asked to speak to her father through you?"

"No. She has not."

"I don't believe you."

"Dr. Noble, I regret that you do not believe me, nor like me, but I am very happy that Clementine and I have become friends. I shall continue to help her in any way that I can."

Ruby LaRue's satchel barked.

Jonathan narrowed his eyes on the brocade bag. "What do you have in there?"

"Nothing for you to be concerned about."

"Nothing sounds very much like a dog."

She heaved a sigh. "Well . . . it is. It's a gift for Clementine."

"Let me see."

She held out the satchel.

He opened it. A small black, shaggy dog with stubby legs and eyes that could barely be seen peered up at him.

"A puppy," he intoned, as if the meddling medium had just shown him a bomb.

Ruby reasserted herself. "Clementine needs a companion while Rand is away."

Jonathan stiffened. "You do not consider me to be a companion?"

"Do not be offended, Dr. Noble, but Clementine is younger than either you or me. A more playful companion will do her a world of good."

As much as he hated to admit it, the haughty spiritualist might have a point. "Where did you get this animal?"

"My children have a dog, and this pup is from her litter."

"Clementine mentioned that you had children. I did not see any evidence of them in your room above the sweet shop."

"Not that it is any of your business, but my children live with friends on a farm not far from here."

"Perhaps, for your children's sake, you should settle down and find good, honest work. You might qualify for a position as a seamstress in Miss Adelaide's shop," he suggested.

Ruby shot him a look that told Jonathan quite plainly that she thought him an arrogant fool. "For your information, I do not know how to sew, nor do I seem to have a talent for it. Just because I am a woman does not mean that I was born with a needle and thread in one hand."

Despite her impertinence, he refused to yield. "Can you bake? Or teach school?"

"Neither pursuit interests me."

"You would make an excellent nanny," Jonathan offered, wildly searching his mind for occupations that provided a woman with opportunities to earn a living. The raven-haired beauty must be able to do something other than communicating with the dead.

Ruby pursed her fine scarlet lips, scorching Jonathan with a fiery gaze. "Whether you like it or not, I have one gift."

A gift for unnerving men. He grunted.

The puppy whined.

"And believe it or not, Dr. Noble, I am able to bring contentment and peace to those who seek my help."

Ignoring her claim, Jonathan blurted, "I know what you can do."

Tilting her head, Ruby eyed him warily. "Pray tell."

"Find yourself a husband."

She gasped. But she only lost her composure momentarily. Balling her free hand on a hip, she lashed into him. "Tell me, where should I look for this husband who will happily support three children who are not his?"

"I . . . I am certain . . . there are men who . . ."

Shaking her head in despair, as if she'd never met such a dull-witted man, Ruby let out another long sigh. "You simply do not live in my world, nor can you understand it. Good day, Jonathan."

He had no choice but to move. The angry glimmer in the medium's eyes told him she would just as soon go through him as around him.

Dipping his head, he stepped aside. "Good day, madam."

The puppy barked excitedly as the woman walked away, leaving Jonathan standing on the street, alone and disgruntled.

She had a way of doing that. Disgruntling him.

The woman was not a medium. She was a witch.

# Nine

*Dear Clementine,*

*I am writing to you from Fort Sumter in the Charleston harbor.*

*Your letters have been welcome. I rest easier knowing that my father is well, that you are faring admirably and that Annapolis remains where I left it.*

*I regret that the dangling legs spoiled your first experience eating soft-shell crabs. You should give our delicacy another chance.*

*So you have taken in a puppy. There is nothing to equal the companionship of a dog, but I would suggest that you discourage Princess from hiding under your skirts. And may I ask why have you named a mixed breed Princess?*

*In answer to your question, as yet there have been no exciting adventures to report. At the beginning of the cruise, I treated the midshipmen for seasickness. Now they come to sick bay with minor cuts and bruises. Fortunately, to this point there have been no unusual medical problems with officers or students.*

*Rand*

Clementine added Rand's letter to the small bundle she'd been keeping. He only answered one letter to every six of hers. Still, with each response she learned something new about him. From the very first moment her eyes met his, she knew she'd married the most handsome officer in the United States Navy. But during the short time that they had together, she'd gleaned little beyond what she could see. And what she could see had been branded in her mind.

Simply envisioning his tall, lusty form and the teasing twinkle in his eyes made her heart flutter like the wings of a sparrow learning to fly. The wry twist of his lips that nearly always preceded a soft, deep chuckle sent delicious warm shivers cascading through her body.

What Rand felt, what he thought, what he liked and disliked had been a mystery to her until now. Now, in the evenings when homesickness and loneliness came upon her, Clementine retired to her chamber and reread his letters. Somehow, as she traced her fingertips lightly over the words he'd written and learned another truth about him, she felt closer to her striking husband. She thumbed through the last letters he'd written.

*Dear Clementine,*

*You asked what my favorite food is. Oysters. Raw oysters. I like to buy a sack fresh from the oyster men on City Dock. You should try them. Have cook mix up some horseradish witOh that new ketchup for dipping and trust me, you shall have a gourmet delight.*

Trust him about raw oysters? Never.

If the information in Rand's responses was not clear, Clementine went directly to her father-in-law.

"Jonathan, what does gour-met mean?"

*Dear Clementine,*

　*Here we are in Key West, Florida. It's one of the navy's major North American ports, but you feel as if you are in an exotic foreign country. Deep green palms reach up to a vivid blue sky. No artist, not even Winslow Homer, can duplicate the beauty found here in the tropics. Cubans arrive each day, fleeing from the revolution at home.*

"How many tropic states are there, Jonathan?"

*Darlin',*

　"*I performed surgery of sorts at sea today. The sail master received an accidental head wound that required twenty sutures. Each day three midshipmen help me to scrub the sick bay cabin down. After reading Louis Pasteur's theory on how germs promote illness, I am certain that cleanliness prevents infection.*

　*You asked how I relax. Currently, I am rereading one of my favorite books, "Twenty Thousand Leagues Under the Sea," by Jules Verne.*

"Jonathan, who is Jules Verne?"

The exchange of letters between Clementine and Rand could hardly be compared to the loving correspondence between Barrett and Browning, two poets to whom Jonathan had introduced her. Nevertheless, the missives marked a beginning. Clementine saved each letter from Rand, no matter how brief.

She had trumped the ghost in one respect. Ellie was in no position to write Rand letters and provide news from home. But whether he enjoyed receiving them or not, Clementine had no way of knowing.

After binding the letters together with pink lace ribbon, she stashed them in the drawer of her bedside table and left the bedchamber. As always, Princess scampered behind, close at her heels.

The house was quiet, the corridors dark. A summer storm had stalled over Annapolis. Most of the windows had been closed against the raging storm. The close air felt suffocating. Thunder rumbled and lightning skewered across the ash-dark sky. Clementine told herself the cries of the house, the creaks and groans, were caused by the pounding rain, not by Ellie.

But it was a perfect day for wandering ghosts, a perfect day to open the door to the mysterious room and discover what secrets it held.

Princess barked up at the window where lightning lashed across the sky.

Clementine held a finger over her lips. "Hush," she warned.

Jonathan had gone out earlier, and she didn't want Millie to come investigating. Alone at last, she could do what she'd been aching to do for weeks.

Sinking to her knees, she stuck the end of the pick into the lock and slowly turned. The ice pick slid out. "Dang."

The cowardly puppy scurried about looking for a way to hide beneath her skirts. Clementine had promised Jonathan that she would eliminate "dang" from her vocabulary, but sometimes it just felt right. Biting down on her tongue, she focused her entire concentration on opening the door of the secret room.

A door slammed downstairs.

She jumped. And bit her tongue.

In a doomed attempt to land in her arms, Princess leaped at her, causing Clementine to lose her balance. She fell backward, hitting her head on the floor.

Whining in apology, the puppy wiggled all about her, licking her face.

Every sound and event that could not be easily explained, Clementine blamed on the ghost of Ellie. Apparently, Rand's dead wife didn't want anyone trespassing in the locked room. But a bump on the head couldn't stop Clementine.

Rising to her knees, she attempted to peer through the small space of the keyhole.

"My dear, whatever are you doing?"

"Dang!" Clementine screamed and threw up her hands simultaneously.

Jonathan caught one hand, preventing her from falling again. He pulled her to her feet, clucking softly. "Forgive me. I did not mean to frighten you."

"Ah . . . ah thought you had gone to the barber."

"I changed my mind. The weather is too nasty. Do you need help?"

"Yes. Ah've misplaced the key." She held out the ice pick. "And ah . . . need to . . . measure for new drapes . . . for this room."

With his gaze pinned on the ice pick, Jonathan hiked a dark brow. "Knowing how to think quickly will take you far in life."

Clementine took his droll remark as a compliment.

But after several minutes of alternating a gentle touch with brute force, Jonathan stepped back. "I think you will have to hire a locksmith to open this door."

Clearly, Ellie was preventing Clementine from gaining entrance to the chamber. The ghost of Rand's first wife was hiding something—which only made Clementine more determined to break into the room.

"Ah will. This is the only room in the house that Ruby and ah have not made over."

"Some things are better left untouched. Undisturbed."

Jonathan's admonishment caught Clementine off guard. She had not considered the possibility of incurring Ellie's wrath by opening the door. The consequences might be truly alarming. Ghoulish moaning during the night. Doors opening and closing without reason. A ghost could retaliate in numerous frightening ways.

Nodding in agreement, she chewed at the corner of her lip. "You never fail to give me good advice, Jonathan."

He smiled. "Age brings a certain amount of wisdom."

She could wait another day to hire a locksmith.

Her father-in-law started to turn away but stopped, addressing Clementine over his shoulder. "Is that woman coming by this afternoon?"

Jonathan always referred to Ruby as *that woman*. "Yes. Ruby has offered to help me dress for this evening's Independence Day celebration at the Markhams'."

"The medium has many talents."

Clementine ignored his snide remark. "Do you think the storm will postpone the gala?" she asked. She hadn't meant to sound so hopeful.

"No. This is a summer squall that will pass soon. What time will Mrs. LaRue be here?"

"She promised to come following her afternoon appointments."

Jonathan groaned. "Do you mean to tell me that the good citizens of Annapolis are actually paying that woman to speak with their dead relatives?"

"Yes. And they feel better for it. Ruby has explained it all to me. You see, when death comes unexpectedly, the things left unsaid and the apologies not made can fester and torture the survivors. When what is needed to be said is said, the spirit may rest in peace and the living can carry on with their lives."

"That woman has an answer for everything," Jonathan offered testily. "She could justify robbing a bank."

"Ruby has been very helpful to me," Clementine asserted, staunchly defending her friend.

"Perhaps. But I fear she aids you for her own nefarious reasons."

"Ah don't understand why you are so cynical when it comes to Ruby. Neither can ah fathom why you have taken her in such dislike. If you don't mind me saying so, Jonathan, you have been unfair to Ruby from the instant you read her notice in the sweet-shop window."

"You are too innocent to understand. And you're the only reason I tolerate Ruby LaRue." He scowled as he said the medium's name. Straightening his shoulders, he started toward the guest room. "We shall leave promptly at seven this evening for the Markhams'."

"Ah shall be ready."

Clementine had mixed emotions about the evening's shindig. As well as marking her official debut in Annapolis society, the Markhams' dinner and summer social was the single most anticipated event of the summer.

She looked forward to seeing Liz Markham but knew that in all probability Sarah Tidwell would be there. Ellie's high-falutin' spinster sister filled her with dread. Sarah literally looked down her nose at Clementine.

Despite her misgivings, she resolved to do her best to make Rand proud of her this evening. She meant to look her best and pattern her behavior after the most circumspect Annapolis lady.

Ruby arrived in the late afternoon to assist with her preparations. She spent hours combing and arranging Clementine's hair in the latest style. The untamable copper locks were tamed, swept back and anchored with pins, combs and bows at her crown, tumbling to her shoulders in a mass of ringlets.

Taking advantage of Ruby's insight, Clementine selected a modest, mint green silk gown with fishtail skirt and train. The snug bodice featured a high collar of delicate lace.

"You will be admired for your conservative dress," Ruby told her.

"Ah had thought to purchase a new gown," she said, viewing the girl in the looking glass with a critical eye. She had decided against spending Rand's hard-earned money on a frivolous gown when he wouldn't even see her.

"You look beautiful," Ruby said.

Clementine whirled away from the mirror. Butterflies had taken her stomach captive. "Please, go over the place settings again."

"If you cannot remember anything else, Clementine, work in from the outside. Start with the last fork and work your way toward the plate."

Clementine did not understand how Ruby knew the many and silly rules of dining and dinner parties, but she was thankful to her friend. Someday she meant to ask. In the meantime, she assumed the knowledge had been derived from Ruby's clients, both living and those dwelling on the other side.

As Ruby made ready to leave, she withdrew a small silk-wrapped parcel from her reticule. "I brought this for you to keep with you tonight."

Clementine unfolded the fabric to find a small evergreen sprig with two white berries. She studied it curiously. It looked familiar, but she could not place the type of plant. "What is this?"

"Mistletoe."

"A Christmas flower?" she asked, bewildered. "Mistletoe in July?"

"The mistletoe promises more than a kiss. It holds magical powers. The legends go back centuries, Clementine. Keeping the mistletoe close to you this evening will protect you from any enemies."

"Like Sarah Tidwell?"

But Ruby did not confirm her fear. "According to legend, mistletoe is Frigga's plant, the goddess of love. The Druids first used it to call a truce with their enemies. All past grievances were forgiven—and forgotten—with a show of mistletoe. No petty cruelty will touch you tonight if you keep this sprig close."

Rather than argue that she had no enemies, Clementine tucked the mistletoe out of sight, into the valley between her breasts. Denying she had enemies seemed senseless in the light of Ruby's gift of insight. She might very well have "seen" something that Clementine did not, could not, know. Unwilling to take any chances, she allowed superstition to rule and thanked Ruby for her gift of mistletoe.

Success tonight was extremely important. With that thought in mind, she dropped her small ivory seahorse into her beaded reticule. She wished to have all available help.

The squall had blown over early in the afternoon, leaving time for the grass to dry. The cool, rose-scented air lent itself to a summer celebration. Jonathan ushered his daughter-in-law up the steps of the Markhams' imposing Georgian mansion. Ablaze with candlelight, the large, ivy-covered brick home sparkled with the jewels of Annapolis's most respected residents.

Laughter, music and the savory aromas of a feast flavored the atmosphere.

"Rand would be proud of you tonight, my dear," Jonathan murmured, hoping to assure her.

"Ah don't want to do anything, or say anything, to embarrass him."

"You won't."

"Ah'm nervous."

He patted her hand. "You know all you need to know. You have been a bright student."

"Do ah still sound like a Texas cowpoke?"

"The soft trace of your remaining accent is like a dash of spice. It adds to your charm," he assured her.

"And ah do know where Havana, Cuba, is . . . if anyone should ask."

When Jonathan first started tutoring Clementine, it was obvious that she had known her figures. She could add and subtract quickly. He'd provided the most help by introducing her to great literature and world geography. She'd devoted long hours to improving her diction. But now she studied by herself. She had no need of him. No one did.

The moment they passed through the drawing-room door, Clementine had turned heads. She was beautiful. Her copper hair gleamed gold in the light, and the soft green shade of her dress complimented her eyes. Jewellike, her eyes danced with excitement.

The freckles that had been pronounced upon her arrival in Annapolis had faded to the point where he almost could not detect them.

Grudgingly, Jonathan silently admitted that Ruby LaRue had been just as instrumental in Clementine's transformation as he. Many times he'd heard her insist that Clementine bring along a parasol on their outings. Roy Calhoun's daughter was not the same tough-as-saddle-leather young girl who had arrived from Oddon, Texas, several weeks ago. In just a short time, she'd blossomed into a lovely, quite remarkable young woman.

Liz Markham greeted them effusively, immediately whisking Clementine away to meet the mayor of Annapolis.

Jonathan watched the ladies glide across the room. When his son returned, he hoped that Rand would appreciate his wife and the changes she'd made for him. Winning Rand's approval meant a great deal to Clementine.

"Jonathan, how good to see you!"

The overly painted woman laid a hand on his arm, effectively bringing a halt to both his progress and his reflection.

"Laverne." He gave her his most charming smile. "What a pleasant surprise. I didn't know you would be here this evening."

She rapped his arm with her fan. "Everyone who is anyone attends the Markhams' Fourth of July celebration."

"Quite right."

"Are you still living with your daughter-in-law?"

"I will be returning to my home tomorrow, as it happens. But if Clementine should need me, I am still close by, of course."

"Clementine appears to have adapted well to Annapolis. But I do find her manner of speaking quite amusing."

He drew himself up to his full, imposing height. "Her manner of speaking is the same as yours, Laverne. Although she does not gossip."

Laverne's winged brows furrowed into a puzzled frown. Within seconds the frown passed, giving way to a shrug and an abrupt change of topic, one closer to her interests.

"Jonathan, it has been too long since you have come to see me. I am entirely well and prepared to make your visit enjoyable." She paused to slant a flirtatious smile. "We will play checkers again, and other games."

Boring checkers. Boring small talk. Attractive, but boring, Laverne. The blood pumping through his veins seemed to still. What was he thinking? Jonathan had never found women boring before. Although he could not blame his strange thoughts on indigestion, he once again feared for his health.

"Laverne, you are too kind," he said, surveying the room for escape. "Ah! You must excuse me for a moment. I see the surgeon who is replacing Rand and must discover how he fares."

Drawing a deep breath, he fled from the widow Hawthorne.

Oysters and soft-shell crabs were served for dinner along with baked ham, corn and fresh hot biscuits. Beer flowed for the men, wine and lemonade for the women.

Clementine longed for a beer. She yearned to roll a cigarette and calm her jumpy nerves. The thought of making small talk tore at her innards. She feared to speak for saying the wrong thing. But she must. She knew she must. Shamelessly superstitious, she counted on her lucky little seahorse and a small, dry twig of mistletoe lodged uncomfortably between her breasts to bolster her courage.

At dinner, she found herself seated between Liz Markham and David Smith, the assistant academy surgeon. Jonathan sat across from her, and Sarah Tidwell perched like a bird of prey beside him. The dour woman appeared ready to spring on Clementine at the very hint of any infraction.

Clementine pressed a hand against her chest, pressed the prickly mistletoe sprig against her skin. She silently invoked the magic of mistletoe to keep her safe from Sarah's sharp tongue.

After dinner the guests retired to the garden to watch the fireworks display. What appeared to be hundreds of candles and flaming torches shed their light over the Markhams' garden, a sloping field of thick green grass overlooking the harbor.

The fireworks exploded over the bay in a glimmering show of light and color. Never having seen fireworks before, Clementine gawked unabashedly. Her heart thumped hard with every boom. She made no pretense of disguising the awe she experienced. If only Rand could be here.

"So, how do you fare without your husband?"

Clementine started. She had not heard Sarah come up behind her. She turned to Ellie's sister, replying quietly and truthfully. "Ah miss him."

"Ellie missed Rand too. He was always away when she needed him."

"It's difficult to need someone and not have them there," Clementine replied. She understood well. There were many times when she'd needed her pa, and he'd been away too. It was the nature of navy men. She'd learned not to need her pa, but she'd never learned not to want him. She supposed she might feel the same about Rand someday.

Sarah's dark gaze gleamed forbiddingly as her eyes narrowed on Clementine. "My sister wasn't tough like you."

*Tough?* "Riding a horse or roping a calf doesn't make a woman tough, Sarah. Ah'm not tough."

"We'll see."

"It's difficult for a man to be in two places at one time. Ah am certain that even while Rand was away, Ellie was always in his heart."

And she still was, as far as Clementine was concerned.

"You can never replace my sister, you know," Sarah sniffed.

Clementine winced in the shadows. "Ellie must have been very extraordinary."

"A pretty girl too. Rand chose Ellie because he loved her. His father chose you," Sarah pointed out spitefully. "Everyone knows about arranged marriages."

The dark, evil woman implied that Rand didn't love Clementine and never would. She needed no reminding from Sarah Tidwell. Tears she refused to shed in front of Ellie's sister welled in the back of her eyes. If she let her tears loose, Sarah would learn she was anything but tough.

Raising her chin, she forced a smile. "Ah shall do mah best to be a good wife to Rand. The type of wife Ellie would have been had she lived."

"You want to be like Ellie?" Sarah sounded incredulous.

"Could ah aspire any higher?"

The spinster's thin lips parted in a half-smile. She appeared puzzled, but pleased, by this turn of events.

"No. No, you could not," she said, and drifted away.

When the fireworks ended, Liz returned to Clementine's side. "Come, I have promised everyone that you will be telling a Texas tale."

"You did?"

"I have been looking forward to this part of the evening all day."

Clementine told her story. She finished to hearty applause, and once again Liz asked her to sing. This time she had piano accompaniment when she sang, "Home on the Range" and somehow it didn't sound mournful.

Flushed with success but still vastly relieved when the dancing began, she tucked her hand in Jonathan's arm as he led her to the floor for the first dance.

"You are an excellent dancer, my dear," he said after circling the floor.

"Ruby taught me to waltz."

He glowered down at her. "Is there anything that woman doesn't know?"

Clementine returned a bright smile. "No. Ah don't think so."

"There's more to Ruby LaRue than meets the eye. And if it's the last thing I do, I intend to discover just what she is hiding."

Before Clementine could reply, the Naval Academy Hospital's assistant surgeon, David Smith, cut in. The handsome young doctor idolized Rand and appeared to admire her as well.

For the remainder of the evening, Clementine did not lack for dance partners. She discovered that French wine tasted better than her brother's home-brewed beer, and the laughter she shared was far more fun than the cigarette she might have rolled had she been alone.

Clementine scored her final triumph of the night by demonstrating and leading a square dance with Dr. Smith. Flying on the wings of her delight, she called as she danced.

The laughing group of dancers clapped and reeled and do-si-doed.

"All the way forward . . . and all the way back!"

One scowling face stood out in the small audience gathered to watch. Refusing to be intimidated, Clementine ignored Sarah Tidwell's obvious displeasure.

At the end of the rollicking square dance, the chorus of "Yahoos!" could be heard all the way down to City Dock. She'd successfully introduced a new form of entertainment and laughingly proclaimed everyone who participated official, "genuine Annapolis dudes."

Shortly after midnight, Clementine left the party on her father-in-law's arm. But her feet never touched the ground. Her spirits soared, and her gratitude for making the evening a success belonged to Ruby LaRue, her lucky seahorse and the magic of mistletoe in July.

Clementine felt certain that Rand would hear of the Markhams' Independence Day gala. The city was small, and its residents enjoyed gossip. Her husband would learn that her formal debut into Annapolis society had been a grand accomplishment—and she'd done it Texas-style. She felt like one of the fireworks, ready to burst and light up the sky.

Jonathan patted her hand as they strolled down the gaslit street toward home.

"You won many hearts tonight, my dear." A ring of pride laced his tone.

"Ah . . . ah hope so. Ah think so."

"I know so," Jonathan stated unequivocally.

A sense of acceptance surged through Clementine, warming her. Yet winning one heart was all that really mattered. His heart. Rand's heart.

# *Ten*

Clementine's success at the Markhams' Fourth of July celebration led to a full calendar of activities. The next six weeks sped swiftly by as she attended garden parties, picnics and ice-cream socials. Enjoying a popularity she'd never experienced before, she accepted every invitation except when asked to sail.

Jonathan and Dr. David Smith both offered sailing lessons. She refused the offers with the same arguments. She could not swim, and sailing did not interest her. Sailboats were known to capsize, and treacherous summer storms came up quickly. She preferred to feel the earth beneath her feet.

Although she enjoyed watching the sailboats on the bay from a safe spot beneath the protective shelter of a parasol, her fear held fast. If she could tame a maverick horse, she thought she might be able to sail a boat . . . as long as it wasn't on water.

Clementine neglected to mention it in her letters to Rand, but with Ruby's help, and keeping to a strict budget, she had completed refurnishing the house. The rooms soon took on a new personality. A warm, light buff shade of paint and whimsical wallpaper replaced purple walls in the sitting room. Airy lace replaced heavy velvet drapes and splashes of Chinese red or terra cotta brightened even the darkest corners. Spool-turned maple furnishings replaced the oversized, overstuffed selections made by the previous mistress of the house.

Rand's housekeeper watched the start of the transformation with a disapproving eye, but by the time the process was completed, Clementine felt she had at last won Millie's approval.

The difference in colors and styles worked like magic. Ellie Tidwell's presence no longer dominated the house. But until the last trace of Rand's first love had been removed, Clementine would have no peace.

The *Manitou* was expected to return to Annapolis any day. The welcome news strengthened Clementine's resolve. Before her husband arrived, she must unlock the only door closed to her. On the chance that something shameful lurked behind the mystery room's locked door, she'd decided against hiring a locksmith.

Millie had gone to market and Princess had been banished to the back garden. Clementine, a mallet in one hand and the ice pick in the other, regarded the locked door for about the one-hundredth time.

At the moment she raised her mallet, the door knocker sounded.

"Dang," she whispered beneath her breath.

"Clementine!"

A smile immediately chased away her annoyance. Help had arrived in the person of Ruby LaRue, a woman who never stood on ceremony.

"Ah'm upstairs. Come up."

"Is it opened?" the attractive medium asked as she reached the landing. "Have you unlocked the door?"

"No. Ah could not call upon a locksmith as Jonathan suggested. And ah have looked everywhere—including places ah should not have been—for the key to open it. Time is running out. There's only one thing left to do."

"What is that?"

"Break down the door."

Frowning, Ruby pursed her lips. "I don't know, Clementine."

"This is the only chamber where Ellie's spirit can hide. Ah can hardly feel her presence in the other rooms anymore. If we open the door, we can hold a seance there, and you can speak to her," Clementine coaxed. "You might persuade her to leave once and for all."

Ruby appeared doubtful. "I don't believe we're strong enough to break down the door."

"Ah have roped and wrestled calves to the ground and run more than one polecat off the ranch."

"Some time ago. You may have lost your strength since leaving Texas," her friend argued.

"If we each put a shoulder to the door, ah'm certain we can push it down. The pick and mallet won't be needed."

"Well, all right," she said, giving a small puff of resignation. "But if Jonathan should come by, you will explain to him that this wasn't my idea, won't you? That man blames me for a change in the weather."

"'That man, that woman,'" she mimicked. "Ah don't understand why you two can't get along."

"He *is* impossible, isn't he?"

"Only when you are about, it seems."

Ruby's only comment was to arch a disbelieving brow. "My shoulder is to the door. What next?"

Facing the medium, Clementine positioned her shoulder against the door. "Ah shall count. On the count of three, push with all your might. One. Two. Three."

Ruby turned red in the face, and the muscles in Clementine's shoulder ached with a biting pain, but the door did not budge. The only results from their efforts were a creak and a crunch.

"Let's try again," Clementine urged. She'd never been one to give up easily.

"I hope what we find will be worth the injuries," Ruby exclaimed.

"One. Two. Three."

A definite splintering rent the air.

Clementine's pulse raced from the exertion, and her body tingled with anticipation. "It's almost open. One more time and the door will give way. Are you ready?"

"How will we explain how this happened?"

"Ah shall hold Princess responsible. One."

"No one will believe you."

"Ah shall claim she chewed on the door so that ah had to have it removed and a new door installed."

"You have never fabricated before."

"Nothing has been this important before. With Ellie gone, Rand and ah can start anew when he returns."

"If he forgives you for breaking down the door."

"Two."

"Where is the puppy?" Ruby asked.

"Most likely digging in the garden. Princess has a bad habit. Three."

"I am sorry to hear that. Would you like me to take her back?"

"Oh, no. Ah love her. Heave."

The door splintered at the hinges and listed open.

"We did it," Ruby whispered in a tone of disbelief.

Clementine sucked in her breath. Her heart hammered against her chest in a jolting rhythm. A sense of deep foreboding fixed her feet to the floor. Transfixed, she regarded the door as if a sack of rattlesnakes waited on the other side.

"Ah'm going in now," she said softly. Taking a deep breath, she slid through the opening, into the unknown.

As she looked about her, she exhaled slowly. The secret chamber was not the shrine to Ellie that Clementine had been expecting.

The room was a nursery, shrouded in cobwebs.

A cradle made of cane sat squarely in the center of the room. Clementine ran a palm over the powder blue quilt, soft as a baby's skin to her touch, and dusty. Not far from the cradle, a lovely dappled gray rocking horse, sporting a genuine horsehair tail and mane, waited for its rider.

An extraordinary feeling of sadness weighed her steps as she walked to the rear window. The secret chamber boasted four windows, and if the panes were not all caked with dirt, it would have been a bright and sunny room. Using her fist, she rubbed a circle in the grime and cleared a bird's-eye view of the garden. The summer garden boasted dozens of tall, yellow, black-eyed Susans.

"Ellie isn't here," Ruby said quietly as she reached Clementine's side.

"Ah know."

And as surely as she knew her own name, Clementine knew that Rand had prepared this room for the son he'd been expecting. The wet heat of tears gathered at the corners of her eyes. She knew he wanted a son, but she had not realized how desperately. Within the walls of the abandoned nursery, she could taste the dreams denied and the bitter disappointment her husband had suffered. Her heart constricted as if it were caught in the folds of an iron curtain.

The musty, barren room held little but dusty dreams.

Clementine would never be able to explain to Ruby or herself what she did next. She withdrew a handkerchief from the sleeve of her dress. After wetting it with her tongue, she wiped away enough of the dirt caking the windowpane to allow a single streak of sunlight to shine into the nursery. And then she pushed up on the window until it opened. A soft summer breeze blew through the open window, bringing a welcome breath of fresh air and into the nursery.

Wordlessly, she turned and hurried from the room.

Ruby pulled the door shut behind them as best she could. "I shall fetch a carpenter to fix the door on my way back to the sweet shop."

"Must you leave? Ah thought you had come for tea."

"I have an appointment with Laverne Hawthorne. Do you know her?"

One of Jonathan's discarded loves. He hadn't been seen with Mrs. Hawthorne for weeks. Clementine expected that was because he'd become too busy fussing and fretting over the medium's continued presence in town—and in his daughter-in-law's life.

"Ah'm acquainted with her. She is an old friend of Jonathan's, though ah do not think he visits with her any longer."

Ruby balled her hands on her hips. "This will be the third woman wanting to know why Jonathan keeps to himself. They suspect a woman and expect someone on the other side is watching for them and can tell them who the interloper might be."

"Evidently his reputation is deserved. They say that Rand is the son of a rake, you know."

The medium rolled her eyes heavenward. "A rake? I believe that is called an understatement."

As they walked down the stairs together, Clementine came to still another important decision. "Ruby, ah would like for you to hold a seance now. Rand will be back at any time. If any trace of Ellie remains in the house, we must send her on her way before he returns."

They had reached the front door. Ruby's gaze settled on Clementine before she nodded. "Do you have plans for this evening?"

"No. This evening would be an excellent time."


Jonathan feared he suffered from some insidious form of dementia. During the past month, he'd neglected every woman friend he had in the city. He'd become obsessed with Ruby LaRue. He'd become obsessed with her undulating hips and scarlet lips. Her attributes occupied his otherwise intelligent mind when he lay in bed at night. He contemplated her enigmatic smile, a bare parting of lips which spoke clearly to him: You have met your match, Dr. Noble.

Clementine believed the sun rose in Ruby LaRue. Nothing he had said dissuaded his daughter-in-law from considering the opinionated charlatan to be a fine woman and dear friend. Clients—mostly women, he'd noticed—continued to flock to the medium. She was too busy to leave town. Without any sign of remorse, she took payment for her imaginings as would any actress. He continued to be appalled.

Jonathan considered the woman a bubbling caldron of contradictions. She behaved like one born to wealth but bamboozled innocents in order to feed her children. If the story of her children was true.

Sons and a daughter may have sprung from her imagination as well. He intended to discover the truth. He wanted to know all about Mrs. Ruby LaRue, the medium. She fascinated him.

This morning he threw off the robes of retirement to become a private investigator, his own Pinkerton Agency. Employing utmost caution, Jonathan followed the raven-haired pretender to his son's home, where she visited with Clementine. The epitome of discretion, he hung back in the shadows as he trailed her back to the room over the sweet shop.

Jonathan was still lurking in the bookstore on the opposite side of the street when Laverne Hawthorne sashayed into the sweet shop. It was one of the warmest days of the year, and yet he felt a chill of alarm shoot down his spine. A few minutes later, when he observed Laverne standing at the window of Ruby's room, he experienced what might be a life-threatening case of heartburn. A moment later, Jonathan consoled himself. His old arrogance had got the better of him. Ruby and Laverne would not be discussing him. Laverne must be seeking contact with her departed husband. After all, the sassy medium conversed with the dead, and he was very much alive.

He thought Ruby would never leave her room. Three more ladies called on her after Laverne. The streets had grown dark when the bell tinkled over the sweet-shop door, marking her departure. Keeping to the dim recesses of doorways and ducking behind trees, Jonathan followed at a safe distance. It soon became evident that she was returning to his son's home, and swiftly.

Shortly after Ruby had been admitted to the house, candlelight appeared in the front drawing room. He moved closer, darting to the bushes where he could keep a close surveillance under the cover of darkness and the dense shrubs. Fortunately, the windows of the room had been opened to let in the evening breeze, and he could hear every word of the women's conversation. With the merest bit of stretching, he could see them as well.

Ruby and Clementine sat across from each other at the small card table in the center of the drawing room. Instead of lighting the lamps, several candles had been scattered about. His quarry placed a single beeswax candle in the center of the table.

"Take my hands," Ruby instructed.

Clementine obeyed, her expression oddly somber. The candle flickered between their arms.

He could make out Ruby's head moving, as if she was surveying the room. "Ellie Tidwell Noble, are you here?"

Son of a gun! Did she expect that poor dead girl to answer? A hoax! It was all Jonathan could do to hold his tongue. The spurious medium dared perpetrate a hoax in his son's home. He should put a stop to it this instant.

"Ellie, we would like to speak with you," Ruby coaxed in a soft tone. "We wish to give you peace."

But he was curious. He edged closer.

"We wish to release you from earthly bonds."

Jonathan heard a thump, as if a book had fallen from a shelf. But he could not see.

"What was that?" Clementine asked in a frightened whisper.

"Ellie," Ruby replied. "Perhaps she's trying to frighten us away."

Or more likely they'd been jolted by Millie the housekeeper walking into the hat rack in the hall, he thought. She hadn't been steady on her feet in months.

"Ah . . . ah think ah felt the table move," Clementine reported in a hushed and quaking voice.

Hah! If she had, Jonathan held Ruby LaRue responsible.

The vixen with the dimpled chin calmly continued, speaking as if Ellie had joined them at the table. "Clementine has married Rand. She has attempted to make this house her home, and she is desirous of making her marriage successful. But, Ellie, you stand between Clementine and Rand."

"Please, Ellie—"

"Let me do this," Ruby warned. After a long, quiet moment—spent, Jonathan supposed, in composing herself or listening to the deceased—she continued. "Ellie, if you love Rand and wish him a life of happiness . . . you must leave and take your rightful place in heaven with the angels."

Jonathan swatted a mosquito. The pesky insects were eating him alive.

As it happened, it would take more than a stern warning and a ghost to still Clementine. She spoke next. "Please, Ellie. Ah know Rand will never love me the way he loved you. But ah want to be a good wife, and . . . and mother. Unless you free his heart by leaving, he'll never let me in. Please, won't you give us a chance?" she pleaded.

Jonathan thought his heart might break. Clementine believed Ellie stood between her and Rand. She wanted children. He might have a grandson at last.

And Ruby took shameful advantage of his daughter-in-law's gullibility. He must put an end to this at once.

Ruby picked up the conversation. "You were a sweet, kind person in life, Ellie."

Another long moment of silence passed. A mosquito buzzed by Jonathan's head.

Ruby finally spoke. "Thank you, Ellie."

He looked up in time to see Clementine lean toward the medium and ask in a hushed voice, "What did she say?"

"She said she will go. She admits that she has tarried too long, but wanted to make certain that you would be a good and loving wife to Rand."

"Oh, ah will. Ah shall be the best wife."

In the dim light of the candle, Clementine's face glowed with happiness. Stunned by the transformation, Jonathan could only stare. She'd honestly believed the house to be haunted, and now she believed the interfering ghost had been banished.

A mosquito settled on his nose. He couldn't risk slapping it and giving away his presence.

"Good-bye, Ellie," Ruby said. "Rest with the angels. Rest in peace."

"Good-bye, Ellie," Clementine repeated.

Ruby LaRue had done nothing but suggest the ghost of Ellie Noble had left the premises.

"Do you think she's truly gone?" Clementine asked in a breathless tone.

Jonathan dashed to the front door and pounded like a madman. Millie, admonishing him with a frown, admitted him and showed him to the parlor.

All the lights were on now, and a deck of cards lay on the table between Ruby and Clementine. The moment of confrontation arrived. Everything looked so innocent, he wasn't certain how to begin. Confessing that he'd eavesdropped did not seem as good an idea as it had when he lurked in the bushes.

Clementine appeared disconcerted, her smile forced. "Ah wasn't expecting you, Jonathan."

Smiling broadly, he blustered, "Just passing by on my way home and thought to stop to inquire of your day."

"Oh?"

"I dined with several of my friends. Male friends."

Ruby arched one dark, flaring eyebrow. "I wasn't aware you had male friends."

"You hardly know me, madam."

"That's true." Ruby stood up. "I must leave now, Clementine. I am staying with my children tonight."

Jonathan seized the opportunity to meet the bamboozling medium's children, if they actually existed. "I shall accompany you. A lone woman should not be walking anywhere after dark."

"I have walked by myself after dark many times."

"This will be one time such a course is not necessary."

"I warn you, Dr. Noble, I do not fancy being berated into ill-humor all the way to the farm."

"We shall discuss the weather," he promised.

"Another time, perhaps."

He had no choice but to follow the stubborn woman home—at a safe distance.

Rand stood on deck as the *Manitou* steamed into the Annapolis harbor. The late summer sunset brushed wide orange-red swaths of color across the sky.

As soon as the ship had been spotted, the townspeople had flocked to City Dock. Relatives of the officers had gathered at the yard's pier. Although he could not see her yet, he knew Clementine waited for him. Her last letters had spoken of how happy she would be to see him. He'd enjoyed her letters. In lonely moments, they'd provided company. Rand looked forward to each new port, knowing there would be mail from his wife waiting for him.

But she wasn't the only one writing letters to him. Sarah Tidwell wrote several times. She'd told him how Clementine had become the belle of Annapolis. She'd reported that some gossips speculated his assistant, Dr. David Smith, had replaced him in more than just one area.

He didn't take Sarah seriously. For one thing, she resented Clementine and would feel the same about anyone who became his wife. Further, his bride had written him loyally, two letters a week without fail. Ellie had never written so often when he was away.

Through the exchange of letters, Rand had learned more about Clementine, about what went on inside that strong-willed head of hers. She was more than a soft drawl, sunset curls and a dead aim. She possessed a generous heart and sharp intelligence.

Happy to be home and feeling more alive than he had in weeks, Rand strode down the gangplank, searching for Clementine and his father.

"Yahoo!"

He'd found Clementine.

She waved a white parasol above her head. His father stood beside her, wearing a wide grin.

In less than thirty seconds, Rand closed the gap. For the first time in memory he felt awkward with a woman. He couldn't suppress his grin, but he waxed as green as a schoolboy, unsure of what to do. Should he kiss his bride, embrace her or politely greet her as he would an old friend? He'd considered the possibilities before, but had been stymied. He had yet to come up with the answer.

Clementine solved his dilemma.

Throwing her arms around him, she gushed into his ear, "Ah'm sorry, ah completely forgot mahself. Ah truly did not mean to yell 'Yahoo!'"

Rand inhaled the familiar scent of chamomile and felt his heart buckle. He wrapped his arms around her slender body.

"Welcome home, son."

His father. Clementine stepped back and Rand reached out to shake Jonathan's hand. "You look well, sir."

"I am well, and I feel so much the better now that you have returned safely to us."

"It's good to be back." And he meant it. He relished the familiar comfort of the firm, green Annapolis earth beneath his feet. But struck by the irony of the turnabout, Rand grinned.

He and his father had reversed roles. When he had been a boy and Jonathan was out at sea, he had worried, feared he might be orphaned. Now it was his father who worried when Rand shipped out.

Clementine locked her arm through his. "Let's go home."

He couldn't seem to stop grinning. "Let's."

Within the hour, he was back in his garden, surrounded by ragged rose bushes. Evidently, Clementine did not clip blossoms or pull weeds. Cooled by a soft summer breeze from the Severn, he and his wife and father sipped sweet pink lemonade.

The new black shaggy puppy positioned herself at Clementine's side and eyed Rand menacingly. Only a glint showed where her eyes should be, covered as they were with wooly black fur. But Rand could feel the dog watching his every move. Whenever he spoke, the puppy bared her teeth. It quickly became plain that if he wished to get close to Clementine ever again, he must make peace with Princess first.

By way of breaking the ice and demonstrating to the puppy that her mistress liked him, Rand's gaze settled on Clementine. "So, you have redone the house."

She smiled proudly. "Mah friend Ruby helped me."

He had seen only a glimpse of the first floor, but all the colors that Ellie had loved so much had been painted or wallpapered over. The new light colors and modern furniture served to brighten the darkest corners of his Georgian home. It was no longer the same house where sickness and death had prevailed. But the refurbishment undertaken and completed in his absence felt like a betrayal of Ellie's memory.

His flesh prickled as if he had rolled in a field of briars. But he held his thoughts and said only, "You have a good and artistic friend."

"Well, I wouldn't be too hasty there, my boy—"

"Jonathan!" Clementine cut off his father with a sharp command and furious glance.

Jonathan raised his hands like a criminal caught in an unlawful act. Something for Rand to look into later. For the moment he only wanted to look at his wife.

Clementine wasn't the girl he'd left behind. She'd blossomed into a beautiful woman. In her frothy white dress, she looked as close to an angel on earth as he had ever seen. His gaze kept drifting to the scooped, lace-edged neckline revealing a tantalizing glimpse of cleavage.

Her eyes were upon him. Meadow green, glistening-after-the-rain eyes promised Rand a cool, plush resting place. To his surprise, all but a few of her freckles had disappeared. Her fair, Dresden complexion contrasted in startling, breathtaking fashion with the cinnamon curls that brushed past her shoulders.

"Millie has made your favorites for dinner," she said.

He had no interest in eating.

"You must look forward to resting," she added.

He had no interest in resting either. He had other plans.

"As a matter of fact, I am rather weary."

His father, scratching at the nape of his neck, took the cue. "And I must be on my way."

His spirited wife set down her lemonade and leaped from her chair. "I'll see to dinner immediately."

Rand and Clementine dined alone by candlelight. He noticed that she barely touched her meal. Hungry for her alone, his food remained untouched as well.

"You look lovely, Clementine."

She beamed with pleasure, a smile that melted his heart. "Thank you. And-and you look very . . . handsome."

After being separated for more than eight weeks, he wanted her more than ever. But could he hold this ache within him at bay long enough to court her as she wished? He barely possessed the patience for small talk. "What happened to your Texas drawl?"

She shrugged, one corner of her mouth turning up in a shy smile. "I've been working hard to lose it. I wanted to sound like everyone else. People used to laugh at the way I sounded."

"No."

"Yes."

"I miss it." And he did.

"Ah thought my accent embarrassed you."

"You could never embarrass me."

He pushed back his chair and stood up. His gaze

never left Clementine's magnificent eyes. He extended his hand to her.

Her lips quivered as she contemplated his outstretched hand.

"Shall we go upstairs?" he asked softly.

# *Eleven*

Jonathan felt like an ant at a picnic, scarcely noticed and immeasurably unwanted—as far as Rand and Clementine were concerned. Even a fool could see that they only had eyes for each other. Their separation apparently had led to a new appreciation of each other. While he was happy for Clementine and his son, he found his role of third party somewhat disconcerting.

After taking his leave, he found himself with nothing to do, nowhere to go. And he itched all over from the mosquito bites he'd received while observing last evening's seance from the bushes. The worst were the bites he couldn't reach.

His choices were limited. He could return to his empty house, or he could walk Ruby home—if she would allow him. He'd learned from following her the night before that she walked a long way to reach her children each evening. The farm, located on the northwestern outskirts of Annapolis, proved to be an isolated destination.

Even though she earned her livelihood in a questionable manner, Jonathan would hate to see any harm come to her. Ruby was an attractive woman, one who should not be walking alone after dark.

Perhaps he could take her to dinner at the Lion's

Inn before setting out for the farm. Warming to the idea, he hurried up Main Street toward the sweet-shop. He had a block to go when he saw Ruby and Lucy, the sweet-shop owner, come out of the shop. After a brief embrace, they parted ways. Ruby headed up Main toward Church Circle, and Lucy returned to her rooms above the shop.

Fearing the fleet-footed medium might quickly out-distance him, Jonathan used the walking stick he carried as a stylish accessory to increase his speed.

The cool evening air marked the end of summer and eased his uphill exertion. Salt from the brackish waters of the bay scented the light breeze. Inhaling deeply, he filled his old sea-dog lungs with his favorite essence.

When he drew close enough for her to hear, he called out. "Wait up, Mrs. LaRue!"

She stopped, looked over her shoulder. Her body stiffened; she tilted her head. Jonathan did not need to look into her eyes to know she regarded his ap-proach with suspicion. A wave of shame swept over him. He'd earned her distrust.

Although he'd never noticed her dressed in any-thing but her forest green walking outfit and the summer gown she wore tonight, Ruby always looked fashionable. A jaunty straw pillbox hat, adorned with a large coral bow, perched atop her dark hair. Her printed eggshell silk dress featured a long bodice that fell below her hips in the current style. Coral pleats bordered the high lawn collar and gave the hem and cuffs of her gown a striking finishing touch. The eggshell and coral colors complimented Ruby's olive complexion in a most breathtaking manner.

In the beginning, Jonathan had been convinced that Ruby was an evil charlatan. But she had proven to be a good friend to Clementine. And when he had followed her to the farm the other evening, he'd deduced by the reception she'd received that Ruby was a good and well-loved mother. He may have judged her too hastily.

Tipping his hat, he smiled to put her at ease. "Good evening, Mrs. LaRue."

Her eyes narrowed. Evidently, he hadn't put her at ease. "Good evening, Dr. Noble."

"I thought we might walk a way together."

Her amber eyes locked on his in a skeptical appraisal. "If you wish to threaten me again, I warn you I would rather walk by myself."

"No, no. As a matter of fact, I thought we might have dinner together."

She hiked a questioning eyebrow. "I thought you would be dining with your son and daughter-in-law."

"They deserve privacy after such a long separation."

"So, you find yourself at loose ends."

"Not at all."

"With no one else to talk with, you sought me out."

Her rather caustic smile did not ease the pain of hearing the truth.

"Madam, there are any number of women who would enjoy my company this evening. I chose you because you are an attractive and intelligent woman."

He realized the truth of the words as he spoke them. Whatever else she was, he found Ruby LaRue an attractive, intelligent woman.

"And when did you come to this conclusion?" she asked in a mocking manner.

"I have always thought you . . . exceptional," he said, scratching an itch at the nape of his neck. "It is your profession that disturbs me."

She sighed, turned and walked away.

He was right behind her. "What do you say to having dinner with me?"

"My children are expecting me for dinner. But if you wish to dine with us, you are welcome."

"Yes," he replied before she could retract her invitation. "I would like to join you."

"Come along then."

He walked in silence beside her, with a thousand questions tumbling through his mind. There was much he didn't know about her, much he would like to know.

Ruby did not seem to mind the silence. She made no attempt to fill it with the nervous jabbering most women resorted to when faced with a lull in conversation.

"You're a widow?" he asked, making his question something of a statement.

"My husband died during the War Between the States."

"And left you to raise your children?"

"My family disowned me when I married Arleigh," she said without the slightest hint of a plea for pity.

"Forgive me for asking, but why has a handsome woman like you not remarried?"

She chuckled softly, as if he jested. But then the alluring spiritualist ticked off the reasons as if she'd recited them before. "There are not enough men my age to go around, since too many of my generation were killed during the war. In my line of work, I do not meet many men. My clientele consists of women for the most part. And the men that I have met are not interested in a woman encumbered with three children."

He scratched a spot by his right ear. "You're a very strong woman."

"I do the best I can."

"Any man would be lucky to have you."

She stopped. Without saying a word, she gazed at him as if he'd grown a second head.

He scratched the back of his hand.

"Why are you scratching?" she asked.

"I-I have somehow received more than my share of mosquito bites."

She gave a bemused wag of her head as if she despaired for him and continued down the road. The five-mile hike to the farm took its toll. By the time they arrived, Jonathan was in need of a rest. Unaccustomed to a great deal of physical activity, he should have learned from last night and hired a carriage.

As he followed Ruby through the door of the rustic farmhouse, the tantalizing aromas of roasting beef, fresh-baked sourdough bread and blueberry pie greeted him. Jonathan's stomach responded by growling as if he hadn't eaten in weeks.

With a natural graciousness, Ruby introduced him to tall, fair-headed Eric and round, blond Gerta Houseman. The young German couple owned the farm and took in boarders. Ruby and her children had been living with them for the past three months.

Jonathan was introduced to Ruby's children next: Harley, the oldest at fourteen; Della, the middle child of twelve; and the youngest, Zeke, who had recently celebrated his tenth birthday. The youngsters regarded him with the same wariness as had their mother. He mustered all the charm he'd accumulated through life in an effort to impress Ruby's healthy young offspring.

Midway through the meal, Della and Zeke relaxed their vigilance and the hardworking farmers welcomed him as if he were an old friend. Only Harley remained aloof and appeared unimpressed by Jonathan.

Noisy conversation reigned at the dinner table. At times everyone seemed to be talking at once, creating a din he'd never experienced with his meals. From time to time, he would look over to Ruby and find her gaze upon him. Relaxed and in her element, she seemed more vulnerable than he ever would have expected. Sensing Ruby required some sort of reassurance, Jonathan smiled each time their eyes met.

When dinner at last ended and he'd scraped the last bite of blueberry pie from his plate, he felt curiously refreshed and ready to take on the walk home.

To his great relief, the Housemans insisted on lending him a horse and carriage, which Ruby would return on the following evening.

Hooting owls and serenading crickets accompanied him on the dark ride home. Rather than being tired, as was usual for him at this time of night, he felt extraordinarily awake and alive.

Ruby's gentle smile as she waved good-bye warmed him. He hadn't had such a good time in weeks—no, months.

Clementine's hands felt safe and natural in Rand's as she followed him up the stairs and into the master bedchamber. But her knees felt unsteady. Muscle and bone had given way to crackers and pudding. She knew what awaited her. Tonight she would honor her marriage vow and the pledge her pa had made. She would become Rand's wife in more than name only.

Before his marriage, Rand gained a reputation as a rake. He'd had many women. He knew how to make love and be loved. She hoped her lack of experience would not disappoint him too terribly.

It occurred to her that perhaps being a virgin wasn't a good thing. Clementine felt as lost and dumb as a heifer trying to swim a stream against the current.

Holding her breath, she followed Rand through the door. He dropped her hand. His eyes darkened; his brows dove into a frown as he looked around, scrutinizing the changes.

"Do you like it?" she asked as the silence lengthened. Her heart pounded like a drum possessed.

"I suppose I shall get used to it in time," he said. "Where did you get the chaise?"

"At Dixon's. It's the new Chinese red shade," she explained, one word tripping over another. "Bright colors are more to mah liking."

His face remained expressionless; his tone, stony. "I see."

He hated it. He hated her. With her renovations, Clementine had destroyed any hope of a happy marriage. Jarringly high-pitched, her voice trembled like an old woman's. "Do you mind? You said you would not mind."

"I didn't realize the extremes you would go to." He gestured to the chaise. "It's an excessively bright red."

"Yes. It's exciting." She sank to the offending piece of furniture and patted the empty space beside her. "And comfortable as well."

He turned toward the fireplace. "What happened to the table and the rocking chair? Did you replace all the furnishings?"

"Most is stored in the attic. Ah donated some to the church."

Staring at the space on the chaise beside Clementine, he ran a hand through his hair. "I'll get used to it in time."

"We have the most stylish rooms in Annapolis. Mr. Dixon himself told me."

"This room resembles a bordello, Clementine."

She didn't know. She'd never been inside a bordello.

"Look, champagne." She jumped up and hurried to the fireplace, where flutes and a chilled bottle of French Champagne waited on the table set between two winged chairs. She hurried to change the topic of conversation. "Champagne to celebrate your homecoming."

"I could use some," he said dryly.

"If you will open the bottle and pour, ah'll just slip into something a bit more comfortable."

For the first time, he smiled. The promise of love softened the hard line of his jaw, brought the twinkle back to his eyes.

Not long ago, Ruby had explained that sometimes it became necessary to assume the role of a femme fatale in order to win a man's heart or soothe his ire.

With a wink that didn't quite work—both of her eyes closed—Clementine disappeared behind the Oriental screen. According to Mr. Dixon, Clementine had gained a certain prominence as the first in Annapolis to own a Chinese red and black lacquer screen. With Ruby's help, she'd become a style-setter.

But Rand's expression had left no doubt that removing all traces of Ellie had not pleased him. Clementine had only done what she had to do. No purple reminders of his first wife remained in the elegant chamber. And hopefully, Ruby's seance had dispatched Ellie's spirit as well. Tonight only two would occupy the bedchamber, Clementine and Rand.

If it was possible, he'd returned even more gloriously good-looking than he when he set off in the old steamer. His skin, darkened by the summer sun to a rich, berry brown, struck an arresting contrast to his sapphire eyes. He appeared more rugged, more virile, more of everything a man should be.

A stream of delicious chills rippled through her.

She slipped off her kid leather shoes.

Did it matter that she knew Rand didn't love her? Should she complain or hold back when anyone could see that he was the most dashing officer Annapolis had ever turned out?

Whenever his eyes met hers, and his lips quirked into a seductive twist, her heart swelled to the size of Texas and her knees turned to molasses. Clementine rationalized that feelings like those must count for something.

Dang. She couldn't get the last few hooks and eyes on her dress undone.

She'd made up her mind to give Rand what he wished: a son. And when at last he held his long-desired boy, he would stop thinking of Ellie once and for all. His love for her would fade, and he would learn to love Clementine.

She'd already placed her good-luck charms beneath the pillow. If her lucky seahorse and the last piece of mistletoe would work their magic, she would be with child before the night ended.

She stepped from behind the screen. "Would you help me with my dress?"

He gave her a slow, crooked grin. Twinkling eyes settled on hers and caused her heart to leap like a mustang jumping a cliff. "My pleasure."

"It . . . it's difficult to reach the hooks and eyes in the back," she explained in a rasp. Her throat felt thick and dry.

"But not difficult for me. This is a husband's job," he said as he handed her a glass of champagne and set to work.

His hands were warm against her spine, and as his fingertips brushed her back, warm ripples of delight followed. She drained her glass.

In the throes of a bubbly glow, she wasn't prepared for what Rand did next. Holding aside the shining mass of copper cascading from her crown, he lightly brushed the nape of her neck with his lips. Goose bumps broke out all over her warm, warm body. The core of her grew hot and moist. And she could not catch her breath.

Clementine's body absorbed the thrilling new sensations, while in her head a chorus of angels struck up "The Battle Hymn of the Republic."

"What's that?" Rand asked.

*He could hear the marching song in her head!*

"A . . . a song," she said quietly, embarrassed.

*Mine eyes have seen the glory—*

"It sounds like your puppy."

The music died. Clementine listened. Locked out of the room, her furry pet growled on the other side of the door. "Princess is used to sleeping with me."

Princess scratched at the door.

"She's not going to be sleeping with us."

"Ah understand, but ah don't know if . . ."

"Tell it to go away, Ellie," he snapped impatiently.

*ELLIE?*

If Rand had taken a scalpel and run her through, Clementine could not have felt more pain. Piercing. Cold. Soul-deep. One word—Ellie—ripped through her, staggered her, took her breath away. She could feel the blood drain from her face, from her broken heart. But she could not move. Immobilized, she gave herself up to unfamiliar, pain-searing emotions. She drowned in them.

His jaw dropped; a frown knitted his brow and cursed his eyes. "I didn't mean that. I . . . I apologize. I know you're not Ellie. I don't know why I said . . . her name."

Clementine stared at him, unblinking.

A fierce silence fell between them. An unseen wall higher, wider, longer than the Appalachian mountain range rose up between them.

If Rand had suddenly taken on the appearance of a fire-breathing dragon, he could not have felt more the monster.

"I think that seeing all of . . . all of Ellie's things gone, brought her to mind," he said, trying once again to apologize.

Clementine opened the door and scooped her growling dog into her arms. The shaggy canine bared its teeth at Rand.

"You are nothing like Ellie. I could never mix you up in my mind or mistake you for her." He swiped at the beads of sweat on his forehead. He shouldn't be saying Ellie's name, but he didn't seem to be able to stop. Each time he opened his mouth, he made things worse.

But he'd been taken unawares. He'd expected a few changes, but not the sweeping alterations Clementine had made. He felt as if he'd stumbled into someone else's home.

Clutching the puppy against her breast, Clementine lowered her eyes. Copper curls released from capture at the crown of her head fell like a thick and glossy curtain to shield her face.

Rand could not tear his eyes from the heart-wrenching vision, at once a melancholy portrait and the most beautiful sight he'd ever seen. The back of Clementine's lovely cloud white gown fell open to the waist, revealing an exquisite creamy path of silken flesh.

In the tension-filled silence, a disquieting combination of remorse and desire descended upon him. Barraged by sensations he could not defend himself against, Rand felt like a battered old man-o'-war going down at sea. He clenched his jaw, attempted to clear his throat of the lump lodged there, a lump as large as an albatross.

Nothing he had yet said had served to soothe her. And he feared nothing he could do would earn Clementine's forgiveness. Remorse and desire ebbed away, leaving him to face his own anger. He'd been an idiot. He'd spoken without thinking and hurt someone who cared for him, someone who did not deserve to be wounded in any way, for any reason.

"I'm sorry, Clementine. It was a slip of the tongue, meaning nothing."

"Please leave." Her voice trembled.

"I don't want to leave you," he said quietly. He wanted to look into her eyes, to comfort her, to hold her through the night.

She refused to look at him. "Ah would like to be by myself."

He nodded.

As Rand left the room, he passed in front of Clementine and the puppy from the land of the damned. As he expected, Princess bared her teeth. But sensing he could not stop to punish her, the shaggy mop growled more loudly than she'd dared before.

Clementine closed the door behind Rand. The room blurred before her, and her tears fell on the puppy wriggling in her arms. Princess licked her face in a failed attempt to cheer her mistress. But nothing in this world could cheer Clementine.

She set the puppy down and flung herself across the bed. Not one to cry, for crying never solved a problem, she sobbed. Unable to stop, she wept with wild abandon. She had done everything possible to rid the house of Ellie and the memories she'd left behind. Even the seance that sent Ellie's ghost on her way had been for naught. Ellie would always be on Rand's mind. If Clementine needed any proof, she'd just received it. He would never forget his first wife. An unpolished gem of a girl from the West could never replace a jewel of an eastern lady.

Clementine cried herself to sleep and woke up with a start after midnight. Princess curled at her side, snoring softly.

She got up without waking the puppy, turned on a light and, giving a slight pull, popped off her gown.

The champagne had fizzled. Her pink satin peignoir lay untouched. Her eyes were puffy, and the tip of her nose was poppy red. But her mind had cleared.

She knew what she had to do. She'd been frugal with the household funds and had stashed more than one found coin in her pouch. Clementine calculated that she'd saved more than enough money to return to Texas. The contents in her red velvet pouch would keep her until she found a way to support herself. First thing in the morning, she would return to Oddon.

The puppy continued to sleep as Clementine dropped to her hands and knees, stretched her arm under the bed and slid out her battered bag.

It had been quite some time since she'd put money away or sought solace in her old treasures. Something about her cache didn't seem quite right. She remembered that she hadn't snapped it shut the last time she'd opened it to deposit a few coins, but neither had she left the satchel wide open.

It was an ominous sign. Her heart slowed to a dull thud. Silently chastising herself for being foolish, she overturned the satchel and gently dumped its contents beside her on the floor. Her shiny little derringer was gone. The swatch of Bay's hair was missing. But most devastating of all, Clementine's red velvet pouch with all her savings had disappeared.

She shook the satchel. Nothing. She searched every inch of the bag with one hand and then the other. The bag was empty save for the tattered cotton lining. Stretching flat on the floor, Clementine peered under the bed in hopes the missing items had fallen out. But no. Her precious possessions and the funds she had counted on were gone. Stolen. And she had no idea when, or who could have done such a terrible thing.

During the past busy weeks, in addition to the regular household help and guests, there had been painters, delivery people and workers roaming the house as the interior renovations were completed. She could not recall one shifty-eyed, suspicious character stalking the halls.

The thief might have been anyone. Chances were she would never know. Although she thought she had cried her eyes dry earlier in the evening, a fresh batch of tears began to flow. For a woman who hardly ever cried, she'd done her share during the past few hours.

The seahorse her pa had given her for good luck remained safely tucked under her pillow along with one—now very small and brittle—twig of mistletoe. Clementine gleaned a modicum of comfort in realizing that she had not been left completely devoid of the instruments of fortune.

Wiping away the tears with the back of her hand, she vowed through clenched teeth that she would find a way back home. She didn't know how, or when, for she was poverty-stricken again. But any doubts she might have entertained had vanished. If she belonged anywhere, if she ever hoped to find acceptance, she must return to the great western state where she'd come from.

Someday, she would ride Bay again. She would fine peace in the beauty and solitary space of the open range. She might even be able to forget Rand Noble.

One way or another, Clementine had to get back to Texas.

# *Twelve*

Rand could not sleep. He couldn't even think about it. Instead, he went to the garden and picked a huge bouquet of black-eyed Susans by moonlight. He left them outside of Clementine's door. He listened with his ear to the door, and when the sniffling finally ended, he quietly stole away. He'd wounded her deeply. If he lived to be two hundred years old, he would never forget the pain in her eyes. His stricken wife had quickly closed the door on him. He might wait a lifetime for her to open it again.

But one door always remained open to him—the hospital door. He left the house and within minutes strode through the academy gates as if an emergency awaited him. Somehow, some way, someday he would find a way to make up his blunder to Clementine.

As he crossed the rickety footbridge approaching the hospital, he saw a light burning in his office. His young assistant must be working late. Administering the academy hospital and practicing medicine was a monumental task. More than likely, David would be happy to have Rand back so that he could resume his assistant surgeon's duties, which were infinitely less taxing.

Rand inhaled the antiseptic aroma that filled the corridors as if it were perfume. The sweet, tarry smell of carbolic acid permeated the hospital. The moment he'd read how Lister used it as an antiseptic to prevent the spread of infection, he'd added the disinfectant to his supply list.

When he reached his office, he paused in the open doorway. Deep in concentration, his hard-working colleague hunched over a pile of paperwork.

"Dr. Smith, I presume?"

At the sound of Rand's voice, his assistant's head snapped up. The deep circles below his eyes seemed to vanish. "Rand!"

"In person." Rand smiled as he sauntered into the office. Removing his spectacles, David jumped up, coming round the desk to pump Rand's hand. "I knew your ship had come in, but I thought you would take a few days of rest before you came back to the hospital."

"Can't stay away. As a matter of fact, from a medical standpoint I've missed the hospital. A far better variety of aches and pains drag into the academy than what turns up at sea."

"Do you mean you experienced no challenges on the cruise?" Smith asked as he returned to his chair.

"None." Rand plopped himself in the hard wood chair on the patient side of the desk. "Once they recover from the initial seasickness, students eager to prove themselves don't complain no matter what. And fortunately, there were no lamentable accidents."

"Sounds as if you were on a pleasure cruise."

Rand grinned. "Not quite. But what about you? How have you fared while I've been away?"

"We have a couple of midshipmen suffering from the ague. And I set a broken arm the other day. As you can see, I've fallen behind in the paperwork, but other than that, everything is under control."

In other words, Rand hadn't been missed. His young assistant had proved himself a good doctor and capable administrator.

"What about the new superintendent?" he asked. "Is Commodore Parker set to make any changes?"

"I don't believe so. Not like his predecessors have, anyway. He's not a well man, Rand. He took command last month, and I've already seen him several times."

"Anything specific?"

David rubbed the bridge of his nose where his spectacles had left indentations. Rand's colleague possessed fine classic features, dark eyes and hair. Dr. Smith had many a young Annapolis maiden setting her cap, but the earnest assistant surgeon seemed oblivious to his attraction.

"Foxhall is an old sea dog who has fought a lot of battles and sustained his share of injuries along the way," David replied thoughtfully. "The aftereffects of his injuries, combined with the natural aging process, have weakened him."

"Well, we shall do our best to keep him alive," Rand said as he stood.

"Are you leaving so soon?"

"I'll be back first thing in the morning." He dipped his head toward the stack of papers on the desk. "I won't keep you any longer."

David regarded the stack and shrugged. "I'm nearly finished. If I'm able to stay awake, I'll clear out of your office before I leave tonight."

"Take your time."

"Wait." The young surgeon rose from the old leather chair and approached him.

Rand waited.

"There's one other thing."

"What's that?"

"Sarah Tidwell. Sarah has attempted to start rumors about . . . about Clementine and me. Word has gotten back to me that she's suggested to several acquaintances that my relationship with your wife is more than a friendship."

While confessing to the current town gossip, David's normally pale complexion had heightened to a remarkable pink hue.

Rand pretended not to notice his colleague's embarrassment.

He waved a dismissive hand. "Don't pay any attention. I don't intend to. Sarah's been unhappy since I remarried. She's not been kind to Clementine, seeking to discredit her at every turn."

Nodding, David swept a hand through his already mussed dark hair. "Clementine has behaved with the utmost propriety, as anyone can attest. You have a charming wife, and if she were free, I won't deny that I would now be courting her."

"I understand. Don't give Sarah and her gossip another thought." Rand slapped his worried assistant on the back. "Good night, David. It's good to be back."

"Good night."

Deflated, Rand left the hospital. Instead of receiving the solace he'd expected, he'd been mildly disturbed to discover all had gone well during his absence. Young Dr. Smith had successfully filled his shoes. Attempting to shake off his disquiet, he reminded himself that he'd just finished a successful cruise, received several commendations for his work and an exciting offer as well. David's success at the hospital meant Rand could take on another seafaring assignment free of guilt.

Except for Clementine. He would feel guilty about

leaving her again. Thoughts of the red-haired, green-eyed Texas woman intruded on his ruminations as he walked home. David Smith had spoken the truth. Rand did have a charming wife. She was not the same spunky girl who had demonstrated lasso tricks to Millie and sang "Home on The Range" at the drop of a hat. She no longer bragged about her aim with a rifle or how swiftly she could roll a cigarette.

Rand had felt an unfamiliar stab of jealousy when Smith admitted that if Clementine were not married, he would be courting her.

From the letters she'd written him, Rand felt certain that Clementine regarded him with respect and a certain affection. Feelings, he suspected, brought on by his absence and their increasingly intimate correspondence.

He had shared his thoughts with her on paper. He had even considered sharing his feelings with her. Writing about how he felt, rather than discussing his emotions like some silly schoolgirl, seemed less inhibiting.

Rand wondered if he could ever regain the trust he'd lost tonight with his loose tongue. It had been a natural slip. Ellie had tried his patience more than anyone he'd ever known. She tested him continually by doing things she knew he would disapprove of. Clementine had done something Ellie might do and it had unnerved him. But Clementine wasn't Ellie.

Even if it proved impossible to regain his freckled wife's goodwill, Rand meant to clear the air between them. He would tell her the truth about Ellie.

The next afternoon, when he returned from the hospital, Clementine was out. But his father had come by to hear about his adventures during the cruise and to catch up on how the navy fared in Caribbean ports.

They sat in the parlor. The formerly dark chamber had evolved to a light and airy room, boasting all-new furnishings.

Oddly enough, Rand felt more comfortable than he ever had in the room.

"The navy is falling apart," Jonathan complained. "Tell me the last time a new ship was built. You can't," he declared without waiting for a response. "You can't because all we have are old ships, relics from the Civil War. If called on today, the United States Navy would be unable to defend Martha's Vineyard."

The navy would never be as good as it was in his father's day; still, Jonathan had a point. "It's true," Rand replied. "We do need modern equipment, but at least we are negotiating for new foreign ports."

"Such as?"

"Samoa."

Jonathan frowned. "Samoa? Where the hell is that, and why do we need it?"

"Samoa is in the Pacific, and we need it for a coaling station," he answered, twisting in the new wing chair in order to see the grandfather clock. "Where could Clementine be?"

Jonathan shifted on the settee as if he were suddenly uncomfortable. "She's probably with Ruby. Those two women spend hours together. They've become good friends."

"Who is Ruby? One of your ladies?"

"No. No, nothing like that," the old man blustered. "Shortly after you left, Ruby LaRue set up her business over the sweet shop. She's a professional woman."

"Ruby LaRue?" For some reason the name amused Rand. "What kind of profession does she practice?" he chuckled. "Is it the world's oldest?"

Rather than join in his laughter as he expected, his

father glared at him. "Certainly not! Ruby's actual surname is Jones. But as she recently confided in me, she believes the name LaRue is better for business. It has a ring. People remember it."

Palms up, Rand quickly apologized but felt relieved to hear the front door open.

"You were a good, good puppy this afternoon," Clementine cooed. She sounded as if she were talking to a baby. "That's why you're my Princess."

"Clementine!" Jonathan called out, and then said to Rand, as if he hadn't heard. "Your wife's home. She was just out taking the rascal puppy for a walk."

Clementine hurried into the room, her puppy nipping at her heels. "Jonathan, I didn't know you were . . ." Her voice trailed off when she spotted Rand.

His heart gave a lurch as if it had not been beating before she entered the room. Rand's hungry gaze swept her still form from head to toe in a swift assessment that left him excessively warm. He ran a finger around his collar and unbuttoned his shirt at the neck.

But he could do nothing about the ache in his groin. Heaven help him. He wanted her. He needed her.

Clementine reminded him of a primrose, sweet and exquisite. Her golden silk gown with its padded bustle and lace-trimmed sleeves displayed her womanly curves to full advantage. Someday, he would hold her full, high breasts. Someday, he would encircle his wife's small waist with just one hand. Someday—before he died.

The red-haired, slender willow was like the autumn wind, cooly slipping through his fingers before he could catch her, caress her.

Princess, sitting at Clementine's side, made no sound. Her round black eyes bore into Rand as she bared her teeth.

"I came by to hear about my son's adventures in the Caribbean," Jonathan told Clementine as he hauled himself up with the aid of his walking stick. "But I must be going along now."

Princess growled.

Clementine plucked the puppy from the floor and cradled the shaggy little beast in her arms the way she might a baby. Perhaps she needed a real baby. Rand longed in the worst way to give her one.

"Oh, Jonathan, don't let me drive you away. Please stay," she pleaded. "Ah am plagued with the most dreadful headache ever and plan to retire. I'm certain Rand would be pleased to have your company."

"Well, perhaps I could stay for a little longer. Do you have a powder you can take for your headache?"

She smiled, a warm, lovely, soft parting of her lips. "Yes."

Realizing it was ridiculous, Rand nevertheless suppressed a twinge of jealousy as he watched his wife kiss his father lightly on the cheek. He wanted Clementine's lips on his cheek, on his lips.

With a careless wave to Rand, she floated from the room.

An hour later he rapped on her door. When she did not respond, he tried the door and, much to his surprise, found it open.

The skirt of Clementine's golden gown spilled off the bed where she lay sleeping. Dozens of white down pillows propped up her head and shoulders, and her rusty curls fanned the stark white eyelet pillowcase in seductive disarray.

As he gazed at her from the doorway, Rand's pulse

spurted ahead of itself. He took a deep breath to calm his body, to bank the fire simmering in the pit of his being.

Clementine belonged in a fairy tale. A genuine Sleeping Beauty, she slept in his bed, but she did not belong to him.

He waited for a sign she was awake, only pretending to be in a sound sleep. He couldn't believe she'd actually fallen asleep when so much needed to be said. She did not move. Her chest rose and fell in a steady rhythm.

The light snoring sound came from Princess, curled up in her own bed in a corner of the chamber not far from Clementine.

Rand moved into the room slowly, as quietly as possible for a man in boots. Not a lash flickered.

He sat on the edge of the bed. Close enough to smell the fresh fragrance of chamomile, close enough to be struck once again by her ripening beauty.

"Clementine, wake up," he urged softly. "We need to talk."

She mumbled in reply and turned her head away from him.

He caught her chin between his thumb and forefinger and gently eased her face toward him. Her skin felt as soft as velvet to his touch.

"I'm sleeping," she murmured, wrenching her chin from his grip. "Go away."

"Let me explain," he coaxed. "There are things you need to know."

"Not now."

"Yes, now."

If he didn't tell her the truth now, he might never find the courage in the future. It might even be easier with her eyes closed. Hell, she was a captive audience.

If necessary he could pin her to the bed. She could feign disinterest, but Rand had a feeling that when he began to talk, she would listen.

Edging up farther on the bed, he took her nearest hand and clasped it in his. The callouses that used to pad her palms had disappeared. Her hand nestled soft and warm within his.

"I was a ladies' man when I was younger. You might have heard." He knew Clementine wouldn't stand for his sugarcoating the truth. If she was to believe him, he had to tell it as it happened.

"My father had been at sea during most of my childhood. I knew him from stories my nanny told me. Most likely, she made them up. And then one day shortly after I graduated from the academy, and after he'd been a year at sea, Jonathan walked through the door and demanded that I marry the daughter of an old friend. Someone I didn't even know."

Rand paused to look at his wife but could detect no reaction. His gaze lingered on her long lashes, gently curled against her cheeks; her lips, moist and slightly parted.

"The daughter was you," he said in a quiet aside. "At the time, I didn't feel as if I owed anything to my father, especially agreeing to an old-fashioned arranged marriage. In those days I was young and stupid. And I never stopped to realize that my father was only human. He wasn't an ogre. He'd made mistakes, hadn't always been there when I needed him, but he'd done the best he could."

Her lashes fluttered. She listened.

He smiled, grateful to realize one small victory. "Between the time I was eighteen and twenty-five, I rebelled against my father and everything he suggested. I left the academy to go to war against his wishes." Rand paused in his tale. Clementine would consider him a total idiot if he wasn't careful. He continued on a lighter note.

"When I returned, I gained acclaim as the oldest midshipman in Annapolis."

She smiled. Rand felt certain that she meant the slight upturn of her lips to be a smile.

Encouraged, he embarked on the most difficult part of his confession. "Not long after graduation, I married Ellie Tidwell in defiance of my father's wishes."

Clementine opened her eyes. A troubled frown lined her smooth porcelain brow.

Rand pulled her into his arms. She attempted to wrench free at first, but quickly realizing a physical struggle with him would be futile, she settled stiffly into his arms. Her dour expression remained wary.

He loved the feeling of her slender warm body close to his, adored her pouting lips. Unwilling to risk having her escape just when he'd come to the most difficult admission a man could make, Rand held her tightly. In a soft, hushed monotone, he disclosed the secret he'd held inside for so long.

"I'd met Ellie at one of the academy hops. She was a town girl looking for a husband, and I knew it. We didn't have much in common as it turned out. She knew how to bake an apple pie and sew samplers. I loved what she represented, sweet and wholesome, but . . . but I might not have loved her."

"Might not have loved her?" Clementine repeated in a whisper.

Rand dipped his head and nodded. "I've never told another living soul about my doubts."

"I would never betray a confidence," she said softly. Her somber pledge drew a smile from somewhere deep inside of him. He'd known instinctively that un-burdening himself to Clementine would be safe. But he'd not done it for himself. He'd chosen to make the confession in hopes the truth would provide her with some sort of peace of mind.

"Go on," she urged.

"Ellie never got over being intimidated by me. She'd wanted to marry an officer, and she did. But I was too . . . too big for her, if you know what I mean. She was an acorn. I was a twenty-foot tree. I filled the house. She kept to the corners. By marrying Ellie, I committed a disservice to her. She would have been happier with someone quiet, a homebody."

Clementine regarded him with wide green eyes but said nothing, forcing him to continue.

"I married Ellie for the wrong reasons. Out of pure, young, hot-blooded spite, I made a terrible mistake. But I intended to honor my vows and be a good hus-band. I never was unfaithful, never broke my marriage vows. Ellie possessed a delicate spirit. She needed someone who would take care of her."

"She sounds quite the opposite of her sister, Sarah," Clementine offered.

"Yes."

"Sarah is as tough as rawhide."

"I know," he said. "And I know that she's tried to make trouble for you while I was away."

"She never succeeded."

"Just the same, I'm sorry."

Clementine's gaze locked on his. "You're an hon-orable man, Dr. Noble."

A shiver of pleasure skipped down his spine, chased by denial. "No. I was impatient with Ellie too often. An honorable man would have been more understand-ing of her weaknesses. But when she was diagnosed with consumption, I tried my best to find a doctor who could make her well. I searched the country for a cure. When guilt tore me apart, I became a good husband."

"You did your best to help her. No one could have been a better husband to Ellie."

"I tried. I spent every minute I could nursing her."

Clementine reached up and laid her hand gently against his cheek. "Some things in life are beyond our control. Fate takes a hand."

He didn't believe in fate, but that was a discussion for another time. "Before Ellie became ill, I spent a good deal of time at sea. Seeking promotion, I signed on at every opportunity. Ellie complained. She acted rashly during my absences, and I was to blame."

"You're much too hard on yourself," Clementine protested.

"I'm not the man I used to be, before marrying Ellie."

"But I like the man you are now. Have I thanked you for the lovely flowers you left at my door? Not many men would make such a thoughtful gesture."

"A poor apology."

"No one expects you to be perfect."

Closing his eyes, he shook his head. "Clementine, I'm far from perfect. I'm trying to tell you that I wasn't a good husband to Ellie. I'm trying to tell you that I don't know *how* to be a good husband. I was born to be the bachelor and rake my father is and will be to his dying day."

"You're wrong," she argued quietly. "You possess all the qualities that make a good husband. You have a generous spirit and a caring heart. When you're ready to be a good husband, you shall be the best a woman could ask for."

Contemplating the somber expression on the beautiful face before him, Rand grinned. He had meant to offer consolation to Clementine. He'd attempted to make her understand his failings and shortcomings, to tell her the truth and take the blame. But she had reversed the roles: Clementine consoled him. Clever woman. Kind, wonderful, brilliant woman.

Relaxed in his arms, she looked up at him as if he were a hero, a prince among men. For an instant, he felt like one. Her light emerald eyes shone with admiration. Her warm smile showered him with understanding.

He did not deserve her.

In fact, Rand had already taken the necessary steps to free her from him.

The silence must have aroused the watchdog in Princess. The seemingly adorable puppy woke, sprang to all fours and barked at him as if he were an axe-murderer intruder.

No, Rand did not deserve the woman Clementine had become, and the puppy from Hell knew it. She attacked him. Growling, once again the shaggy animal bared her teeth. But this time her sharp-toothed mouth opened—and clamped shut around Rand's wrist.

"Yeow!"

Clementine rolled from his arms. She took an inglorious bounce on the bed before her gaze narrowed on Rand's wrist. "Oh. Oh!"

Princess had drawn blood.

"Don't faint," Rand warned. "It's not much. Just a few drops. Don't look."

Blood splashed from his wrist as if it had been caught in the jaws of a shark. A painful throbbing fired from his wrist to his shoulder. A small vein had been punctured.

"Let go, you naughty puppy!"

He didn't know whether to laugh or cry as Clementine scolded her Princess demon. Averting her eyes from Rand's bloody wrist, she grasped the puppy's midsection and tugged, attempting to dislodge the canine's death grip. "Let go!"

Princess responded to Clementine's angry tone in the nick of time. The puppy released him just as Rand prepared to retaliate.

Considering the countless ways in which to kill the evil animal, he headed for his office in need of antiseptic and bandages.

Clementine followed close on his heels, apologizing all the way. "Ah don't know what came over her. She has never bitten anyone before."

"If you wish to keep her, keep her out of my sight," he ordered.

"Let me help bandage your hand."

"I can manage."

"Very well," she sniffed.

The moment she stormed from the room, Rand regretted snapping at her. The dog bite hadn't been her fault. And it took him an hour to bandage his own hand.


Jonathan met Ruby as she left the sweet shop. It was cold and growing dark, and he considered it an unfit afternoon for walking alone. She did not appear surprised to see him and gratefully accepted his offer of a ride. He helped her into his rented carriage and ordered the driver onward.

"Did you see Clementine today?" he asked.

"Yes."

"I suspect things may not be well between Rand and Clementine." Jonathan knew Clementine confided in Ruby and hoped Ruby would pass on any information she might have gleaned.

"I suspect you're correct," Ruby replied primly.

She forced him to be blunt. "What did she say to you?"

"Jonathan, I do not share confidences. I am shocked that you could even ask. I thought you'd come to know me since you started escorting me to the farm."

"In fact, I don't know you, not as much as I'd like."

Startled by his directness, she whipped her head around in his direction.

Jonathan pretended not to notice. "For instance, I don't know where you were raised . . ."

"In Boston."

"Or who your parents were."

"My father owned a textile mill. My mother's side came over on the *Mayflower*. I come from a wealthy New England family and have had the best education," she said as if she were reciting her qualifications for a position.

"Do you have siblings?"

"I have a brother and a sister. Neither of whom wished to speak with me after my parents disowned me."

"Lord, Ruby! How could anyone turn their backs on a good woman like you?"

Inclining her head, she raised a brow. "Have you come around to believing that a medium might be a good woman?"

"I said *you* were good. I did not mention how you earned your living."

"Of course not."

They lapsed back into the same familiar old argument. It seemed he would never convince Ruby of the error of her ways. He shifted tactics. "Well, I don't expect you'll be talking to the dead forever. You're still young, and someday you'll meet a man who will wish to support you in the style to which you once were accustomed."

"Jonathan, I am forty-eight years old. I'm far too old for romance."

"A man my age considers a forty-eight-year-old woman little more than a babe."

"A babe?" Her luscious berry red lips quirked in amusement. "You continue to astonish me."

"Romance is not only for the young. Hearts can catch fire at any age."

"Your reputation attests to your prowess with fire," she quipped with a raised brow and faintly ominous edge to her tone.

He'd irritated her, but that hadn't been his intention. He moved quickly to smooth over the rough patch. "Do you think you might have dinner with me this evening?"

"The children are—"

"You have dinner with the children every night," he interrupted.

Ruby sat a little straighter on the bench beside him, but she appeared to be considering his request. "If I agree to have dinner with you, my profession must not be discussed."

"You have my word. I shall not mention it."

"Very well then."

Although she didn't sound thrilled with the idea, Jonathan experienced a moment of triumph. Before Ruby could change her mind, Jonathan ordered the driver to stop at the Maryland Inn. For the following two hours, he enjoyed one of the most pleasant and diverting dinners in memory. He and Ruby argued about the worth of Edison's phonograph, the policies of President Hayes and the future of the telephone. Although they held opposing views, he found her points thought-provoking. She kept herself well informed—for a woman.

He didn't bring up what vexed him until after dinner, over coffee, when his astute dinner companion fairly demanded that he do so.

"Something is on your mind, Jonathan." Ruby leveled a steady, keen-eyed, amber gaze. "Something is troubling you."

There were times, like this, when he wondered if she might indeed possess clairvoyant powers. Although he always doubted her ability to communicate with the dead. And still did.

"Jonathan?"

"On the way to meet you this evening, I ran into Dr. Smith."

"Yes?"

"Smith thought I knew and asked how I felt about Rand's next assignment."

"And?"

"It seems my son has accepted orders dispatching him to Pago Pago."

# *Thirteen*

Rand's revelations stunned Clementine.

She'd been thunderstruck to learn that he questioned his love for Ellie. She'd been astonished to hear that he was convinced he'd been a poor husband to his first wife. And she still felt the dazed shock of discovering Rand believed he could never be a good husband. For any woman. For her. A belief based on his experience with Ellie.

Clementine knew Rand's confession had been difficult for him. He was a proud man, a man used to being admired for his achievements.

Ellie Tidwell still stood between Rand and Clementine, just not in the way she'd thought. If the young town girl had been the proper wife for him, Rand wouldn't feel the way he did.

In Clementine's opinion, having the courage to admit his failure demonstrated Rand possessed the instincts and the heart to make a first-rate husband. If she could prove his value, she might yet save her marriage. She might not need to return to Texas.

"If I were you, I would make peace with the man," she scolded Princess. "For I am the wife Rand was meant to have. I am the best and most suitable wife for him."

She only wished she felt as confident as she

sounded. Whenever she thought of him, whenever his face popped into her mind—which happened more and more frequently—the twinkle in his eyes suggested seduction would never be sweeter. When her imagination locked on the bold invitation in his eyes and the enigmatic smile on his lips, returning to Texas lost its appeal.

Princess barked, effectively breaking the spell Rand Noble had cast upon Clementine from afar. The puppy's dark, doleful eyes peered from behind its shaggy mop, begging for release. Since biting Rand on the previous afternoon, the bit of black fluff had been confined to the outside doghouse. Determined to remain firm, although she didn't have the heart to muzzle her puppy, Clementine set down the bowls of food and water.

She issued a stern warning. "Until you learn to get along with the master of the house, I fear you will stay a yard dog."

As if she understood what had been said, Princess whimpered, slowly lay down and turned her shaggy head away from the bowls.

"For your sake, I hope Rand's wound is healing well," Clementine added as she marched away.

She would find out shortly. She had yet to visit the academy hospital, and this seemed as good a day as any. Snatching a cloak to protect her from the cool autumn air, she set out for the sick bay. Knowing her aversion to the sight of blood, Rand would never expect a visit from her at the hospital. She intended to surprise him.

And she did.

One of the new female nurses directed her to Rand's office. But as she passed an open door on the way, she heard his voice and stopped to look. Carefully.

Seeing no sign of blood, she made a sweeping survey. The large room boasted twelve beds but contained only two patients. One midshipman slept at the far end of the room. Rand stood at the bedside of the second boy, his back to the door. He wore a surgeon's traditional white linen sack coat, which identified him as a doctor at once, but also, Clementine noticed, emphasized the invincible breadth of his shoulders.

A warmth spread through her. Gentle, tingling.

The boy confined to the bed appeared to have a broken leg.

Evidently Rand had been examining the leg. "How are you doing this morning, son?"

"I'm fine."

"No pain?" he asked. "You don't have to be brave in a hospital, you know."

The young man bit down on his bottom lip. "I'm not . . . Well, there's a little pain."

"How did this happen?"

"I climbed the Herndon Monument. I was about halfway up when I fell. Landed the wrong way, I guess." The poor boy slanted his doctor a sheepish grin.

Rand laughed, and the sound strummed Clementine's heart. She hadn't realized how much she had missed his deep rumble of laughter while he'd been away.

"Son, when I was a fourth-classman, I had a similar mishap with Herndon. Fortunately, I walked away with no broken bones. However, I bruised my rump and my ego." He lowered his voice to a conspiratorial tone. "I couldn't sit down for a week."

The boy grinned, and Clementine realized that Rand had accomplished what every excellent doctor strove to do. For a few brief moments, her husband, the good Dr. Noble, had banished his patient's pain.

"Gosh, Doc. I didn't know you were a midshipman."

"And proud to have been. I graduated in 1869. Even then, back in the dark ages when I was a student, the academy provided a fine education."

The boy nodded in agreement. "I'm anxious to get back to class, sir."

"Maybe we can arrange that sooner than you think. I'll be back later."

"Thanks, Doc."

Rand turned to leave but stopped in his tracks when he saw Clementine standing in the doorway.

She smiled.

He smiled.

And then the man who made her stomach loop-de-loop hurried to her side. "Clementine, what brings you here?" he asked in hushed tones. "Has something happened at home? Is my father all right? Did the evil dog gnaw on someone else?"

"No. No. No!" Laughing, she hooked her arm through his as he started down the gleaming white corridor. "I'm a curious creature, you know. I've never been inside a hospital before, and I've wished to see where you do your healing for a long time."

"But you knew there might be bleeding patients."

"I felt up to taking the risk this morning."

"Good. No one is bleeding today—yet." He shot her a teasing grin that caused her heart to melt.

"Then I have come at the perfect time."

"And I shall take you into my office where you can feel relatively safe from the possibility."

"Is your wrist healing?" she asked, sneaking a peak at his still-bandaged body part.

"Yes, I believe so."

"Is the wound painful?"

"Not any longer," he replied, adding with a grin, "but your concern is appreciated."

"Of course I'm concerned." Did he think she had a cold heart or was oblivious to his charm?

"I'm glad to hear it."

"You're my husband."

"But have you shot the dog?"

Coming to an abrupt halt, Clementine gasped.

Rand laughed. "I didn't mean it." Placing his hand in the small of her back, he guided her from the hall into a spacious sunlit room. "Come into my office."

Clementine's first look at Rand's hospital office reminded her of his office at home. But on closer inspection, the similarities ended with the skeletal figure and instrument case. While Millie kept his home office clean, his hospital office gleamed. The walls, the floor, the glass, even the furniture revealed not a speck of dust or trace of a finger mark.

"How—how clean," she said, knowing Rand awaited some sign of her approval.

"Every room in the hospital is clean. Each afternoon we scrub from floor to ceiling. I've read Dr. Lister. He was on to something ten years ago. Bacteria, germs," he added, "don't proliferate in a clean hospital. Therefore, patients suffer from fewer infections."

Clementine felt a puff of pride. No one could be a wiser doctor than her husband. "And what is that?" she asked, pointing to the strange instrument on his desk.

"It's a microscope. With the microscope I can see bacteria. *You* can see bacteria. Come, sit at the desk."

"No, thank you."

"They're just little specks that appear to be swimming."

"Perhaps next time." She sank into the chair opposite his desk, away from the microscope, and initiated a swift change of subject. "Tell me, did Dr. Smith do well while you were away?"

Any disappointment he might have felt for Clementine's lack of interest in bacteria, Rand concealed with a ready smile. "Yes. David proved more than up to the task."

"Excellent. Rand, I have had an extraordinary idea."

He leaned forward, steepling his hands, fixing his sparkling blue eyes on hers. "What is that, darlin'?"

When his smiling eyes settled on hers, she felt like the only woman in the world. She took a deep shaky breath before she felt able to continue in a steady voice. "You proposed once before that we take a proper honeymoon. I should like very much to accept your gracious offer."

He appeared startled. "A honeymoon, now?"

"Yes."

"After all I told you last night? Knowing I'm ill-equipped to be the husband you deserve?"

"I'm suggesting nothing more than a journey together. Think of yourself as my escort, rather than my husband, if you wish. I've been nowhere except for Texas and Annapolis. There is so much more of this world ah would like to see, and there is no time like the present to start."

She'd said it all. She'd rushed to get the words out, fearing she might get cold feet halfway through.

He angled his head as if studying her. "How would you like to travel to Key West with me?"

Key West. Rand had visited the port city on his summer cruise. And she remembered from Jonathan's lessons that water surrounded the town. "Can we reach Florida by land?"

"Yes," he responded eagerly. "And there's no better place for a honeymoon. Key West is a tropical paradise."

Satisfied that she'd accomplished her mission, Clementine stood. "Very well," she said, bestowing her brightest smile. "We shall honeymoon in Key West."

As Rand nodded, his gaze flitted over her shoulder. Clementine turned to see Dr. Smith striding into the office.

The handsome young doctor saluted Rand. "Dr. Noble."

Rand stood and returned the salute. "David."

"Clementine! I mean Mrs. Noble." Rand's assistant reddened as he held out his hand. "It's good to see you."

"Thank you, David, it's been too long," she responded. "You must have dinner with us before we leave."

"Ah, so you're going to accompany our good doctor to Samoa?"

Puzzled, Clementine shifted her gaze from David to Rand and back. "Samoa? No, Key West."

"Key West is the embarkation point for Samoa," Rand told her in a quiet voice.

Smith stuttered. "Ha-have I said something that I should not?"

"No, not at all. I was just about to tell Clementine that Key West was the first stop on the way to Pago Pago."

"I . . . I . . ." Confused and hurt, Clementine's heart raced as if she were running from a stampeding herd of cattle. "It was nice to see you, David." She hurried to Rand and offered a wifely peck on the cheek.

"You aren't leaving?" he asked, protesting. "You haven't had a tour of the entire hospital yet."

She met his gaze directly. "But I've already learned so much this morning."

He felt lower than a bilge keel. Rand hadn't meant for Clementine to find out in the way she had that he'd taken the opportunity to ship out again. The prospect of establishing a port in the Pacific promised a great adventure.

He'd first been approached during the summer cruise but didn't sign on for what might be a dangerous journey until the day he'd finally faced the truth about himself. It was only then that he was able to honestly tell Clementine that he would never be a good husband. He didn't possess the character or ability to be the man any woman would desire in her mate. With Rand away for a year or more, she could establish a life of her own, and no one would question her. But before leaving, having his longed-for son in mind, he'd hoped to consummate their marriage.

For Clementine to come to him and propose a honeymoon had seemed too good to be true. But that hadn't stopped him from immediate planning. Once in Key West, he could make love to her during lazy afternoons, shaded beneath swaying palms. He would make love to her on balmy, moonlit evenings beneath star-studded skies. Before he shipped out for Samoa, his spirited, green-eyed wife would be with child.

Everything had changed in a flash. Rand's honeymoon plans had been dashed by David Smith's ill-timed disclosure.

Still, when he reached home, he'd attempted to persuade Clementine that things weren't what they seemed.

She refused to listen. Through the closed door of her bedchamber, he explained he'd been a hairbreadth from telling her the entire story. He failed to convince her. She maintained an icy silence.

For most of his adult life, Rand's charm had prevailed in such circumstances. He could talk a woman into almost anything. But he was unable to sway his wife in the week left before his departure. She refused to talk, and successfully avoided him thanks to the devil's own dog. Princess had him at a disadvantage. She could smell him coming. The puppy growled and barked whenever he was within striking range.

Rand's time ran out. He needed his father's help and went to Jonathan's cavernous home.

The old man appeared pleased to see him as he was shown into his study. He poured a brandy for each of them before asking, "To what do I owe this honor?"

"Will you look after Clementine for me?"

"It will be my pleasure." Jonathan's eyes narrowed on Rand. "I hope you are not at odds again."

"She's upset with me at present," he admitted. "She'd agreed to go to Key West for a belated honeymoon. I was about to tell her about Pago Pago when David came in and unwittingly spilled the beans."

His father sighed, shaking his head as he had long ago when Rand was caught playing some childish prank. "Did Clementine agree to travel to Key West by ship?"

"No. But I think I might have persuaded her."

"How long will you be away?"

"A year." Rand shrugged, feeling small beneath his father's increasingly disapproving gaze. "Maybe two."

"You're newly married," Jonathan barked. "How could you sign on for a lengthy journey? Is this my fault for insisting that you marry Clementine?"

"No. My choice has nothing to do with you. I allowed myself to believe that if I married Clementine, I might prove to be a better husband than I was to Ellie. I hoped a marriage arranged by older, wiser men would be a better choice than the one I'd made."

Blowing out a sigh, Rand swiped a hand through his hair as he made his way to the nearest window. "But I was wrong there too. It's in our Noble blood. You and I were meant to live a single life."

"What makes you think that?"

"Look at you," he said, turning. "Mother died more than thirty years ago. During that time, you've courted many women and never loved and settled on one."

Jonathan lifted his head and gave a yank to his vest. "I never married, because I never found my match."

Rand met his father's eyes. "Do you believe Clementine is my match?"

"She could be. If you allowed her to be."

That wasn't the answer Rand wished to hear. He started toward the door. "I shall write. Perhaps in time, she will return my letters. She writes well."

"Don't make my mistakes, Rand."

The gruff warning caused Rand to stop, to regard his father with renewed interest.

"Don't follow in my footsteps or you will end like me, Son. Yes, I've looked at myself. I'm an old man rattling around in a big old house. When I'm alone, I talk to myself just to hear a voice."

Rand couldn't quite believe what he was hearing. He suspected a ploy of some sort. His father had been, and continued to be, a role model for bachelorhood. To all outward appearances, Jonathan led the ideal life.

"Father, I have never known you to be without companions. For six months a year, you race your sloop against your old sailing cronies. And every Tuesday and Thursday, summer and winter, you're playing darts at Reynolds Tavern. You have never, never been without a lady, or two."

"What you say is true, but the hours that I spend alone are three times as long as the hours spent with friends and acquaintances."

"I suggest you marry one of your female admirers."

"I am too old."

"Laverne Hawthorne will marry you in less than a minute."

"I meant that I am too old for the only woman I would consider marrying."

Again, Rand felt himself taken aback. He thought he knew his father very well, and yet the old man continued to astound him with unexpected disclosures. "There is someone, then?"

Jonathan shook his head. "Never mind. It cannot come to anything. The lady in question only tolerates me."

"Women find you charming!"

"As they do you."

"Clementine is not interested in me or having a family with me."

"If you stay, you can make her change her mind."

He shook his head. "Even if I could, I wouldn't. I'm not good enough for her. She deserves a better husband than I'll ever be."

"Is becoming a widow good for her?" his father shot back.

"What do you mean?"

"Yellow fever has been breaking out all over the south. I still keep up with the medical papers. By the time you reach Key West, the chances are good that the disease will have reached the city. You'll be putting your life in danger."

"Not if I don't get bitten."

"Bitten? Bit by what? What are you talking about?"

"If you've been keeping up, you'll know there's a new theory that proposes yellow fever is caused by a mosquito bite. Mosquitos carry the disease from one person to the next."

His father's blue eyes blazed. "Preposterous! A poor attempt to explain the unexplainable."

Rand knew an impasse when he'd reached one. "I'm going. My ship leaves tomorrow from Baltimore. If absence makes the heart grow fonder, perhaps Clementine will be glad to see me when I return," he bit out. He'd never get over her refusal to talk with him.

"When you return in two years?" The old man made a sweeping, dismissive gesture with his hand.

"Good day, Father. I'll come by in the morning before I leave."

"Two years," Jonathan muttered. "By then Clementine may have forgotten you."

But Rand dominated Clementine's thoughts every waking minute. And when she slept, she dreamed of him. She had not given him the benefit of the doubt. He may well have been ready to tell her that he had signed up for the great adventure. If she loved him, as her heart insisted, she would be happy for him, happy that he'd been chosen for such a great journey. He'd received a great honor.

Still, her heart felt heavy. She'd let him go without making peace. By refusing to settle their differences, she'd thought to punish him but had only succeeded in punishing herself.

Rand had been gone less than a week, and Clementine missed him terribly. The days grew colder. The leaves turned colors, from green, to gold, to brown. She watched from her window as, withered and dry, they fell to the ground. She felt as barren as the poplar branches, as brittle as the leaves that crunched beneath her feet.

She released Princess from the yard and allowed the puppy back into the house. But she needed something else to occupy her time other than taking her pet for a walk. She required something else to occupy her mind so that she would not always be thinking of Rand. He'd asked her to be the mother of his child. What kind of fool had she been to deny him? To let him go without loving him?

Awake, he filled her consciousness; asleep, he filled her dreams. The tall, handsome doctor had offered her his love. The passion that she rejected glimmered deep in his ocean blue eyes. His wry, crooked grin hinted at pleasures she could not even imagine but had let slip through her fingers. In the quiet gloom, Clementine could hear Rand's laughter, full of joy, echoing in the corridors.

Shaking off the memories of Rand that haunted her more surely than the ghost of Ellie ever had, she grabbed Princess's leash and whistled for her puppy. Training Princess had become one of the ways in which Clementine filled her empty hours. The shaggy dog responded to her whistle and stopped growling at the snap of her fingers. But there was still work to be done.

The cold air invigorated Princess and tore through Clementine, biting at her cheeks and nose. Pulled along by the excited dog, who had gained ten pounds, she tugged on the leash when they reached Jonathan's house. Clementine decided to make an impromptu call on her father-in-law. Her temperamental dog liked the old man, and he, in turn, appeared to enjoy Princess's antics.

His butler answered the door. "Come in, Mrs. Noble. Dr. Noble is in his study."

Alvah, stiff as a whalebone and more than refined, ushered Clementine into Jonathan's study.

He looked up from his reading.

"Am I interrupting?" she asked.

"Not at all, my dear." Smiling, he rose from behind his desk and came around to take her hand. "It's always a pleasure to see you, and you," he added, with a glance at Princess.

"I hope you don't mind. When I'm reading, I dislike any interruptions."

"But this reading isn't for pleasure; it's medical material," he said, leading her to the overstuffed, olive green sofa. "I may be retired, but I shall always be a doctor. And a doctor never knows when he may be needed in an emergency. As a matter of principle, I try not to fall behind."

"What is the medical news you are reading today?"

"There is a controversy brewing about yellow fever."

"Yellow fever? Is there a case in Annapolis?"

"No. There are several areas of the country experiencing outbreaks, but—"

"Florida? Key West?" Clementine questioned as alarm shot through her in icy flashes.

Jonathan shifted uneasily on the sofa beside her. "There may be—"

"Is Rand in danger?" she asked, interrupting once again.

"I don't think so. No." Her father-in-law got up from the couch. Clasping his hands behind his back, he crossed to the fireplace. "Rand knew there had been a few cases recently but decided to take the risk."

"He risked his life?"

If something happened to Rand when so much had been left unsaid, when she had locked him out of her life, Clementine would never forgive herself. He hadn't told her of any risk from disease.

Neither had Pa disclosed the dangerous voyage he'd embarked on to a strange land. The voyage that ended his life. Just as her brother hadn't told her when he corresponded with Jonathan to rearrange her arranged marriage.

Time and again, she'd been kept in the dark by the men in her life. She'd had no knowledge or control over the events determining her destiny. A sad fact she determined must change, starting now.

Jumping up, Clementine marched to the desk and snatched the paper her father-in-law had been reading. The word "epidemic" screamed from the page.

"I must go."

Jonathan swivelled around from his study of the fire. "Where?"

"Key West. What is the quickest way to travel?"

"By ship, but—"

Alvah, standing at the threshold, rapped sharply on the door, interrupting the elder Noble's protest.

"Begging your pardon, sir. You have another caller. Marshal Downs," he announced stoically. "He insists on seeing you at once."

Clementine seized the opportunity. "I must leave, Jonathan."

"No, stay. I'll take you to Ruby; she's at the church. Her ladies' group has made a project of Christmas baskets for the poor this year. But she'll take time to talk some sense into you."

"No. I love you both, Jonathan, but I know what I must do."

From now on she would be living life on her terms. She did not require counsel from others. Clementine meant to follow her heart.

# *Fourteen*

Jonathan watched in fist-clenching frustration as Clementine hurried away. She passed Marshal Downs as he strode into the study. The marshal, a large man with thick fingers and carrying a worn felt hat, halted in the middle of the room.

"Dr. Noble, I've come about a boy. His name is Harley Jones, and he says he knows you."

Frustration became anxiety, constricting the pit of Jonathan's stomach. "Yes. I know Harley. Is he in trouble?"

"He stole a shawl from Dixon's Dry Goods Emporium. Said it was for his mother, for her birthday."

"Harley would never steal anything," Jonathan declared in righteous indignation. "This is a misunderstanding, Marshal. Take me to him. We'll straighten this out within the hour."

If the fastest way for Clementine to reach Rand was to travel by ship, she must overcome her fears. Her adventuresome husband had exposed himself to double danger. If anything were to happen to him, she would never forgive herself. Before another nautical knot separated them, she swore on her last twig of mistletoe to make peace with Rand. She'd behaved as stubbornly as a ranch mule toward the man who made her pulse quicken and her heart jump through hoops. The lusty male who filled the blue and gold uniform to perfection might look like a mythical god, but he was not immortal.

When Rand was forced to confess he'd signed on for the long, hazardous voyage to Samoa, Clementine had been beside herself. Caught up in a painful tangle of wounded pride and anguish, her anger simmered within her. In retaliation, she'd tried to shut him out. But in the end, she found denying her love impossible. Rand faced grave dangers in the months ahead, and she wasn't ready to give up on him.

The Pacific Ocean was vast, and the voyage to Samoa would take months. Anything could happen during the lengthy journey, from a typhoon to a mutiny. Or he could fall ill in Key West and be taken by the fever.

The same fate could await her.

Clementine's ship could sink. She might contract the fever. But if she remained a prisoner of her fears and superstition, she would never truly live.

After she had seen Rand once again, after they had come to a meeting of the minds and resolved their differences, there would be more than enough time to think about returning to Texas.

When Jonathan's dire warnings about the possibility of contracting yellow fever could not dissuade her, he agreed to keep her dog and even advanced Clementine the necessary funds to purchase passage on a civilian cargo-and-passenger steamer. She found consolation knowing that the *Sea Gull* was a newer ship than any of those the navy owned. Extraordinarily seaworthy, the steamer made only one stop, in

Savannah, Georgia. With good weather, the ship would arrive at the southernmost tip of the United States within seven days.

In her darkened room above the sweet shop, Ruby held an impromptu seance. With Clementine by her side, she contacted Roy Calhoun. Ruby related that Roy promised his daughter a safe voyage. He would be with her. She had nothing to fear.

Clementine feared everything from the moment she stepped upon the deck. Still, until the *Sea Gull* set sail, she believed she would survive her sea voyage. Ruby and Jonathan gifted her with a bon voyage basket containing a half-dozen bottles of champagne. The doctor in her father-in-law prescribed alcohol. If she felt faint of heart during her sea voyage, he advised her to take a bottle of champagne and retire to her bed. To further ensure a successful journey, Clementine had the foresight to pack a fair supply of her favorite Saratoga chips in case they were not available in Key West.

Two hours into the journey, the seasickness started. Even though a lakelike calm settled over the indigo ocean, her stomach tossed and churned like a sack of beef jerky in a chuck wagon. Curling in her bunk, Clementine rubbed her lucky sea horse between her fingers until she feared the creature would disappear from wear. Champagne was out of the question. Death seemed inevitable.

She'd brought along her banjo for company and comfort, but her fingers trembled too much to play. For the first two days, she could keep nothing on her stomach, and when she looked in the mirror, a green girl with hollowed eyes stared back. Frightening.

According to Ruby, Clementine's beloved pa watched her from on high. Keeping that thought in mind, she told herself again and again that nothing worse than the awful seasickness would befall her. Pa would see to it that her voyage ended safely.

When the steamer stopped in Georgia, she remained on the ship, fearing if she disembarked she would never reboard.

On the eighth day of the journey, which seemed never-ending, the *Sea Gull* at last reached Key West.

"Land ahoy!"

Clementine had never been so happy to see a city in her life. Standing on deck as the ship steamed into the picturesque harbor, she felt as if she might jump out of her skin. Tingling excitement scampered through her veins, threatening to burst from her in a big old western "Yahoo!"

But weeks ago she'd promised Rand not to shout out again. Beginning her Key West visit, her honeymoon, by embarrassing him with a holler and a Texas hoot would not make for an auspicious start.

The tropical surroundings captivated Clementine at once. She viewed the coral reefs in the distance and the aquamarine Atlantic with undisguised wonder. The clear blue-green water allowed her to see small fish swimming near the surface. She could see sand and shells.

Tall, slender palm trees, heavy with coconuts, spread their deep green fronds toward a rich blue sky cluttered with puffs of white clouds. Seagulls and blue herons circled in an ever-climbing pattern above. The salty, moist air bathed her face and transformed her tight curls to cinnamon frizz.

When the crew lowered the gangplank, Clementine's swiftly beating heart thumped loud enough for all the keys they'd passed on the way to hear. Her body hummed with edgy anticipation.

She envisioned Rand's surprised expression . . . an image she credited with keeping her alive on the darkest days of the journey. When she felt so ill that she could not get out of her bunk, she thought of the handsome officer she'd married, pictured his enigmatic smile, the twinkle in his eyes.

A childlike joy of anticipation bubbled throughout her body as she picked up her old satchel and made her way down the gangplank.

Approaching the first uniformed sailor who caught her eye, she asked directions to the hospital. He obliged by escorting her. Along the way, Clementine passed up a coin on the sandy dirt path. Too anxious to stop, she walked right over the nickel cent winking in the sun.

Within minutes, they arrived at a three-story house with quaint gingerbread trim and a railed widow's walk high atop the roof. The grand home had been converted to a makeshift hospital. She ran up the steps, but paused when she reached the foyer.

The sick moaned, the overworked snapped at one another and a strong smell of death shrouded the rank, wet air.

Closing her eyes, Clementine clenched her jaw, summoning whatever courage lurked beneath her skin. She opened her eyes in time to see a young doctor scurry by.

She clasped his arm to stop him. "I'm looking for Dr. Noble."

"Back there. He's caught the fever. He's in quarantine." The doctor pointed to the rear of the house and then added in a hurried, distracted tone, "We don't have enough help to go around. You shouldn't be here, ma'am."

"I shall be careful," she promised, rushing in the direction the beleaguered doctor had pointed. "Ah'll help."

She quickly found Rand's sickroom, a small wooden shack separate from the house. He'd been left to die in a room with dirty windows, a dirty floor and furnishings so sparse that a jail cell would provide more comfort.

At first sight of the strong, compelling man who had left Annapolis, her heart sank.

An obviously weakened Rand lay motionless on the narrow iron-railed bed, drenched in perspiration. He was too tall for the bed, and his feet dangled over the end. He'd lost several pounds, and his complexion had taken on an unhealthy yellow hue.

A strangled cry escaped her as Clementine ran to his side. Dropping her satchel, she sank to the bed beside him. He did not stir at the movement; not a lash flickered. She studied his tall form in swift assessment. He wore nothing but cream-colored knit underdrawers rolled up to just below his knees.

Beads of sweat dotted the crisp mat of dark hair that spread across the muscular width of his chest and narrowed near the center to form a virile trail. Her gaze followed the dark path that disappeared beneath his drawers into forbidden territory. But the outline of his manhood clung to his damp underwear.

Clementine stared. Neglecting to breathe, she gaped open-mouthed, until her lungs grew tight from lack of oxygen. She would never have dreamed. He was magnificent. Thoroughly male magnificent. A man made for lusty passion.

Oh, mercy! Silently chastising herself for succumbing to lascivious thoughts at a time like this, she tore her gaze away and placed a hand on his forehead. He burned. Although ragged, the rhythm of his breathing seemed normal.

A crude square table at bedside held a washbasin and rag. She squeezed the cloth and then used it to gently bathe his forehead, then his cheeks and jaw. The stubble of his beard cast a dark, spiky shadow across his features. He groaned.

"Am I hurting you?" she whispered, alarmed.

"Feels . . . feels good," he murmured.

Wishing the water was cooler, she rinsed out the cloth and dabbed at his neck, tenderly applying the liquid along the solid column of his throat, the slight bump of his Adam's apple. After rinsing the rag again, she pressed it against his chest. Not even a Texas cowboy could hope to compare to the rigidly corded muscles, the unbridled, rugged strength Rand's physique suggested. A warm flurry of butterflies chased the wonder within her heart.

She must keep her mind on the nursing. She must help him regain the strength to work those muscles again.

When Clementine finished bathing him, she began again. When day turned to dusk, she found a nurse to bring her fresh water and started over again. When dusk turned to darkness, she continued to cool Rand's fever by lantern light. At midnight he moved. His eyes opened.

"Da-darlin'?" He peered up at her through narrowed eyes, dark and dull. His raspy tone grated. "Is that you?"

She smiled. "Yes. Ah'm here."

"I'm hallucinating."

"No, it's me," she insisted, forcing cheer. "Ah've come to be with you."

Groaning, he rolled his head to the side. "I'm sicker than I thought."

"No. No, I'm going to nurse you. You need me. The hospital staff is short handed."

"No. Clementine would never board a ship."

"Yes, I would . . . for you."

He blinked and looked again. His flat gaze fixed on her. Deep purple circles underscored his eyes. After a long moment, he reached up and tenderly traced her jaw with the back of his hand. "Clementine."

"Ah'm going to be your one and only nurse."

"I'll be . . . fine." His eyes fluttered. "I'm a . . . doctor. Protect yourself from . . ." His voice trailed off as he sank into unconsciousness.

"From mosquitos," she said, quietly finishing the sentence for him. "I know."

Clementine bathed him with cool water through the night. To keep awake, she sang "Home on The Range" over and over, sometimes sweetly, sometimes with gusto. Shortly after drawn she fell asleep in the hard pine rocking chair she'd drawn close to his bedside.

"Who are you, one of the ladies from town?"

Clementine woke with a start. An older man of forty years or more stood over her. He regarded her with a jutting chin and deeply wrinkled frown. The stranger's skin had been darkened to the shade of cowhide by the sun. She judged his creped flesh to be the same tough texture as well. He appeared haggard, wore spectacles and possessed a full, thick head of silver hair. The stripes on his uniform jacket identified him as a navy surgeon.

"Well?" he demanded.

"I'm Dr. Noble's wife, sir. Ah've come to nurse him."

After a moment, he nodded approval. "Good. That's good. But you must move aside and give me room to bleed him. I'm dr. Stock."

"Bleed him?"

"Yes. We bleed the poison out of our patients."

"No." Clementine rose from the rocker, fixed her gaze on Stock and squared her shoulders. "I will not allow you to bleed my husband."

Unused to being less than revered, the doctor's eyes widened and his mouth twisted with arrogance. *"You* won't allow it?"

"He needs his strength. Bleeding him will diminish—"

"I would advise you to listen to the lady, Dr. Stock. She may be hiding a derringer beneath her skirts."

Clementine swung her gaze down to the man she defended. Rand's voice might be soft and weak, and his lopsided smile barely there, but he'd made his opinion known.

The doctor appeared angry. He shifted his glower from patient to nurse.

"I know you have many patients requiring your attention," Clementine said soothingly. "I'll care for Rand as he wishes."

Stock directed his sharp question to Rand. "Is that what you want, Dr. Noble?"

"Yes."

With nary a nod to Clementine, the silver-haired navy surgeon turned on his heel and stormed off.

A small victory, but sweet.

Clementine made certain to keep herself covered at all times to protect herself from mosquito bites. According to Jonathan, who scoffed at the theory, it was thought a mosquito bite passed along the tainted blood of the already infected victims. In case it was true, she wore a dress with long sleeves in the heat of the day, a stifling situation but just bearable in the tropical fall weather.

Clementine found an empty cot in the attic of the hospital and moved it into the room beside Rand's bed. She spread netting around both beds to protect against mosquitoes and any other flying insects. Within hours of her arrival in Key West, she'd seen bugs that defied description, insects larger than Princess—with wings. Smudge pots and mosquito netting were commonly used at the tropical naval base.

She put into practice what she'd learned from Rand and his father, scrubbing the floors, walls and windows of the shack with carbolic acid that she'd brought from Rand's office. She added water to stretch the antiseptic, which smelled to her like an unpleasant combination of iodine and rubbing alcohol. But if Rand believed in it, she would too.

Her experience on the Texas range served Clementine well. She'd made many a campfire in her days rounding up strays. Now she prepared and cooked chicken broth over an open fire just outside the house.

Spoonful by spoonful, Clementine fed Rand the rich broth, slowly restoring his strength. She shaved him slowly and carefully every day. Cooled him with wet compresses over and over again. For ten days and nights, she nursed her husband around the clock. When he opened his eyes, when he saw her, he would smile. Not his usual mocking smile but a soft, grateful parting of his lips. A smile that stirred the music in her soul.

Sometimes he would speak, a sentence, a word.

"Stay with me."

In the evenings she often would play her banjo in a soft bedside serenade.

Occasionally, Dr. Stock would look in to see if her patient still lived. Upon finding Rand no worse for not being bled, he would mutter something unintelligible and leave.

Although Clementine stayed close to her patient, she had to leave the room for supplies. On one of these forays she came upon a patient with a nosebleed. Living so close to sickness and death had toughened her. In the last few days, she'd learned through grief and compassion to swallow her fear. She no longer ran from the sight of blood. Dr. Stock explained that in the last stages of yellow jack, as the disease was frequently called, bleeding from the nose and eyes was common. Clementine gave a word of encouragement to the patient before returning to her husband.

On the twelfth day, Rand sat up in bed. She had been outside warming broth over a fire. When she entered the shack, she found him upright, grinning like a fox who'd robbed the henhouse. Alarmed that he might be suffering some odd effects of the fever, she hurried to his bed. "Should you be sitting up?"

"I should," he declared. "Or I shall be so weakened that I'll not ever be able to leave my bed. Which might not be a bad thing if you would join me."

His rakish smile brought a bubble of laughter to Clementine's lips. The man she'd known had returned to his body. Rand had survived the fever.

For the first time in almost two weeks, when she put her hand to his forehead she felt no fever. The yellowish cast to his complexion had faded.

"I brought you warm broth."

"I cannot take another swallow of broth."

"Why not?"

"I want steak."

"You shall have it."

"A steak and a shave."

The hospital gave her a steak, which she cooked over the open fire and shared with Rand. What he wanted and what he could eat turned out to be two different matters.

She shaved him by lantern light, lathering his beard, gently and carefully running the razor along his jaw. Wiping away the foamy residue, she stroked her fingertips along his smooth jaw.

"I think I have learned to be an excellent barber," she said, satisfied with her work.

"And I am thankful that you learned while I was, for the most part, unconscious."

She scowled.

"Would you trust a woman who wrestles grown men to take a razor to your throat?"

Clementine gave in to his teasing and laughed.

Rand's gaze met hers. "If I were just a little stronger, you wouldn't have been able to finish the job tonight."

"Why not?" She could not drag her eyes from his. He held her locked in azure depths of possibilities.

"I would have you in this bed with me, and I would be making love to you," he replied in a husky timbre.

Clementine fought to retain her composure as chills of delight raced up and down her spine. "Do you make love to all your nurses?"

He shook his head. "Females are new to nursing. I've never had a female nurse. And no one but you has ever saved my life."

"I don't think I sav—"

He clasped her hand in his, squeezing it tightly. "I do. You saved my life."

Filled with a joy she'd never known, Clementine could not breathe, could not speak. She felt as if she'd been given wings to fly, to fly to places she'd never been before.

Rand continued to gaze into her eyes. She could not move, immobilized by an unspoken message she could not be certain of, not even to wipe away the tears that gathered in the corners of her eyes. Dang.

"There will never be any way that I can repay you for what you've done," he said.

She was accustomed to a certain arrogance from him. She'd never heard the humility underlying his tone. "You don't need to repay me. You're my husband."

"And you make me want to be a husband, a good husband."

The sweet fragrance of jasmine scented with a salty tang wafted on the evening air. Creatures of the night sang their songs to the rustle of the palms and the rhythm of the waves lapping the shore.

Rand's heart swelled to a point where it hurt to be confined in his chest. Clementine made him feel like a green, infatuated boy trapped inside a man's body. The warmth infusing him came from her smile, not the Key West climate. He still could not believe that she had braved the ocean and the risk of contracting yellow fever to be with him.

At one time during his recovery, he feared he was at death's door, and, in his feverish condition, he'd given the angel who had come for him Clementine's face and form.

Soon, determined to be strong, he began to walk. Leaning on Clementine, they would make several small forays a day, until he finally strolled to the beach with her. Within days, it became a ritual to spread a blanket and sit side by side under the shade of a palm tree, quietly watching the water change colors. They wiled away the hours talking, delving into any subject but the future. Clementine confessed that she missed her horse, Bay, more than she missed her brother, Junior. Rand admitted that he'd grown up determined to emulate his father. A man admired by men and women alike, a man with an independent nature, an island of a man. Together, in the heat of the afternoon when no cooling breeze stirred, they speculated on the prospect of an early snow in Annapolis.

Two weeks after taking his first shaky steps, Rand escorted Clementine on a walk into town. He stopped at Maloney's Inn on Duval Street. "You have cooked enough for me. Tonight you will be treated as you should be.

"And how is that?" she asked.

"Like a queen."

She laughed, but he'd meant it. The woman he'd been forced to wed had risked her life for him. But his admiration ran deeper. He didn't know exactly when it happened, but Clementine had assumed an aura of confidence; she moved like a loving princess among unruly peasants.

Rand being one of the peasants.

During the six months of their marriage, she had grown more beautiful. Her curves had softened, her lips turned up and even her eyes smiled more often. Only a trace of her Western drawl remained. Since coming to Florida, she'd clipped her bundle of springy curls to the top of her head. He knew she'd fashioned the new hairstyle to keep her neck cool, but she looked like a prim schoolmarm. The schoolboy in

Rand ached to release the fiery mass from its confining pins.

The funny, sweet freckles that marched across the bridge of Clementine's nose had returned. She'd been a victim of the constant Key West sun. Unable to carry a parasol while cooking over an open fire, she accepted her freckled fate with a shrug. She tolerated his teasing with good humor. It didn't faze her that the once-faded spots reappeared darker than before. And it certainly didn't faze Rand. Except that many times during his recovery, he'd longed to trace the freckle trail with his fingertips. He'd daydreamed of lightly kissing each and every dot.

When they first met, Clementine fainted at the sight of blood. Now she assisted in the hospital, helping fever victims without even noticing the stains of blood upon her apron. Rand held unbounded admiration for the woman she'd become. She'd changed.

Perhaps he had as well.

After an exotic dinner of turtle steak and Rand's first wine since the fever, he guided Clementine home, strolling back by way of the beach. A full golden moon shimmered on the water and provided a glistening path along the sand, lighting the way to the palm tree where they kept a blanket.

His strength had returned, his recovery complete thanks to the woman at his side. Since the fever, he'd felt far more appreciative than ever before of nights like this. He filled his lungs with the salty air, savored the light breeze ruffling his hair. Shimmering silver stars fanned across the sky as far as the eye could see.

"It's a marvelous night for moongazing," he said.

She raised jeweled green eyes to gaze above. "It is," she said softly.

If Rand could dive into the deep, luminous pools of

Clementine's eyes, he knew he would find heaven. The peace and happiness that always seemed to elude him waited there. He knew it as surely as he knew his name. Sparks of fire shot through his veins, warming him.

"I'll get the blanket."

She agreed with a smile. Her dark rose lips, kissed by the stars, were moist and beckoning.

Tearing his gaze from the lips he longed to cover with his, Rand unfolded the blanket. The sand was still warm to his touch as he spread and smoothed the cotton square.

Clementine sank to the center. He folded his long frame down beside her. An invisible fire crackled between them.

"How do you feel?" he asked.

"I feel quite full of food. It's difficult to think that Jonathan and Ruby may be shivering in the cold while we are gloriously warm."

Rand hardly heard what she said. He folded his arms across his chest, concentrating on keeping his hands to himself when he wanted them to be all over Clementine.

"And," she continued, "I am astonished by the beauty of this night, and this place."

"As am I. Beautiful." But Rand wasn't looking at the moon or the stars or the ocean; his gaze had settled on Clementine.

The tropical moonlight enhanced her copper curls with ribbons of gold. It wasn't her beauty alone that took his breath away. It was the goodness shining in her eyes. The keen intelligence and determination the girl from the Wild West possessed set her apart from every woman he'd ever known—including Ellie.

Clementine turned to him. She fixed him with a

soulful gaze that caused his heart to slam against his chest. His throat felt drier than the sand beneath the blanket.

She lifted her chin and whispered, "Kiss me . . ."

Rand wasn't certain he'd heard correctly. He feared her soft command was only the echo of his own desire.

"Kiss me . . ." she repeated in the same breathless voice as she leaned up and into him.

He kissed her. He'd meant it to be a tender kiss, but when his lips touched hers, when he tasted her, he wanted more. His body demanded more. Gathering Clementine into his arms, Rand held her with the need of a man who refused to let the woman he held escape. Ever.

Releasing a soft, deep sigh, Clementine wrapped her arms around his neck and melted into him, and the simmering ache in his loins grew intense. The heat that enveloped Rand, swiftly and surely, had nothing to do with the climate and everything to do with the woman in his arms. His wife. His sweet, funny, smart, precious wife.

He would make love to her. Now. At last. He would make certain that she would never forget this night. He would warm her gently, love her in every way, transport her beyond this tropical paradise to another.

# *Fifteen*

Clementine surrendered herself to the warm, welcome shelter of Rand's arms. The fierceness of his kiss left her feeling light-headed. Frightened and emboldened. Eager and tentative. A tempest of conflicting emotions brewed within her, flowing warm, rushing hot.

She opened her eyes to the face imprinted on her heart. The striking face of her daydreams, the strong angular face that invaded her dreams at night. Rand's face. From inches away, his breath tickled her cheek, teased her sensitive skin.

Narrow streaks of moonlight shot through his dark, coffee-colored hair. His locks had grown long and curled at the nape of his neck. The blue gaze that she'd come to know as well as her own fixed on her. Desire glazed his eyes.

Clementine ached for him. To have him and hold him until the tide came in and swept them from the sand. She needed his kisses more than her beloved bluebonnets needed the Texas sun.

He smiled.

And her heart clamored with love.

She loved the man she'd married. The feeling had come slowly. It slipped in through her pores and settled deep in the essence of her being, shedding its light like a candle. A candle destined to burn for eternity. Silently acknowledging her love, Clementine felt filled with the sweetness of summer rain falling on dry range.

Rand. Her love. For life. She loved him in ways that she'd never imagined. She loved his belly laugh, his carefree saunter, his ability to heal the sick with both skill and humor. She loved his mischievous, lopsided smile and, most of all, she loved his humanity.

"What are you thinking?" he asked.

"Ah'm thinking of you," she replied, lulled into the old familiar drawl.

His lips curved up into a satisfied smile as he gently lowered her to the blanket. "The night is made for lovers."

"And I shall be your lover," she promised breathlessly.

His lips came down upon hers. Burning. Bruising.

The walk-in-the-spring-woods scent of him wrapped around Clementine. Spruce and musk filled her senses. The stubble of his beard scraped lightly against her chin. His raw masculinity.

Her lips parted in an involuntary, instinctive response to his kiss, a kiss deeper than the Atlantic. When he slipped his tongue into her mouth, Clementine lost the ability to breathe. Her heart pounded like the bass drum in a traveling medicine show.

Did Rand feel what she felt? She had no idea how to explain the fire racing through her body or how to share it. She could only give herself up to the glorious, giddy feeling of rising, floating, buffeted on a hot, wet current. She was swept away like a dandelion cluster in the wind. Her body buzzed in bristly awakening. Clementine came alive and realized she'd never been truly alive before.

Rand raised his head, gazed down upon her.

Her lips felt bare and swollen.

"Make me your wife tonight," she whispered urgently.

His mouth covered her ear, and he whispered, "Are you certain that you want me, darlin'? Are you certain?"

A series of hot, delicious waves flooded her body clear down to her curled toes. There was nothing in this life that she wanted more than Rand.

"I want you. Oh, how I want you."

Rand did not hesitate. His tongue gently traced the sensitive shell of her ear, triggering a fresh onslaught of fiery tremors. And as he fumbled with the buttons of her bodice, he brushed tantalizing kisses along her neck.

"I can help," she whispered.

He released her with obvious reluctance.

Clementine quickly straightened, unbuttoned, discarded, until she wore nothing but her chemise. Simultaneously, Rand rose to his knees, pulled, yanked and discarded. He plopped down on the blanket and again pulled, yanked and tossed off both his trousers and underdrawers.

Overcome with equal parts wonder and shyness, Clementine sighed. Rand grinned.

She had never seen such a splendid sight as Rand naked in the moonlight. Sculpted muscles gleamed like steel for all eyes to see. With renewed, pulse-pumping admiration, her gaze skimmed over his broad, matted chest and brawny, wide shoulders. Motionless in the moonlight, his virile form could be mistaken for a bronzed god of astounding proportions.

His eyes twinkled in the old magical way, the

crevices at the corners deepening with his pleasure. This was the Rand of old, a healthy, lusty rake. Astonishingly uninhibited, he radiated raw masculinity and . . . happiness. His joyful laughter resounded on the deserted beach.

It was his laughter that enchanted Clementine. The laughter that echoed in her heart.

But his laughter faded as, drawing closer, he gathered her into his arms and lowered her to the blanket. Mesmerized by the fierce passion in his eyes, she abandoned thought to feeling. She felt his heat as he gently rolled down the sleeves of her chemise. And his heat fueled hers. Clementine burned with a fever she'd never experienced before. His lips grazed her shoulders and slowly claimed as his each newly exposed area of her flesh. Shudders of delight rippled through her like rivers of thick, liquid gold.

As the simmering ache between her thighs intensified, Rand's exploration slowed. He slipped her arms free, planting a sensuous caress in the soft crook of her elbow, feeding on the soft palms of her hands.

With painstaking care, he freed Clementine from the confines of her modest white linen garment. His gaze never wavered as he rolled back the fabric.

"You are exquisite," he said in an awed, husky timber. His gaze lingered on her breasts.

"Delicate," he murmured.

Clementine could barely catch her breath.

His gaze fastened on her hips. "You're perfect. You're far more lovely than I imagined."

Every nerve within her body tingled. She must do something. What must she do? She didn't know. She longed to touch Rand, feel him, love him in whatever way would bring him pleasure.

"Tell me, tell me what to do."

But he didn't answer.

She listened to the waves lap against the shore, the rustle of the palms overhead.

"Do nothing. Just be mine," he said at last in a tone barely audible but filled with longing.

Clementine reached out. Rand swiftly pulled her into his arms. Her breasts crushed against his steely chest. The simmering ache within her became a torrid blaze.

He slipped one leg between hers. She became a firestorm.

Lowering his head, Rand covered one breast with his mouth while his thumb gently brushed the nipple of the other. Speechless, mindless, Clementine could only utter a whimper of ecstasy. She'd never felt ecstasy, but knew this was it. Her nipples hardened, tingled, as he suckled. When she feared she would explode from the ache and the excitement, he switched to her left breast, to cover and suckle again.

She rocked beneath him, her body demanding release from the relentless ache that threatened to tear her apart.

"Be patient, darlin'," he murmured, lifting his head, stroking her thighs.

But Clementine was beyond patience, beyond rational thought. She felt like a flower petal tossed in winds, constantly changing directions. Unable to control her feelings or the liquid heat rushing through her veins, her fingers dug into the muscles of his back.

Rand sprinkled a trail of light kisses along her belly. He paused briefly at her navel and then continued, finding the entrance to her core with a gentle, probing finger.

"Oh mercy!" she croaked.

Clementine reeled in a pleasure so extreme, wet and hot and raging, she thought she would explode.

"Help me . . ." she pleaded in a breathless sigh. She didn't know how he could help, but innately understood that he could.

And then Rand parted her legs, hovered above her. His flesh brushed against hers, igniting still another fire. Strangely, she could not feel his weight, barely heard his anxious assurance, "I will not hurt you, would not hurt you for the world."

He entered her with a gentle thrust. He filled her. She gasped at the strength of him, gasped at the pain that lasted less than an instant. The rapture had just begun.

With each thrust, Clementine soared higher. With each thrust, Rand guided her with surety toward a great unknown.

The blanket of stars sparkling above them appeared closer and closer. Rand sped her toward the stars, faster and higher.

Aroused beyond human endurance, she feared she would burst. Clinging to Rand, she splayed her hands against the pebbled flesh of his back. Higher. Faster. She could not explain what was happening to her, but she made a raspy attempt.

"I'm . . . I'm . . . Oh! Oooh."

She'd reached her star. Shining. Blinding. Beautiful.

With a final thrust, Rand cried out, a deep, triumphant release.

Clementine had no doubt. He'd reached his star. Smiling, she collapsed beneath her husband. She drifted in languid peace as warm and sweet as melting sugar.

Rand broke the silence. "I believe I now can say that

I am completely recovered. You've proved to be an excellent nurse, Clementine."

Holding each other fast, they laughed together in the moonlight.

Jonathan had been invited to dinner at the farmhouse, an invitation he'd accepted with uncommon alacrity. Ruby shivered beside him during the drive to the farm. Riding against the wind, the cold late-October air penetrated even his fine cashmere overcoat and muffler. He couldn't help but notice his companion's worn wool cloak and wondered how he could replace the garment without wounding her pride. Ruby possessed far too much pride for a woman. A roaring fire in the kitchen fireplace welcomed them and served to ward off the cold. The seven diners who gathered around the table generated a good deal of body heat through their energy alone.

Rather than the landlords they were, Eric and Gerta Houseman behaved more like the revered young aunt and uncle to Ruby and her family. The hardy couple obviously took great pleasure in their four boarders.

As did Jonathan, although he found it difficult to follow the dinner conversation. Each time one of the three children spoke, he or she changed or skipped subjects. Livelier than dinners he'd shared with former lady friends, he found the hour challenging and often confusing. And it passed much too quickly.

He wasn't ready to leave.

"Jonathan, would you like to have coffee with me in the parlor?" Ruby asked as she rose from the table.

"I would be delighted."

Her smile made his heart beat faster—a phenomenon that had frightened him at first, thinking he was about to have an attack. But now, as it occurred with increasing frequency when in Ruby's company, he understood and accepted its implications.

"I'll join you as soon as I have tucked Zeke and Della into bed. Say goodnight to Dr. Noble, children."

Zeke bobbed his head from where he stood at his mother's side. "Goodnight, sir."

"Goodnight, son."

But Della took Jonathan by surprise. A sweet child with long, dark sausage curls and large, golden eyes like her mother, she sidled shyly up to him and proceeded to plant a firm kiss on his cheek. "Goodnight, Dr. Noble."

Slanting him a Mona Lisa smile, Ruby raised a marveling brow.

Shocked into silence, words failed him. The small spot on his cheek where Della had placed her kiss warmed and delighted him. Struggling to recover, he offered a smile and a hushed, "Goodnight, my . . . my dear."

Gerta, in the tone of a woman used to giving orders, spoke first to Ruby. "Tonight I shall clean up. You need not come back to the kitchen."

"But I always—"

Gerta waved her off, "Go. And you, Harley, show the doctor to the parlor."

"Yes, ma'am."

No one dared argue with Gerta, it seemed.

Certainly not Jonathan, a guest. After thanking her profusely for another delicious meal, he followed the tall, gangly boy into the parlor. Smelling of lemon polish, the room was not much bigger than his foyer at home. The furniture consisted of a sofa and two slat-backed rockers flanking the fireplace. Nothing but embers burned there. Choosing a seat closer to whatever heat was left, Jonathan eased himself into one of the rockers.

"I 'preciate what you did for me, Dr. Noble. Saving me from jail. My mother likely would have killed me. Or cried. Or both."

"Don't mention it."

Hanging his head, Harley shifted nervously from one foot to the other. "I didn't know what to do. I give my mother the money I earn at odd jobs after school. It helps pay our room and board here."

"I understand. You don't have to explain again. I'm glad I was able to help."

Unable to look Jonathan in the eye, the boy tugged at the sleeve of his flannel shirt. "I like the new job you found for me at the newspaper and—"

"One more payment and we will be square," Jonathan interrupted, unwilling for Ruby's contrite son to suffer any further embarrassment. "You need never bring the incident up again. You meant well, and we men have to stick together and help each other out. Your mother never need know."

"Yes, sir."

Jonathan felt inordinately pleased with himself. He vaguely wondered if any of the other children had a problem he might help with. "Would you mind stirring that fire a bit before you leave, Harley?"

"No, sir. I'll put a fresh log on."

"Good. You know, I was thinking that I would like to take the whole family to dinner at the Maryland Inn on your mother's birthday. She seems to like the place. Do you think she would enjoy a family feast?"

"Yes, sir. She would, sir."

"Very well, I shall extend the invitation this evening."

"She never complains, but it's been hard for my mother since our father died. She won't ask for help. Never has."

"Your mother is a remarkable woman."

A throaty chuckle from the doorway brought Jonathan up short. Ruby stood there in full glory, gloating—if he wasn't mistaken.

"How sweet and insightful of you, Jonathan."

Quickly bounding to his feet, he cleared his throat several times.

"And I appreciate you reminding my children of my value," she continued, sashaying into the room. "They believe me to be a she-devil, insisting on school and work and chores."

"Madam, they could not possibly. I'm certain that you exaggerate."

"Off with you, Harley. It's time for study."

"Yes, ma'am."

In a swirl of silk skirts, Ruby sank wearily to the sofa. She pulled her shawl more tightly around her.

"Are you cold?"

"A little. It grows colder each day. Before we know it, Christmas will be upon us."

"Yes, Christmas," he repeated absentmindedly. As one of the town's most eligible bachelors, he always celebrated Christmas in the homes of friends. He hadn't observed the holiday in his own home since Rand was a boy. No matter where he was or how many people he joined around the piano to sing carols, he felt lonely. He likened himself to a marionette, the façade of a man with a hollowed-out body.

"Christmas is one of my favorite holidays," she added.

"Mine too," he lied, adding quickly, "Harley just put another log on the fire. You shall warm up soon."

"He's a good son," she said.

Jonathan removed his jacket and draped it over her shoulders. "Yes, he is. You have a fine family, Ruby. You've done an excellent job of raising your children by yourself."

She gave him a tired smile. "I haven't been able to give them as much as I would like, but I believe they will be solid citizens eventually."

"You are a woman to be admired."

"Jonathan, you don't mean that."

"But I do," he protested, mildly insulted.

"You do not admire my occupation and have made no bones about it."

Sitting beside her, he crossed his arms over his chest. "Your choice of occupation is another matter."

"Jonathan, I've studied people and know their hearts and minds. When I found myself widowed and estranged from my family because I had married a Southerner, I was lost."

"I cannot fathom such a position," he admitted.

Folding her hands in her lap, Ruby inclined her head. Her eyes fixed on his, seeming to insist on his understanding. "As you can guess, I was not trained to work. I had no skills or special talents. But I possessed a gift that set me apart. I had an innate knowledge of how people think, how emotions influence and in some cases rule their lives. Almost by accident, I discovered that I could support my children by giving peace to troubled souls and hearts."

Jonathan had a bad feeling. "Why are you telling me this now?"

"Because, despite your disapproval, you have been a good friend. I want you to understand so that perhaps you will at least accept that what I do may be beneficial to some, even if you do not approve."

"Ruby, you don't require my approval."

She nodded. "I know. But listen. Like you, I heal people. I'm a doctor of a different sort, healing invisible wounds. I treat scars formed on troubled minds and hearts. I listen to fears, to guilts and to hopes, and I offer absolution. My clients hear what their loved ones would like to say if they could. Is that so bad?"

Jonathan felt a moment of shame. A weight settled in the pit of his stomach. He had judged her and been wrong. He should never have chastised Ruby without a true understanding of what she did. "No. No, your work is not harmful or bad."

"Everyone needs something to believe in. Consider the happiness of children who believe in Saint Nick. Is it wrong?"

"No."

She flashed a great, warm smile. "I have said my piece, and that is all there is to that."

"Please accept my apologies. I may have trouble with how you achieve your . . . healing, but the fact remains you have offered solace and strength to those who've sought your counsel—like Clementine."

"Speaking of Clementine, how does her dog fare, living with you?"

"I have trained Princess," he announced with pride. "She no longer growls or bares her teeth at strangers. Hopefully this will hold true for Rand when he comes home."

Jonathan had been happy to take the pup when Clementine left for Key West. Training the rascal had helped to fill his empty hours.

"I'm glad to hear it. I received a letter from Clementine today."

"What did she say? Is Rand continuing to grow stronger? Is she still getting on with him?"

"Glowingly!" Ruby declared. "And she has learned to roll cigars from a Cuban cigar maker."

"What?"

"Well, because of Cuba's current political strife, there are many Cuban exiles in Key West, and from what Clementine tells me quite a cigar industry is flourishing there."

"Why would my daughter-in-law wish to learn how to roll a cigar?"

"She is an expert at rolling cigarettes."

He was appalled. "You don't mean that Clementine smokes?"

"No, but she did when she first arrived in Annapolis. Every chance she got."

"You modern women are quite beyond my understanding. Why must you do what men do?"

"To prove that we can." Her amber eyes sparkled with pleasure. "We are a shameless lot, are we not?"

"You certainly are," he agreed with a grin.

But as his eyes met hers, Ruby's sparkle faded. Hugging his jacket to her, she rose and crossed to the fireplace. Standing with her back to Jonathan, she jabbed at the fire with the poker.

"Is something wrong?" he asked.

"No, I have . . . Yes, there is something you must know that I can no longer put off telling you."

"Get on with it then, you've never hesitated to speak your mind to me in the past."

She turned from the fire. Her gaze locked on his. "I fear what I have to say may distress you."

"That never stopped you before either," he scoffed. But his bravado was but a bluff.

A hodgepodge of fears tumbled through his mind. Ruby had contracted a deadly disease, or she had received a marriage proposal from a suitor who recognized her beauty and brains. Jonathan pushed himself up from the sofa to stand like a man. "Tell me what is on your mind and let me decide if I shall be distressed."

"My work here in Annapolis is done. I must move on."

In the dead silence, he could hear the tick, tick, tick of his pocket watch. "No. How can your work be done?"

"I have healed all of the lost souls who have come to me. It's time to move on to another town. I shall be leaving for Baltimore."

Jonathan felt himself falling, as if a ladder he'd been climbing had suddenly been jerked from beneath his feet. His stomach filled with hot, sizzling acid. "When? When do you plan to do this?"

She lowered her eyes. "Next week."

"Next week?" he repeated. "You can't!"

"You have been very kind to me, Jonathan," she said softly. "Your friendship has meant a great deal, and I hope that you will write to me as you do to Rand and Clementine."

"I . . . I don't know what to say. I never thought you would leave. The children appear happy here. You and Clementine have become staunch friends—"

Moving quickly to his side, Ruby took his hand, attempted to comfort him. "Everything you say is true, but I cannot earn a living in Annapolis any longer. I have no choice. I must move on."

An overwhelming desire to take the lovely medium into his arms and hold her prisoner took hold of Jonathan. But he recognized his need as an old man's dream. She said he'd been a good friend. Being a woman of her words, clearly that was exactly how she regarded him. As a friend. He could not hope that he meant more to her. He was older than Ruby by more than ten years. Why would she want him?

But how could he let her go?

"Would you have dinner with me before you leave?"

No longer his antagonist, all pretense of discord melted away. She smiled softly. "Of course I will."

"With the children?"

"Are you certain?"

"Yes. At my home."

If he set his mind to it, perhaps he could think of a way to make her stay.

# Sixteen

Rand made love to Clementine every day and evening. If he'd had his way—and the stamina—he would have loved her every hour of every day. His wife had become his obsession.

Instead of slackening off, his desire for her grew. As one lazy, sweltering day slid into another, he only wanted her more.

Rather than shirking from his touch, from all physical contact as Ellie had, Clementine enjoyed making love. Any and all inhibitions she might have had fell away on that first night they spent together in the moonlight. In whispered, whisky-voiced passion, she urged him to teach her what gave him pleasure. Soon he knew more sensual excitement than he'd ever experienced before. Clementine took to exploring with great gusto. In her loving hands, he found release and the peace of a man whose questions had all been answered.

And she never withheld disclosing her own joy, sometimes reverting to her Texas roots with a wild cry.

"Yaaaahoo!"

His bride's enthusiasm acted as a galvanizing force. Hot and aching for her, Rand became Hercules, powerful and potent. His heart roared and his body temperature climbed to dizzying degrees. Joined with soft, spirited Clementine in a frenzied dance of love, he became whole. The flurry of needles and pins that skittered through his veins found release as he reached undreamed-of heights. He soared to the top-mast and fell to earth in the arms of an angel. Serenity claimed him, invading muscle and bone like a sweet, warm syrup.

Rand owed her his life. His swift recovery.

Within days of being declared well again by Dr. Stock, Rand and Clementine moved into a cozy three-room cottage provided by the navy. Their honeymoon house came complete with gingerbread trim along the roof and veranda. They enjoyed a breathtaking view of the sunset from their porch, which overlooked the Gulf of Mexico. Late in the afternoon, Rand held Clementine's hand and watched the brilliant orange-red globe slowly descend into indigo waters until it vanished below the horizon.

The cottage furnishings were ancient and ugly, but Clementine found ways to add beauty in unlikely places. Crimson hibiscus blossoms sprouted from the spout of an old teapot; shiny conch shells marched across the windowsills.

Too soon for his liking, Rand returned to work in the hospital, but at every opportunity he stole away to be with his bride. If he could find her.

She'd taken to visiting the island school and entertaining the children with tall tales of the West. Mixing her stories with a good dose of actual history, her lessons were accompanied by a song or two on the banjo. In mere weeks, she'd become the belle of Key West.

Life in the tropical paradise was as perfect as possible. Once merely a word, happiness had become a way of living. Rand relished his joy and the feeling it gave him of being able to conquer the world single-handedly. Thanks to Clementine, he had reverted to the carefree man he used to be.

Shaking off his reflections, Rand hurried down Greene Street, snapping bougainvillea blossoms from the bushes as he passed. By the time he reached the cottage, he carried a bouquet screaming with bright scarlet red, shocking pink and lemon yellow flowers.

"Clementine, I'm home!"

"I'm in the kitchen," she called. "The indoor kitchen."

He barreled into the back room, holding the flowers behind his back. The small plank table had been set for dinner, with linen napkins and a beeswax candle between the tin plates.

A picture of domesticity, Clementine stood at the pine counter peeling shrimp. The window above the small space offered a view of the Gulf. At the sound of his approaching steps, she looked over her shoulder and greeted him with a radiant smile. "Welcome home."

"I slipped away as soon as I could." As he'd grown in the habit of doing every day. "This *is* our honeymoon."

Tendrils of copper frizzle framed Clementine's face and dangled at her nape in charming defiance of any brush or comb. He'd come to admire with great fondness the haphazard direction of her curls. She wore a narrow, striped taffeta bodice and skirt in a shade similar to blue china. The trim of blue fringe that circled the small padded bustle especially fascinated him. With the slightest movement of her hips, there was a swish of fringe. He considered it a profoundly provocative motion for an enamored man like himself.

Unlike most women in his past, Clementine was no slave to fashion. She bowed to the warm weather and chose comfort over fashion. Rolling up the sleeves of her gown to her elbow, she'd left the snug bodice unbuttoned to reveal a tantalizing peek of luscious decolletage.

She looked too good to resist. He tossed the flowers on the table.

"You are delicious," he growled, coming up behind her. Wrapping his arms around his hard-working wife, Rand sprinkled kisses behind her ear and all the way down to her tasty nape.

She wiggled in his arms. "Oooh, that feels so good."

"If you think that feels good, just wait." Stepping back, he whirled her around to face him, tipped up her chin.

"But dinner is ready," she protested in a breathy tone.

"Can't it wait?" he asked, lowering his head, aiming for her lovely rosy lips. Even to his own ears, his voice rasped thick with desire. "I came home early to give you a swimming lesson."

"I guess the shrimp can—"

His lips locked on hers, preventing Clementine from finishing her sentence. He kissed her deeply, completely.

When she gasped for air, he tore his mouth away. Growing warm, growing hard, he forced himself to disrobe her trembling body slowly. The painful ache within him demanded release. The pounding of his heart grew heavier, faster until, at last, the garments lay pooled at her feet on the kitchen floor. She stood before him in nothing but her chemise. His hungry gaze drank in Clementine's proud form, the luscious curves that drove him wild.

He tore off his own clothes. Down to his drawers, he extended a hand. "Come with me, Mrs. Noble. I shall show you a sunset that you will never forget."

She said nothing, but one corner of her lips turned up in a plainly seductive smile. And that said everything.

Hand in hand they walked into the clear aquamarine water. Ahead, the huge crimson ball of sun hovered above the horizon, preparing to set.

Rand stopped when he'd reached a point where the water lapped just beneath his chest. Clementine's generous breasts were covered but clearly outlined against her chemise beneath the crystal water.

Enfolding her in his arms, he ducked into the water. As long as he held her tightly, Clementine showed no fear. She'd reached the point where she confessed to enjoying the sensation of the tepid water rolling over them.

"It's like taking a bath together," she declared.

Wet, warm and pressed flesh to flesh, Rand's arousal swiftly reached a point where he feared losing control. He guided her to an upright position. But once her feet were planted in the sand, she splayed her palms against his chest, triggering a parade of chills that ricocheted down his spine.

He plucked the hairpins from the top of her head, marveling as the mass of her hair tumbled down in fiery disarray. Twisting one of the curls around his finger, he brushed his lips against the silken strand. Hearing Clementine's ragged sigh, he freed the unruly lock to join the rest caressing her glistening shoulders. The ache within him intensified to unbearable proportions.

Curling her arms around Rand's neck, Clementine dipped her head to gently nibble at his chest. Unable to speak, to even catch his breath, he groaned at the touch of her lips. He didn't know how much longer he could keep at bay the soul-galvanizing, white-hot need to be one with her. He peeled down her wet chemise and cupped her bare, creamy breasts in his palms. His loins caught fire. The kind of throbbing pain he experienced had but one release.

He carried Clementine to bed.

An hour later, her hair still damp and curling round her shoulders, Rand sat across from his beautiful wife, dining on shrimp and champagne. Thanks to his father's generous prescription for Clementine, their supply of champagne had just begun to dwindle.

Reaching across the small table, she popped a large shrimp into his mouth. "A king-sized morsel for the king of our little castle."

"Open wide," he commanded with a grin, and returned the favor.

He fed her shrimp and wiped the juice with his fingertip when it trickled down her chin.

Interlocking her arm through his, Clementine sipped champagne from Rand's glass, and he from hers.

Satiated, at the end of the meal he led her to the bedroom, where he would make certain they would be satisfied again.

A knock sounded on the door just as Rand pulled Clementine down on the bed.

"Aargh!" He had no patience for an interruption now.

"Someone needs a doctor." Her tone was as much a lament as a statement.

He pushed himself off the bed and hurriedly slipped on his trousers. "If they do, I shall make an excuse by saying that at the moment my wife requires my undivided attention."

"Which is quite true," she said, flashing a seductive smile.

But when Rand opened the door, the sailor waiting there simply handed him an envelope, saluted sharply, turned on his heel and left.

The orders had come. The orders he'd been expecting.

Ice washed through his veins. He froze to the spot.

He wasn't ready to leave yet. Forcing himself to tear open the envelope, Rand scanned the contents. He had five days to prepare before leaving for California. After arriving on the West Coast, his orders directed him to join the expedition that would establish the Navy's first base in Samoa.

"What is it, Rand?"

Clementine stood in the doorway. Barefoot, unmindful that her copper crown had become an enticing, tangled mass, she waited for his reply.

Her gaze fixed on the paper he held.

And his locked on the exquisite rise and fall of creamy mounds. Almost translucent, and swollen with desire, her breasts rose above the square neckline of her chemise, beckoning him.

Rand sucked in his breath. Never had he seen Clementine appear so wanton, nor so lovely.

She gestured toward the orders. "What does' it say?"

"I've received my orders. I am to leave for Pago Pago in five days' time."

Her body reeled and her expression folded in pain as if she'd received a blow. Feeling helpless and wretched, he watched tears spring to her eyes. Her lips quivered.

"Five days," she repeated in a rasp.

Rand hurried across the room, gathering her into his arms. "You will come with me. We'll ship out to California and from there cross the Pacific to Samoa. An officer's wife is able to accompany him on long deployments."

"Is this a dangerous mission?"

"And when have you run from danger?" he asked, unable to deny the risks. "A woman who goes after cattle rustlers."

"I knew the land and the thief. This is much different."

Clementine's body felt listless in his arms. She spoke quietly, but he heard resignation in her tone. "How is this different?" he demanded, determined to change her mind.

"Despite what their leaders have agreed upon, the Samoan natives might object. You know what happened to my pa in Korea."

"There will be no fighting. The Samoans are welcoming us. There is nothing to fear. We shall be explorers, you and I. We shall see and experience new lands and new people. We'll be traveling where few Americans have been before. How can you refuse to be a part of such an exciting event?"

"How can you ask me to cross two oceans?"

He set her back from him, gripping her forearms, locking his gaze on her misty eyes. "Because you can do it. Because the chance to make a voyage like this may never come again."

"How can you be so certain?" she protested.

"Because I know how unpredictable an officer's life can be. An opportunity like the one I've been given is rare and in all likelihood will not be offered again. Life in Annapolis and all that goes with it will always be there for us."

"Will it? Will you always have a position at the hospital?"

"As long as I return in time. My orders call for an absence from the hospital of eighteen months."

"Then you must go."

"And you must come with me," he insisted. "You traveled the Atlantic on a steamer by yourself. On this journey, you'll have me at your side."

Shaking her head, Clementine lowered her eyes. "No."

"Why?" he pressed. His blood had begun to boil. Her stubbornness gnawed at the edge of his already frayed patience.

"Why must you go?" she countered, blinking back her tears.

She sounded just like Ellie. Ellie all over again. Just when he'd come to believe Clementine was so different, she opposed him. She refused to accompany him on the greatest adventure he would ever know. Just like Ellie, she preferred to cling to him at home.

"This is a once-in-a-life time opportunity," he argued, struggling once more to make her understand his feelings. Rand lived for adventure. To reject his passion was to reject him.

"How many men, or women, have the opportunity to settle in a foreign land and establish a presence for their country?"

"Not many, I expect." She raised her gaze to his. "You must go."

Rand read resolve in the depths of her spring green eyes but refused to accept her decision as final. "And you'll be with me," he vowed, as much to persuade himself as her. "You'll change your mind, Clementine. You have before."

She turned and padded back to the bedroom. He didn't follow.

Three days after Rand received his orders, Clementine waited on the dock. Passengers were boarding the launch that would take them to the ship headed for Maryland and Boston. She dreaded the return journey to Annapolis, but she had no choice.

From the corner of her eye, she glanced at Rand, who stood rigidly at her side. Her heart skipped at the sight of him as it always did. Tall and striking in his blue and gold uniform, with his cap tucked beneath his arm, he seemed more naval officer than doctor this morning. For who knew how long, perhaps forever, she must carry this picture of him, with his jaw clenched tightly and his eyes focused on the horizon. Unyielding.

They had argued for two days, until, when it became plain that neither would budge, they fell into a tense silence.

Clementine cried inside, giant sobs that seared her lungs. Her heart felt so bruised and swollen she could hardly bear the pain. At any moment she feared it would shatter. She could not understand Rand's need for adventure when a good life awaited him back in Annapolis, where he was loved and respected. Plainly, he could not understand her refusal to embark with him on his great adventure.

Several passengers had already boarded the launch that would take them to the ship anchored in the harbor. Clementine's time with Rand was running out. Her knees had no more substance than the Gulf breeze.

She briefly closed her eyes when the young officer

approached her, attempting to close him out. She knew he'd come for her. "Mrs. Noble, are you ready?"

"Yes." Her lips quivered as she looked up at Rand. "It's time for me to go."

His blue eyes no longer sparkled. They were dark with shadows. His gaze settled on hers. "Have a safe journey . . . sweetness."

Taking his hand, Clementine pressed the object she fingered into his palm. "My Pa gave me this seahorse for luck. He said it was the only kind of horse he ever liked."

Slanting her a puzzled frown, Rand looked down.

"My pa carved it himself," she explained, "on one of his voyages. He promised it would bring good luck."

"I can't accept—"

"Hush," Clementine interrupted. She closed his hand around the small, delicate seahorse. "I'm counting on this little horse to keep you safe and bring you back to me."

His eyes squeezed shut as he drew in a sharp breath. "I . . . Clementine . . ."

She pressed a finger to his lips. "We won't say goodbye."

"Please, come with me. Stay," he pleaded in heart-wrenching anguish.

"Be safe, my love." Raising up, she kissed him on the cheek. Before she could weaken, Clementine turned on her heel and fled to the tender, unable to look back.

She could not tell Rand the real reason why she chose to return to Annapolis. Ellie would have. But if Clementine revealed her secret, her deserving husband might miss what he believed to be the adventure of a lifetime.

\* \* \*

Jonathan paced nervously as he waited, waited for the night and the moment that might change the rest of his life. He'd sent a letter to his son announcing his intentions, explaining what he was about to do. If Rand were here, he might attempt to stop him. But Jonathan could not be stopped. He could not think of anything else to do. It was the only course open, the only one he wished to take. And, in all likelihood, his plan would be rejected. He did not entertain high hopes.

Ruby and her children arrived for dinner precisely at seven o'clock. She didn't realize that he knew it was her birthday. According to Harley, who kept Jonathan informed, his family had packed their belongings. They were prepared to leave the next day for Baltimore.

Unbeknownst to Ruby—which proved she could not see and know everything—Harley and Jonathan had become friends since he'd rescued the boy from the law. He'd taken to counseling the lad as he had been unable to do with his own son. While Rand was growing up, he'd been away at sea.

Jonathan greeted Ruby with a slight bow and kissed her hand with the flair of a gallant. Which earned him a raised bow and a long moment of questioning contemplation. But she took his arm, and he led the family into his drawing room.

Unlike the farmhouse parlor, his spacious drawing room boasted ample and comfortable overstuffed furnishings of spool-turned black walnut. A soothing terra-cotta color dominated, supplying warmth to the chamber, along with fire from the hearth.

The three children scrutinized the plush surroundings, making no attempt to disguise their astonishment. They appeared stunned into silence. While Jonathan and Ruby were served brandy, Harley, Della and Zeke perched on the edge of their chairs and sipped ginger beer.

Jonathan felt an unusual tension between him and Ruby. It stretched between them like the endless sky as they strained to make conversation.

"Are you packed and ready to depart for Baltimore?" he asked.

The thick sausage curls that fell from Ruby's crown to her nape took a bounce as she bobbed her head. "Yes, we are."

"Do you know where you shall be staying?"

"Certainly. I have contacted a preacher and his wife. We shall be boarding with the Reverend Fleming for the first week."

"I see." She had taken care of everything, as Jonathan knew she would have. Ruby had no need of a man to take care of her.

"On a trial basis," she added.

Even when they argued, the words always flowed between Ruby and him. This stop-and-go, forced discussion made Jonathan uncomfortable. His skin prickled. His neck felt warm beneath his shirt collar. Uncharacteristically uncertain of his course, he talked in circles.

When his butler finally announced dinner, relief poured through him like Poor man's punch, relaxing rigid muscles and soothing frayed nerves.

He could use the interlude, and a glass of wine, to shore up his courage.

# *Seventeen*

Jonathan's dinning chamber approximated the size of a ballroom. Bathed in light from fireplace, wall sconces, chandeliers and candles, the room gave off a warm glow.

His heart gave off a similar glow as Jonathan presided over the sumptuous dinner from the head of an imposing black walnut Renaissance table. The classic table accommodated a dozen diners comfortably, but in this instance his guests numbered four.

It was the first occasion in his memory that anyone under the age of eighteen had dined in the spacious, high-ceilinged dining chamber.

None of Ruby's offspring appeared intimidated by the luxurious surroundings. Harley, Della and Zeke set a lively conversational pace. Unlike many mothers, Ruby did not hold to the old saw that children should be seen but not heard. Jonathan found it rather refreshing that the young trio was encouraged to express their ideas and opinions at the table. Oddly enough, their conversation, which skipped and jumped from one subject to another, helped calm his nerves. He also credited several glasses of wine with restoring his confidence. Heaping portions of beef and Yorkshire pudding did not hurt his feeling of well-being either.

Following the meal, the small group returned to the drawing room. The fire hissed and crackled, warming the room in defiance of the increasingly cold night. Before sitting, Jonathan rested his hand briefly on a windowpane. Ruby and her brood would have a long, cold ride to the farmhouse tonight, even in the closed hired carriage. Unless he could convince her to stay.

Ruby and Jonathan were served tea under the watchful, restless eyes of her children. The medium sat beside him on the sofa, dressed in the same dark hunter green skirt and bodice that she'd been wearing the first day he laid eyes on her. He realized now that meager funds allowed her only two choices in gowns: one for winter and one for summer. When Ruby leaned toward him, he inhaled deeply. Her rosewater fragrance seemed especially sweet tonight.

"Is something wrong, Jonathan?" she asked quietly.

"Not at all." He took a deep breath. "Your perfume is delightful. Have I told you before?"

Tilting her head, she slanted him a small, pleased smile. "No, but thank you. I make the rose water myself."

"You are a woman of many talents."

"Yes," she declared, wagging a finger in his direction. "And one of my talents is knowing when a dear friend is troubled."

"Well, no. No, I'm not troubled," he grumbled, denying her insight. "But I am . . . I am disturbed. We have just shared our last meal together, after all."

"You might come to visit me, you know," Ruby pointed out quite logically. "Baltimore is not on the far side of the world."

"Neither is it a brief carriage ride away." He hesitated to add, like the farmhouse.

"Ah. I see. Traveling to visit us would be inconvenient for you."

"Which does not mean that I would not," he shot back.

"In any case, the children are looking forward to a new school."

"Not me," Zeke pouted.

"Never mind." Ruby leveled a glance at her youngest son that plainly admonished him, no words needed. But in the next instant, the light in her eyes suggested she'd had a grand idea. "Children, would you like to play with Princess while Dr. Noble and I talk?"

Eager nods revealed their fervent desire to escape drawing-room confinement and boring adult conversation.

"Yes, ma'am," Harley croaked.

"Where is she, Jonathan?"

"I expect the pup is begging for leftover scraps in the kitchen. Through the door and to the left."

"I'll watch them, Mother," Harley promised with a toss of his head toward his younger brother and sister.

"Thank you."

As her children fled the room, Ruby sipped her tea with the air of royalty. Her scarlet mouth hugged the rim of the cup, and, not for the first time in her company, Jonathan felt a warm stab of desire.

He was too old for these feelings. The impulse to smother Ruby's lips with his own was preposterous. Months ago, he'd blamed his loss of desire on age, not Laverne Hawthorne. But since meeting Ruby, he'd been wrestling with physical longings of greater magnitude than he remembered from his youth. If she could indeed read his mind, the medium beside him would be shocked beyond measure. On the slightest chance she possessed other worldly powers, Jonathan hastily wiped clean the lecherous slate of his mind.

He cleared his throat like a nervous, callow boy. "A new client right here in Annapolis wishes to consult you," he said.

Her amber eyes narrowed warily. "Who would that be?"

"It is I."

"You?" She choked on her tea.

"I must speak to Roy Calhoun," he stated firmly.

"Clementine's father?"

"Yes, I require old Roy's guidance."

"Why is that?" she asked, hiking a speculative brow. The woman possessed a suspicious mind.

"Clementine is as stubborn as is my son," he said, fumbling with his explanation. "I need to know how Roy handled—"

"Nonsense," Ruby interrupted. Never one to mince words, she continued in a terse, almost scolding manner. "And why would you expect me to change my plans and stay for one client, one conversation with you and Roy?"

Jonathan was not off to an auspicious start. "I believed that you might, as a favor to me. You and I have become good friends. I thought."

Shaking her head, Ruby rolled her eyes and released a heavy sigh. "Forgive me for speaking plainly, but that's a cock-and-bull story if I ever heard one."

As she had a way of doing, Ruby's forthrightness caught Jonathan off guard. "How in the world do you keep clients with an attitude like that?" he barked.

She set her cup down and reached for his hand. Her eyes softened as her gaze fixed on his. "I shall miss you too, Jonathan."

She knew!

He nodded. Slumped.

The clever medium understood how much he'd come to look forward to her company, to enjoy her startlingly honest way of speaking, and how much he'd learned to adore her inviting gypsy lips.

Jonathan resisted the desire to draw Ruby into his arms and hold her close to his heart. He could not shock her, nor place her in a compromising position. Instead, he straightened his shoulders, stood and crossed to the other side of the room, where he tugged the bellpull.

"There is more to this evening than saying good-bye," he announced.

"I cannot imagine what more you might have planned. It's been a wonderful evening." Ruby patted the empty spot where he'd been sitting. "Come back and sit with me."

Quite happy to oblige, he smiled. How had she become the queen and he her humble servant?

The bell had served to summon his cook. Mary appeared carrying a mouthwatering dark chocolate concoction. As preplanned, Zeke, Della and Harley followed, singing the birthday song. After placing the three-layer cake on the side table, Mary quietly slipped from the room.

Ruby's eyes filled with tears. Rising, she gave each of her children a warm embrace, ignoring the tears streaming down her lightly rouged cheeks.

"Make a wish, Mother," Della coaxed, tugging her mother toward the thickly frosted cake decorated with a long candle.

Bestowing a loving smile upon her daughter, Ruby sent a questioning gaze to Jonathan over the girl's shoulder.

"I could blow out the candle if you want," little Zeke offered. "Do you want me to blow out the candle?"

"Thank you for your kindness, but this time I shall blow it out myself." The fetching spiritualist made good by easily extinguishing the flame with one soft breath.

Jonathan applauded with the children. He would give his navy pension to know what Ruby had wished for.

Della volunteered to cut the cake, and Ruby acquiesced. As soon as she'd returned to Jonathan's side, Harley presented a box to his mother.

"This is from all of us. From Della, Zeke and me," he said as a bright red blush stained his fuzzy cheeks.

Once more, Jonathan caught the gathering of fresh tears in Ruby's eyes. He'd never seen her like this, glowing with happiness, emotional and vulnerable.

"Thank you, children." Her long, elegant fingers trembled as she opened the box.

While Zeke and Della regarded Ruby expectantly, Harley hung his head.

On a swift intake of breath, she lifted the cotton paisley shawl from its box. "Oh! It's beautiful," she exclaimed.

"I hope you really like it," Harley said.

"I have never liked anything as much in my life!" she replied. Jumping up again, she embraced Harley and sank to her knees to give his smaller siblings a hearty hug.

Love filled the room. Jonathan could feel it, see it in the smiles of the family surrounding him. Their eyes shone with deep, abiding love. His throat felt thick. Incapable of speech, he savored the moment.

Once more, the children took up their chatter, and when they had finished the cake, Ruby collected them

in her arms. "I cannot remember when I have celebrated such a wonderful birthday. Thank you,
children." She looked over their heads. Her golden
eyes gleamed with gratitude as they met Jonathan's.
"Thank you, Dr. Noble."

Her gaze locked on his, and he realized that the
gentle smile that settled on her lips was the smile
she'd dazzled the world with as an innocent girl of
eighteen. A smile that dazzled Jonathan at the moment.

He must do it now.

"There is one more gift, Ruby."

Jonathan reached inside the breast pocket of his
brown wool tailcoat and removed a small black box.

Releasing the children, Ruby silently approached
him, stopping inches away.

Without saying a word, for he couldn't yet trust
himself to speak, he placed the box in Ruby's hand.
He counted on the gift to speak for itself.

Poking a finger into the dimple on her chin, she regarded the box with a puzzled frown. After lifting a
questioning gaze to his, the most remarkable woman
he'd ever known opened the box.

In the silence, waiting for her reaction, Jonathan
feared his heart might give out. The old organ beat
too furiously, hammered against his chest with frightening force for a man his age.

Ruby's mouth formed a silent "Oh," and she shifted
her wondering gaze from the box to Jonathan and
back to the box.

"What is this?" she asked in a stunned whisper.

"It's a ring, Mother!" Della exclaimed.

"Yes," Ruby agreed in a hushed, reverent tone. "I
see." She stared at the ring for a long moment, re-

garding it as she might a secret weapon she feared would explode at her touch.

"Do you think it will fit?" Jonathan asked. But then he was struck by the thought that size might not be the problem. She might not like the ring's design.

Ruby removed the sparkling object from the box. "Jonathan, it's beautiful. But it's—it's too much."

"I want you to have it," he replied more gruffly than he'd intended.

"But it's a ruby! A beautiful ruby encircled by sparkling diamonds." She shook her head as if she could not believe her eyes.

"I thought a ruby would be fitting because you are, after all, a . . . ruby."

He thought he detected the hint of a smile on her lips, but he couldn't be certain.

"Children, leave us for a moment," she ordered softly. "Go find Princess."

Jonathan watched in dread as the two boys and lively girl obediently left the room. He wasn't certain he wished to be alone with Ruby. The courage he'd summoned to fight enemies and heal the sick completely failed him. The palms of his hands grew clammy. He'd not often heard the word "no" for any reason in his long bachelor history. He wouldn't have feared rejection had he launched a proposal with any other woman in his acquaintance. But Ruby was not like any other woman.

His heart slammed against his chest again and again. He'd been a fool to think she could care for him.

Ruby shut the door.

They were alone. Fleeing was out of the question.

She stiffened. Head held high, she sailed across the

room and held out the ring to him. "I am too weary for games."

Baffled, he asked, "What game do you think I play?"

"At first glance it appears that you are bribing me to be your mistress."

"No! Not my mistress!"

The rigid set of her mouth softened, but, obviously perplexed, her brows dove toward the bridge of her nose. "What then? What does this mean?"

She held the ring up between them.

She was forcing him to say the words he hadn't said to a woman in thirty years. But he could not say them. "I-I am an old man, and I have no right asking a woman who is as young and vibrant as you to be my wife."

"An old man? Not you!" she scoffed. "Young and vibrant?" she dissolved into peals of laughter. "Not I! Although I am flattered that you think of me that way," she added hastily.

"Well, yes, I do."

"You realize that I come with three children, who eke the youth and vibrancy from me each day?"

"I realize you come with a family. You . . . would you consider becoming my wife?"

Her eyes met his in a penetrating golden gaze. "Why are you asking, Jonathan? Because it is the only way you believe I shall stay in Annapolis? Or because you have feelings for me?"

He should have known Ruby wouldn't make this easy for him.

"Because . . . because I have feelings for you, madam."

She sank to the sofa. "Say it, Jonathan, dammit."

Dammit? Ruby appeared distressed.

Swallowing a lump in his throat the size of a submersible, Jonathan went down on one knee. A trifle arthritic, he wobbled a bit but made it with a grateful sigh.

Clasping his true love's hand, he gazed up at the strong, lovely face he'd come to adore. "I love you, Ruby Jones LaRue, and I would be honored if you would accept my hand in marriage."

She favored him with a smile as wide as the Severn. "Jonathan, I love you too. And I would be honored to marry you. You are a man among men."

She loved him? He could scarcely believe it.

"Even after all I've said about your . . . profession?"

"You didn't mean those things," she said, pooh-poohing his previous insults. "I understood from the start that it was your way of capturing my attention."

"You did?"

"I knew at once what a loving, kind man you are," she insisted, helping him to his feet.

"You did? Of course you did. You have the gift."

"I heal hearts." She grinned. "You are not the only healer in the room. You have met your match, sir."

"More than my match," he declared, slipping the ruby-and-diamond ring onto the third finger of her left hand.

"Aren't you forgetting something, Jonathan?"

Most likely he had. His mind whirled like a topsail in a monsoon. "What? What have I neglected?"

"You've never even kissed me. Never even tried. I've waited for weeks."

"You have?"

Apparently unwilling to wait another minute, Ruby encircled her arms around Jonathan's neck and kissed him as he'd never been kissed before. His pulse raced dangerously fast. He felt more light-headed than when he'd received his first boyhood kiss. At first he thought it might have been his age that caused his dizziness, but he quickly changed his mind, believing it more likely to be the impact of Ruby's passionate kiss. The woman had no shame.

Clementine fared even worse on her return journey to Annapolis than she had on her voyage to Key West. At least then she had been traveling to join Rand rather than steaming away from him. Physically spent and emotionally drained, she struggled to retain her composure. It became a daily battle. Her nausea remained constant from the time she woke in the morning until she fell asleep at night, lulled by the ceaseless rocking motion of the ship.

She'd sent a brief telegraph to Jonathan and was relieved to see him waiting on the dock along with Ruby when her ship docked in Annapolis. In contrast to the tropical climate she'd recently left, the morning air felt bitterly cold. A dark, gray sky threatened snow. Shivering, Clementine pulled her cloak closer against her body.

Once down the gangplank, she flew into Ruby's open arms.

"Welcome home, Clementine. I've missed you so."

"And I've missed you," she replied with a sniffle. Fighting back tears had become a daily battle for her.

"Did Rand really sail for Samoa?"

"Yes. He'll be away for at least a year, perhaps more."

Jonathan angrily struck his walking stick against the cobblestones. "What's wrong with him, running off when he has a wife at home?"

Clementine defended her husband. Forcing a smile, she laid a soothing hand on her father-in-law's arm. "Rand has dreamed of an exploration like this since he was a boy."

"That's no excuse. He has a responsibility to you now."

"My husband knows I am capable of taking care of myself."

Jonathan took exception. "Be that as it may, you shall move in with me, my dear, until my irresponsible son returns."

"What a wonderful idea," Ruby said, giving Clementine a great, warm smile. "I shall like having you close by."

"I don't understand."

"Ruby has agreed to be my wife," Jonathan told her. His voice rang with pride, and his delighted grin erased years from his face. He'd become a young man in love. "Fortunately, you have returned in time for our wedding."

Tears, always close at hand of late, splashed freely down Clementine's cheeks. But these were tears of happiness. She embraced Ruby and bussed Jonathan on the cheek. "I'm so happy for you both."

Wedding plans were discussed during the carriage ride home. For Ruby's sake, Clementine put aside her grief. It seemed hours until she was left alone with just Millie and the rest of the household staff. Ruby and Jonathan insisted on seeing her properly settled.

"We shall discuss this state of affairs with Rand tomorrow," Ruby whispered before taking her leave. "Take heart. I don't see this situation being as dire as it seems."

Clementine appreciated her encouragement but held little hope. "Perhaps."

"I promise that you will be too busy to dwell on your husband's absence. Your help is needed filling the church Christmas baskets for the needy. And we are already behind in making the rag dolls."

"You know I shall be glad to help."

"Good." Ruby's warm smile and sparkling eyes reflected her happiness. "Until tomorrow."

Ruby's engagement to Jonathan pleased Clementine. They were perfect for each other. Ruby's life would be infinitely less difficult, and her children would benefit from the love of two parents. In turn, she felt confident that Jonathan would be cared for as if he were a king by his new wife. They deserved their happiness and did not need a third party living with them as they started their life together. Clementine graciously declined Jonathan's offer to stay with them until Rand returned.

While she'd been away in Key West, Jonathan had worked wonders with Princess. The "puppy" weighed more than fifty pounds, and from every indication the dark-eyed clown remembered Clementine. Having the shaggy dog's companionship had become even more important. After sharing weeks of wedded bliss with Rand, being completely alone would be unbearable.

Before retiring, she took Princess out to the garden. The frosty air stung her cheeks and the tip of her nose. If she still smoked, it would have been a good time to roll a cigarette. Peering through the night, she could just make out the crumbling stalks of the black-eyed Susans. The rose bushes looked dead, and the trees were bare. In contrast to feeling the warm sand sifting through her toes just weeks ago, the ground beneath her feet felt hard and cold. As cold as her heart.

Apparently Jonathan had not been able to break Princess from digging. The big puppy pawed at the packed earth by the picket fence like a creature possessed.

"Come, Princess," Clementine commanded.

Princess looked up at her and barked.

"Come at once," she ordered, forcing a deep pitch and grave authority into her voice.

Giving a pitiful whine, the dog followed her back into the house.

Too weary to do much else, Clementine retired early. For lack of anything better to do, she searched her chamber once again for the missing velvet pouch. Thinking that she might somehow have overlooked it in her previous searches, Clementine tore the room apart. If the pouch indeed had been stolen, she held out hope that it might have been returned as the result of the thief's guilty conscience.

Both possibilities proved erroneous. But even if she found the money, she could not go back to Texas now.

# Eighteen

Rand stood on deck as his ship, cruising at full sail, crossed the Gulf of Mexico. Congress had cut funding so deeply that coal-burning steamers were rarely used. The old naval vessel headed toward New Orleans, where it would make its first stop.

The sails slapped in the wind and a salty spray blew up from the Gulf. Rand loved the taste of the warm breeze on his face, the feeling of the wind riffling through his hair.

Fingering the smooth ivory seahorse in his trouser pocket, he understood that Clementine had given him her most precious possession. She'd also given him the most complete happiness he'd ever known during their time together in Key West.

On those long, leisurely evenings they shared, Rand realized that he hadn't made love to Clementine for the sake of creating the son he desperately wanted. He'd made love to her because he could think of nothing else. Overwhelmed by his desire for her, for her passion, he wanted only one thing—to make his wife the happiest woman in the world. Rand's ability to give her the stars and moon in sweet release had been all that mattered.

He never thought she'd leave him.

The despair he'd felt ever since they'd parted was

worse than the anguish he suffered when losing a patient. He tried in vain to shrug the feeling off. Clementine wasn't dead. She was more alive than Ellie had ever been. Comparing the two women was one of the most foolish things he'd ever done.

Rand put aside his troubling musings as a young officer approached.

"Dr. Noble, sir."

"Yes, Lieutenant. At ease," he ordered, bracing himself for word of a medical emergency.

Instead, the officer extended an envelope to him. "This letter was found in the bottom of the mailbag. Apologies, sir. It should have been delivered to you before we left Key West."

He took the envelope from the lieutenant. Since navy mail had a way of getting lost, receiving it late was better than never. A glance at the scrawl told him that the letter was from his father. His troubled heart reacted to the disappointment as if it had been pierced by one of his surgical probes. Rand had hoped to see Clementine's familiar handwriting.

"Thank you, Lieutenant."

With another sharp salute, the young man turned on his heel and strode away.

Jonathan was not one to write often. Rand opened the letter with trepidation.

*Dear Son,*

    *There is no way to break this news but in a straight-forward manner. I have decided to marry. In the hopes that Ruby Jones will accept my offer, I plan to ask for her hand in marriage this evening. By the time you receive this letter, I may be a married man with a family of three young children.*

    *Before you rail that this is a foolish thing that I am*

*doing, let me admit to you what a lonely life I've led for the past few years. A bachelor, or rake, as I have been, must keep up appearances. He purports to have life by the tail. He crows like a rooster about the joys of freedom. He can never confess to the loneliness that cuts sharper than a scalpel. He does not admit to talking to himself, to hearing his voice echo in empty rooms.*

*Beautiful women don't flock to an old man's door. Intelligent women are even more difficult to meet. And I have less to offer with every passing year.*

*I am settling down as I should have done years ago. Not only for your sake, but selfishly, for mine as well. If Ruby rejects my hand, I will accept my fate like a man. But be warned: Do not follow in your father's hapless footsteps. Do not come to the end of your life as a lonely old man. You have the opportunity to create a good life with Clementine. She will provide you with more adventure than the navy can ever hope to equal.*

*My deepest regards to you both, your father*

Rand reread the letter several times. He could scarcely believe his father intended to give up his bachelorhood and settle down with a wife and family. But Rand liked Ruby and felt that the clever medium would be a good wife to his father. She would bring Jonathan the happiness he sought.

Although he should feel happy for his father, Rand's spirits plummeted even deeper. He folded the letter and shoved it into his pocket with the lucky seahorse. The seahorse brought his thoughts back to Clementine. In all likelihood, she would be on her way back to Texas soon.

He'd ruined his chance for happiness. During their too few weeks of bliss in Key West, Clementine frequently had claimed that Rand made the perfect husband. He'd begun to believe her. Perhaps he'd only needed the right woman all along. Clementine.

But then, he'd behaved much less than perfectly when he'd let her go.

Clementine expected Ruby and Jonathan to come calling for her at any moment. They'd insisted she accompany them on a Christmas tree hunting expedition, assuring her that Jonathan's butler had already been charged with chopping down a pine tree for her as well. Although celebrating seemed unthinkable without Rand, she resolved to go through the motions on this bone-chillingly cold December day.

Unable to refuse her dearest friend, she'd also agreed to help with Ruby's wedding preparations. Her own wedding to Rand had been planned by others, and Clementine was uncertain how much assistance she could offer.

Before she left for the afternoon, Princess required her attention. Donning her long, black wool cloak, she walked as far as the rear veranda, where she released her eager pet for a fast run in the garden.

But Princess didn't run. The diabolical pup pranced to her favorite spot beneath the hickory tree next to the fence and began to dig.

Clementine stamped her foot in frustration and shouted, "Come! At once!"

Princess never even paused.

"Stop your digging! This instant!"

The misbehaving pup succeeded in breaking ground.

"Dang." Resigned to pulling the dog back into the house by her ear if necessary, Clementine dashed from the veranda to the spot near the fence where the dirt flew. "What do you have down there, an old bone?"

While she did not expect a reply, she did not expect a mouthful of dirt either. Angry, she pushed her pet aside and glared down into the small hole Princess had dug. A shiny object caught her eye.

The shaggy dog impatiently whined behind her as Clementine fell to her knees. She hadn't bothered to wear gloves for a trip to the back veranda. Scooping up the dirt with her bare hands quickly became a torturous task. But when she had finished, she discovered her missing derringer buried in the dirt. Princess had been the thief!

On the chance Clementine might find her velvet pouch with her life savings, she dug to the right of the weapon and then to the left. And then deeper. Paying no mind to her cold, numb hands, she clawed the hard ground and scooped away the dark, solid earth.

There!

With a cry of joy, Clementine snatched up the dirty velvet pouch. She pulled open the drawstring with trembling fingers. The coins, the bills, her entire savings remained intact. She sat back on her heels, curling her fist around the pouch.

"Princess, all we need to return to Oddon is right here in the palm of my hand."

The pup barked in reply.

"Never mind, you thief. If you weren't such good company, ah should send you to live with Sarah Tidwell."

The dog ceased her whining and cocked her head.

To Clementine's surprise, she did not feel the elation she expected if ever she recovered the pouch. "We can't return to Oddon. Not now. First, I must help Ruby with her wedding. And the church Christmas baskets have yet to be finished."

Princess responded with a snort and a lick on Clementine's cheek. The warm, wet smooch almost toppled her. Laughing, she continued to share her thoughts with her canine companion. "You know, with the money in this little pouch we could purchase mittens, mufflers and gloves to add to the baskets. An extra gift to help every man, woman and child keep warm this winter might be most welcome."

Clementine slipped the derringer and red velvet pouch into the pocket of her coat and pushed to her feet. "Now, that's a thought," she said, as if it had come from someone else. "Come, Princess. We can't be dawdling out here with all there is to do."

Her busy schedule had been devised to fill her time, to prevent her from thinking of Rand and the happiness that could have been theirs.

Thankfully, Clementine never felt Ellie's ghost in the house anymore. But the essence of Rand occupied every room. The soap-and-spruce scent of him lingered in the nooks and crannies. She often paused in the same spot where he'd been standing when she first heard his deep, contagious laughter. By closing her eyes and concentrating, she could almost hear his laughter again, warming and enclosing her in its comforting cocoon. She envisioned the twinkle in his eyes lighting every chamber. And sometimes in the stillness she could hear the sound of his footsteps as he strode down the corridor.

Every night at dusk, in a purely symbolic gesture, Clementine placed a candle in the front window to light Rand's way home.

As she hurried back toward the house, Ruby sailed

onto the veranda. "Jonathan is waiting in the carriage. Hurry, Clementine."

"Tell me again. Why do I need a Christmas tree?" she asked, as she reached her friend's side.

For a long, cold moment, Ruby studied her as if she'd lost her wits. "Where shall you place your Christmas gifts if you do not have a tree?"

"I do not expect to be receiving gifts. "

"What? You have not written to Saint Nick?"

"No. And I never have. We did not observe Christmas often when I was a girl. We were much too poor."

"We must make up for lost time then," Ruby declared in her usual impervious manner.

"No, we must not," Clementine insisted, adding firmly, "and I shall not be trimming a Christmas tree by myself. It would be far too lonely a task. If you force me to have a tree, you and your brood shall have to come to my tree-trimming party."

"What fun. We shall be delighted!"


A light snow fell the night of Clementine's tree-trimming party. The white lace flakes glistened beneath the gaslights as they floated from the dark sky, settling on the cobblestones and the barren branches of the maple trees.

Only ten days remained until Christmas; five days until Jonathan and Ruby's wedding. Clementine had no time to indulge in melancholy or self-pity. For her first foray as hostess, she'd invited everyone she knew in Annapolis to the party. Just about everyone had accepted her invitation, including Sarah Tidwell.

Not one but two Christmas trees greeted her guests. One stately tree stood in the foyer, and the other, a smaller tree, filled a corner of the drawing room. The fresh scent of pine wafted throughout the downstairs rooms. Each fireplace boasted a roaring, crackling fire to which a pinecone or two had been added.

Garlands of deep green holly studded with red berries wrapped around the staircase bannister and nestled atop each fireplace mantle. Bright red velvet bows and white candles snuggled amid the evergreen boughs, and oversized balls of mistletoe dangled from the doorways, inviting Christmas kisses.

The guests were offered eggnog and hot rum toddies as they looped strings of popcorn and cranberries around the trees. The dining buffet came close to buckling beneath a holiday feast. Tantalizing aromas of a ten-pound baked ham, hot Maryland biscuits and steaming baked beans wafted through the house. After-dinner treats of nuts and gingerbread men, mince pies and a fruitcake supplied sweet temptation. Indulging herself, Clementine made certain heaping bowls of Saratoga chips could be found in every room.

The house swarmed with guests. Dr. Smith, Rand's replacement at the hospital, hovered at her side throughout dinner.

"I know you must miss Rand," he said, commiserating with Clementine as the guests gathered in the drawing room for caroling. "Have you had word from him as yet?"

"No. The mail is exceedingly slow. I may not hear from him for months." Clementine forced a light reply along with a smile.

The absence of any word from Rand distressed her greatly, but she refused to let anyone know. She wrote to her husband every day and hoped that her daily visit to the academy mail facility would reward her with a letter from him. To date, her trips had been to no avail.

As soon as the caroling began, she slipped away, intending to see if Millie required assistance. But Sarah Tidwell waylaid her in the foyer.

"So, Dr. Noble sent you back, did he? I warned you that you could never measure up to Ellie."

Clementine's chin shot up. "My return had nothing to do with your sister."

"Is that what you tell yourself? How do you explain the doctor's trip to the other side of the world?"

"Rand is following his heart."

"He's put the most distance possible between you and him. That's how it appears to me—and most others."

"I don't care how it appears to you or anyone else, Sarah. Rand will assist in establishing the first United States Naval coaling station on Pago Pago," she bristled. "What sort of wife would I be if I prevented my husband from taking part in this great adventure? I am terribly proud of him."

The dark-eyed woman snickered. "Are you now? Well, here's a bit of advice. A man with Rand's reputation should have his wife beside him at all times."

"Sarah, you're a guest in Rand's home. How dare you say such a thing? Rand was never unfaithful to Ellie."

"Even the devil wouldn't betray an ill woman."

"I'm afraid you have no understanding of Rand Noble, and if you cannot join in the spirit of the evening, perhaps you should leave."

Vastly affronted, Sarah gasped, then scowled. Her narrow lips stretched in a tight white line beneath her nose.

Before the spinster had the opportunity to retaliate, Ruby sidled up to Clementine. "The hostess is needed in the drawing room."

With a curt nod to Ruby, Sarah turned sharply on her heel and stalked from the room.

Clementine loosed a sigh. "Thank you for saving me. I'm afraid that I lost my patience and put Sarah in her place."

"She's had it coming for years. How does it feel?"

"It feels . . . wonderful."

"You didn't tell her how long Rand would be away?"

"No. Of course not."

Her friend hiked a caustic brow. "Two years. I just don't see it."

"You may be losing your powers."

"And he asked you to go with him?" the bride-to-be asked, repeating a question she had asked before and to which she very well knew the answer.

"Yes. But I am not yet brave enough to travel all those oceans without a strip of land in sight. I had to return," she insisted. "Now, enough of this. It's time to sing."

Ruby leveled a probing gaze. She looked directly into Clementine's eyes, as if the truth could be detected there. "There's something you're not telling me," she said at last.

"Would I dare keep anything from a seeress?"

Five days later, Clementine stood in front of the looking glass. In just a few minutes the carriage would arrive to take her to Saint Anne's Church, where Ruby and Jonathan were to be married. The beautiful Anglican church had been Annapolis's first church. The first wooden structure had burned to the ground, but it had been rebuilt on the same site three times.

Clementine had joined Ruby, her children and several of the medium's satisfied clients in decorating the church yesterday. A sense of joy and underlying excitement prevailed as the women worked. Unwilling to ruin Ruby's happiness, Clementine forced a merriness she did not, could not feel. But the results of their efforts were breathtaking. Boughs of fragrant evergreen looped the altar rails, and white satin bows adorned each end of the pews. The simple ornaments of Christmas eloquently contributed to the atmosphere of love and peace.

Jonathan invited Clementine to spend Christmas Day with Ruby, the children and him. But the prospect of celebrating without Rand seemed bleak. She worried that she could not keep up her pretense of happiness much longer. Miserable without him, she desperately missed her handsome, devil-may-care husband.

But it was no time to be thinking of Rand. Taking a deep breath, Clementine dragged her mind back to the present. Harley and Zeke prepared for the wedding with Jonathan at his home, just down the street. Ruby and Della were here with her. The young girl spent most of her time playing with Princess in the guest chamber. But up until a few minutes ago, Ruby and Clementine shared her more spacious chamber, giggling like schoolgirls as they dressed.

The day after Ruby agreed to marry him, Jonathan had hired a maid for her. With Liza's assistance, Clementine and Ruby had fashioned each other's hair, bathed in rose water, sipped hot cocoa as they dressed and applied rouge and powder to their pale winter faces.

Like most brides who married for love, Ruby glowed. But her mind was as scattered as Clementine had ever known. Her friend had just dashed off to look for the garter she planned to wear as something old.

Studying the reflection of the woman in the looking glass, it was clear to Clementine that she was not the same frightened and angry girl who had arrived from Texas seven months ago.

The emerald green satin gown she wore complimented her fair complexion more than any dress she'd ever worn. The bane of her life, her fiery curls, had been swept back and held at her crown by countless pins and combs of pearl.

Ruby had chosen the same elegant style as her wedding gown for her bridesmaids, but the rich Christmas color promised a splendid contrast to her bridal gown, a pale, creamy beige, encrusted with pearls.

Clementine's gown was far more beautiful than the one she'd worn when she married Rand. *Rand.* Whenever she thought of her husband, she wondered if she had ever truly left Annapolis. The love she'd shared with him in Key West seemed more like a dream.

Unlike her, Jonathan and Ruby lived their dream every day. Their love touched Clementine daily. She'd never seen a couple as happy as this man and woman who had discovered love late in their lives and come close to letting it slip through their fingers. To date, Jonathan displayed absolutely no regret over relinquishing his title of rake about town.

Clementine started as Ruby bustled into the room. "Are you ready?" she asked, all in a dither. "It's time to go."

"I'm ready." Clementine nodded and clasped her friend's hands. "Ruby, you look so beautiful."

Because this was her second marriage, wearing traditional white had been out of the question for Ruby.

But the elegance of her simple gown was stunning. The boned bodice buttoned up the front to a small standing collar, trimmed with Honiton lace, at the throat. The same delicate lace trimmed the narrow sleeves and trailed behind her in a long, elegant train. Exquisite pearls sprinkled the gown, including the slender skirt that hugged Ruby's ample hips and gathered in a small bustle in the back. A cluster of pearls formed a circular crown from which her veil of Honiton lace fell.

Ruby beamed. "And you, Clementine. You are more beautiful than you've ever been. I wish Rand could see you."

And so did she.

But before Clementine could slip into wistful thinking, Della skipped into the room, her eyes alight with excitement. "Mother, the carriage is here."

"The time is near," Clementine whispered to her friend.

Ruby's eyes grew misty as she confessed, "And I never saw it coming."

Jonathan waited at the altar, resplendent as a peacock in his custom-made two-piece double-breasted dove gray suit. A white brocade waistcoat, white shirt and white silk tie completed the most visible of his wedding attire. He'd gone all out to make this wedding unforgettable.

Contrary to what he'd expected, he didn't feel at all nervous. He'd never been so certain of what he was about to do.

The gossips had been shocked when the invitations were mailed. The old rake, marrying the medium? In a matter of hours the news, embellished and widely speculated upon, traveled from tongue to wagging tongue. Jonathan heard and enjoyed the stir.

Ruby eloped when she'd married the first time, against her family's wishes. Jonathan wished to give her the dream of every woman: a lavish church wedding. At first she'd protested, but before long became caught up in his plans, altering them and offering her own thoughts.

Early on, he'd made certain that she had a maid, a wedding gown and a new wardrobe. Following the ceremony this afternoon, he'd arranged a grand celebration in his—no—*their* home. In the spring they would take a honeymoon tour of Europe.

The magnificent old church filled rapidly. When at last the organist finally struck up the wedding march, Jonathan's heart swelled to a size too large for his chest. He gripped the rail behind him to steady himself. He shifted his gaze to the far end of the middle aisle.

The procession began with a grinning Della, followed by Clementine, who smiled demurely. They glided slowly down the aisle—too slowly for him. He wanted to see Ruby, to clasp her hand, to look into her eyes, to promise her his love until his dying day.

He gave Della an encouraging smile. He knew she feared tripping. The lovely gowns she and Clementine wore rustled softly as they approach. His new daughter and daughter-in-law carried small bouquets of mistletoe tied with white velvet ribbon.

Over Clementine's shoulder he at last caught sight of the woman for whom he'd been waiting most of his life. His love, his soul mate. Ruby floated slowly down the aisle, escorted on either side by Harley and Zeke. Lacking a father or brother, she'd chosen her boys to give her away, a nontraditional but loving gesture. And the boys' eyes shone with obvious pleasure.

A vision in satin and lace, Ruby took Jonathan's breath away. When she described her work as treating the scars left upon troubled hearts and minds, he accepted her explanation as true. He'd gained respect for what she accomplished as a medium. He'd been one who had benefitted from her gifts. For his bride-to-be had taken his troubled, lonely heart and filled it with love.

The term "luckiest man on earth" had previously held no meaning to Jonathan. Until this moment.

"Dearly beloved, we are gathered . . ."

Only one person was missing.

# Nineteen

If he'd had to wait another minute, Rand would have jumped ship. The snow didn't slow him down as he raced from the pier to Saint Anne's Church. He ran at breakneck speed, as if he were running for his life. In fact, he was.

Hell-bent on reaching Annapolis as quickly as possible, he'd taken three ships, a train and ridden horseback since coming to his senses in New Orleans.

Snowflakes stung his face, melted on his cheeks. His heart pounded from exertion and excitement. The muscles in his legs ached. But he ignored the physical drain. He arrived at the church in record time. Sprinting up the steps, he stopped only to pause for breath. Hard, ragged gasps thundered through his body as Rand composed himself. Breathing restored to normal, he quietly opened the door and slipped into the rear of the church. Every pew was filled.

Ruby and his father faced each other, exchanging vows.

Rand had never seen his father look so happy. But there was another person he was even more eager to see than his father. Clementine. Rand's frantic gaze swept the wedding guests until he spotted her.

Clementine stood to one side of the altar, a member of the wedding party. She smiled softly. Her gaze was fixed on the beaming bride and groom. But the bride was not the most beautiful woman in the room. It was his darlin', his Clementine.

Her emerald green splendor took his breath away. He'd never seen her look so lovely. Her pale ivory skin presented a lustrous contrast to the exquisite green satin gown she wore. His fingertips tingled at the memory of her fair, silky flesh warming to his touch.

When would she see him?

His gaze drifted to her honeyed lips, to her sea green eyes and up to the coppery curls he loved to twist around his fingers. The springy tendrils had been tamed and captured by pearl combs atop her head in a flaming sunset crown.

His heart roared like a wildcat. Mustering every ounce of self-control, Rand clenched his jaw and fists. Exercising the strict discipline of a naval officer, he stifled the urge to race down the aisle and take her into his arms.

When would she notice him standing in the rear shadows?

"You may kiss the bride." The preacher's words echoed in the church, bringing the ceremony to a close.

Rand tore his gaze from Clementine to watch his father kiss the glowing Ruby LaRue. The rake had met his match. As had the son of the rake.

Once again he turned his attention to Clementine. He found it impossible to keep his eyes off her for long. At last, at almost the same moment, she looked up from the kissing couple. Raising her chin, she gazed dreamily out into space, to the back of the church. To where he stood.

Her eyes locked on his.

He grinned.

She blinked.

Clementine blinked twice, but the mirage remained. Blue eyes, familiar blue eyes, deeper than the sky and lighter than the ocean, riveted on hers. A soft, crooked grin reached out to her, swirling 'round in her head like a soft Texas breeze.

Her heart bounced against her chest hard and fast. Once, she'd heard an old desert rat tell of mirages he'd seen in the desert. And Rand had confessed to seeing a mirage during a long ocean voyage early in his navy career. Illusions. A phenomenon of the mind, enabling a person to see what he or she wished to see. Water, land, and in Clementine's case, Rand. She longed to see him so much, she'd conjured him up.

Hoping to rid herself of the disturbing image, she closed her eyes again and silently counted to ten before opening them. Nothing had changed. The twinkling gaze fastened on hers. Her heart slowed to a near stop. Without realizing, she held her breath.

The mirage of the man standing in the rear of the church possessed the same firm, narrow lips and strong, angular jaw as Rand. Laugh lines etched his sun-darkened skin, framing his mouth and crinkling the corners of his eyes. Clementine's pulse kicked like a bucking mule. But Rand could not be in Annapolis.

The eerie resemblance proved true down to the smallest details. She lifted her gaze to thick, nut brown hair. Hair like Rand's, which always smelled of soap. But it could not be her husband standing in the rear of Saint Anne's.

The gleam of brass buttons caught her eye. In a frenzy of desire, she'd once ripped the brass buttons from Rand's uniform jacket, eager to love him. She'd learned slowly how to love her husband, but she had learned well.

"Mrs. Noble."

Lost in her wonderful mirage, she heard the voice as if it came from a very great distance. Her knees felt like wet Key West sponges. She reached for the support of the altar rail.

"Mrs. Noble. Take my arm," Harley demanded beneath his breath.

"What?" She turned to Ruby's son. Two Harleys, side-by-side blurs, spoke to her.

"It's time for the recessional," he hissed quietly, never moving his lips. "Take my arm. We're leaving the church."

She heard the organ music then. Mendelssohn filled the church, rose to the rafters and penetrated her consciousness for the first time.

Clementine nodded. Grateful for Harley's support, she slipped her arm around his. Unable to trust her eyes, she chose to gaze straight ahead, at the solid forms of Jonathan and Ruby. Still, her heart bucked like a penned mustang.

"Mrs. Noble, are you all right?"

"Yes, Harley."

*No, Harley.* Catching a full breath proved impossible. Her lungs ached with the trying.

The man remained her mirage alone. No one else in the wedding party seemed aware that Rand hovered in the rear of the church.

Clementine and Harley were halfway down the aisle, directly behind the bride and groom, when she decided to risk another look. With a fair amount of trepidation she directed her gaze to where the mirage had appeared. He'd vanished. The wedding guests were all standing, making it difficult to get a clear view, but even craning her neck, searching between bodies and over heads, she could not find him.

"Mrs. Noble, are you sure you're all right?"

"Yes. I'm fine," she assured Harley. But the young boy seemed unconvinced. "It—it's exciting, isn't it?"

"Yes, ma'am."

And then she heard the confirmation of all her heart had been telling her. A shout of joy rose above the music, above every sound in the church.

"Rand!" Jonathan's voice boomed above the music and chatter.

Clementine swung her attention from Harley to that spot just ahead of her where Jonathan and Ruby had come to a sudden halt. Her father-in-law took two steps forward and threw his arms around the man standing directly in the center of the aisle. Her mirage. Rand.

The buzz in the church grew louder. The dizzying buzz within Clementine's head immobilized her. Silently, she watched father and son embrace.

Dazed and confused, Clementine feared moving. Her heart flew. Rand may have returned only for his father's wedding. He might still be angry with her for refusing to accompany him on his great adventure.

Ruby rushed to her side. Clasping Clementine's hand, she squeezed tightly. "You see, he came back to you. I knew I didn't see two years. Rand could never stay away from you for that long."

When Jonathan and Rand stepped back from one another, she nudged Clementine forward, whispering, "What are you waiting for?"

Looking over his father's shoulder, Rand's eyes settled on Clementine's. Her lips trembled as she attempted to smile, sudden tears splashing down her cheeks.

Taking two swift strides, Rand gathered her in his arms, crushing her to him. He murmured her name in a husky whisper. "Clementine, Clementine. Dear God, I've missed you, darlin'."

He held her as if she were his anchor in a storm, held her as if he would never release her. Engulfed in the musky scent of him, the faint salty fragrance clinging to his jacket, Clementine came close to swooning. When his lips came down on hers, she melted into him like butter on hot bread. Warm. Wonderful.

The church echoed with applause, the thunderous sound causing the floor to vibrate beneath her feet. With a triumphant grin and a rakish wink, Rand released her. Evidently unwilling to let her go, he circled an arm around her waist to steady her. The entire wedding party, participants and invited guests, still applauded. Clementine felt the heat on her cheeks, felt the blush push all the way down to her toes.

Impatient to be alone with her husband, she pulled him out onto the church steps and into the snowfall.

His laughter warmed Clementine's heart as he gathered her into his arms on the church steps. "You need your cloak. I'm not going to lose you to frostbite."

"I want to be alone with you," she pleaded breathlessly, immune to the icy air. "There is so much to say, so much to know."

Rand rocked her in the warmth of his arms. "We'll have time alone soon. I promise you. The rest of my life is yours. But this is my father's day."

Rand knew his father would expect him to attend his wedding party, and he didn't have the heart to spoil the old man's happiness.

Festive Christmas decorations cheered the somber bachelor's mansion. Garlands of holly, balls of mistletoe, and bright red ribbons festooned doorways and chandeliers. In the parlor, strings of popcorn and cranberries wound around a twelve-foot-tall pine Christmas tree. Toy soldiers and sugarplum candy dangled from the branches in a colorful display. Rarely used by his father during his bachelor days, the room had been cleared of all furniture to become a dance floor. A pianist and violinist played a rousing waltz from a small platform in the far corner.

Holding fast to Clementine's hand, Rand teased her. "Will you join them to play your banjo?"

"Ah will if you wish," she replied earnestly.

"No. My greatest wish is to keep you by my side." Rand didn't have the heart to tell her that while she might enjoy playing her banjo, he didn't enjoy its tinny sound.

Her eyes sparkled like precious gems as they gazed up into his. "At your side is where I want to stay."

Rand brushed the tip of her nose with his fingertip. He couldn't get enough of her, not in this crowd of wedding guests. He feasted on her natural beauty. Her cheeks sparked pink, and not from the cold. Eleven fireplaces warmed his father's house.

"We'll escape as soon as possible," he whispered.

She nodded eagerly. Her smile struck his heart.

"I still cannot believe you're here. I thought I was seeing a mirage at the back of the church."

"You mesmerized me," he admitted. "I have never seen you look more beautiful than you do today."

"I wish I could always be beautiful for you," she said softly.

"You are."

Her cheeks grew hot pink again, and a dangerous warmth settled into his loins. He would have taken advantage of any excuse to hold her in his arms, but dancing offered the first genuine opportunity since they'd arrived. Jonathan and Ruby invited Clementine and Rand to join them on the floor for the first dance.

With the first steps, he learned that his square-dancing wife had learned to waltz very well. She danced with him as if they'd been waltzing together for years. He held her closer, inhaling the familiar, soothing fragrance of chamomile, superior by far to the salt of the sea. The warmth within him deepened.

Unwilling to wait, Rand waltzed Clementine to the nearest doorway and kissed her beneath the mistletoe. He kissed her quite thoroughly, stopping only for air.

"I love mistletoe," she murmured.

"As every man and intelligent woman must," he agreed. "But we most likely have shocked the children."

"Ah would be pleased to shock them again."

Within minutes Rand maneuvered her to the same mistletoe spot and tasted lips far sweeter than sugarplums.

After another dance, genuine hunger forced him to leave the floor. "I'm afraid I need something to eat. I've not had anything all day, and if memory serves me correctly, I shall have need of my strength before this day is over."

Her laughter filled his heart. "But dinner will not be served for another hour."

"I cannot wait an hour. Certainly Ruby and Father will understand." Seizing her hand, he guided her into the kitchen where the cook and a hired staff bustled about administering final preparations to the meal.

He filled a plate with roast turkey and mashed potatoes fresh from the mashing pot. Clementine rooted around until she found Saratoga chips, which she liberally piled upon her plate.

"Surely you'll have more than that," he said. "Where is the woman I know with the appetite known to put ten large men to shame?"

She gave a little shrug and a pert, upward turn of her lips. "It's the excitement of having you home. My stomach is a bit unsettled."

"Hmm." Feigning a frown, he bit down on the corner of his mouth. "I never considered that my return might give you a bellyache."

Grinning, she curled her fist and gently poked him in the arm. Gripped by an overpowering urge to drop his plate and pull her into his arms for more than just a kiss, Rand lowered his voice. "Do you think we can find a quiet spot to . . . to have our meal?"

"I know the very one—one you probably never knew existed. Follow me." She led the way to the staircase in the foyer, stopping in front of the wall beneath the stairs. "When we were decorating the house yesterday, Zeke showed me this secret room." She pushed on a panel.

A long, narrow storage space beneath the stairs opened.

"It's a hiding space, built during the Revolution in case the British attacked," she explained.

"A candle, matches and a stool. More than we need," he said, taking inventory as he entered behind her, crouched as low as he could go. He was too tall to stand upright in the small, dim space.

After pulling out the stool for Clementine, he plopped on the floor to wolf down his meal.

One small candle flame glowed in the darkness.

"When I didn't hear from you, I thought you were

too angry with me to write," she said in a hushed voice.

"I was angry at first. I told myself you were behaving just like Ellie. But halfway to New Orleans, I realized there was no comparison."

"No comparison?"

"You are more woman than Ellie could ever hope to be. She needed someone to cling to, someone who would give her a life. She never had the courage to make a life of her own or to become my partner in carving out a life together. It wasn't her fault. She just didn't have it in her. I expected too much from her."

Rand had been slow to understand what went wrong in his marriage. For years, he'd blamed himself, assuming responsibility for its failure. He'd made Ellie a martyr in his mind.

Owning up to his mistake didn't come easily. The only person he trusted to keep his confession locked in her heart was perched on the stool across from him. He put down his plate. "Ellie wasn't the proper choice. My father was right all along. You are the woman meant for me."

Clementine's clear green gaze settled on his. She spoke in a hushed, solemn tone. "From the start, I've worried that you would never be able to love me as you loved her."

"Darlin', I couldn't live without you."

"But what about your great adventure?"

"Samoa would have brought no pleasure without you," he admitted quietly. "You're my great adventure, Clementine."

"And you're mine." At the slight, seductive upturn of her lips, his mouth went dry as medicinal powder.

It was all he could do to resist the demanding, powerful desire to tear the pearl combs from her hair. "I should have returned to Annapolis with you," he confessed in a voice strained from his losing struggle with self-control. "I'm sorry, Clementine. You'll never know how sorry. Will you forgive me?"

"Forgiven." In one sly, swift movement, Clementine slid from the low stool down onto Rand's lap, where she straddled him.

He groaned softly and closed his eyes, opening them just in time to see Clementine pull up her skirt. The rustle of her gown and the warm shift of her body pitched Rand to the last thread of his restraint. The searing ache in his loins demanded a remedy.

The pink tip of Clementine tongue circled her lips, moistening the mouth he craved like children craved candy. She lowered her mouth to his. His blood fired.

Abandoning all restraint, Rand rained feverish kisses, hot and wet, upon her dear, adorable face, and the long, fair column of her neck. Through the soft, folds of her dress, he cupped her soft lush breasts. "I want to be inside you, buried deep inside you," he whispered hoarsely.

Her response came on shallow gasps of air. "Come . . . come, be one with me."

Desire so long denied released itself in a flurry of frantic need. Rand rolled Clementine from his lap to the floor. As she hastily wiggled from her lace drawers, he swiftly discarded his trousers.

Pushing her skirt up, Rand entered his wife with a kiss as deep and fierce as the darkness surrounding them. Buried in her warm, moist depths, he danced on the wings of a bold, relentless rhythm. He danced higher and deeper than he'd ever gone before. Too fast, too fast. He was unable to temper his need, when what he needed was the woman in his arms.

Arching her back, Clementine drew in a breath and cried softly in his ear, "Oooh, yaaaahoo."

Her shuddering sigh hastened Rand's release. Gritting his teeth to smother a loud outburst of joy, he spilled into the universe. Again and again. Until, at last, he slowly floated to earth.

"Welcome home," the wondrous woman beneath him whispered.

He rolled to his side, looming above her, reveling in the glazed contentment in her eyes. "I hope your stomach has settled and that you're feeling much, much better now."

"I am sooo much better, Dr. Noble. Your bedside manner is unmatched."

"And you are just what the doctor needed, darlin'," he proclaimed, sealing her lips with a tender kiss.

After long, quiet moments drifting in sweet contentment, Clementine asked, "Do you think we've been missed?"

"No, but we should get back to the festivities before we are."

"How can we leave? Look at me. My hair, my gown . . . I'm all undone. I think we should stay hidden beneath the staircase until everyone leaves."

"Don't worry. All eyes will be on the bride and groom. And I'll help straighten your hair."

"My face will be flushed."

"Your face has been flushed since the moment you spotted me in the rear of the church," he chuckled.

"Truly?"

"Truly."

"Oh, mercy."

\* \* \*

Clementine and Rand joined the wedding party as the fifty invited guests sat down to dinner. A dozen circular tables spread with white linen cloths had been installed in the spacious dining room. Rand was asked to give the champagne toast.

"To my father and his lovely bride. I cannot wish you both any greater happiness than what I've found. Every day is like Christmas with Clementine, full of joy and shining with the greatest gift of all. To your love, to your happiness, we celebrate."

Loving green eyes met his as Rand finished his brief toast.

Shortly after Ruby and Jonathan cut their enormous wedding cake, Rand approached the ceaselessly grinning bridegroom. "Father, you've chosen wisely. You'll have a lifetime of happiness with Ruby."

"Well, maybe not a lifetime, not at my age. But I caught myself before it was too late, stubborn old fool that I am. At least you discovered what's important early."

"If it hadn't been for you and Clementine, I'm not certain that I ever would have been the wiser," he replied.

Pursing his lips, Jonathan studied Rand. "I expect you might wish to go home now. You're probably tired from your journey."

"Yes, I guess it's obvious," Rand responded, relieved.

"Go along. I understand." His father leveled a lop-sided grin. "Don't want you to have to resort to my hidden stairwell again."

Rand experienced the same sinking feeling as when he'd been a boy, caught by his father after smoking one of the old man's cigars.

"You knew?"

"I intend to use that place one day myself, Son."

* * *

The wedding party lasted until after midnight. By the time Jonathan carried his bride over the threshold—which he thanked the good Lord he was still able to do—he looked forward to bed.

Although Ruby hadn't slept here yet, she had arranged for new drapes, a new carpet, installed a screen and ordered two large vases of fresh flowers. Jonathan felt as nervous as an eighteen-year-old virgin. With her eyes all aglow and her gypsy lips gleaming like juicy berries, Ruby looked no older than he felt.

"What's wrong, Jonathan?"

Stalling, he cleared his throat. "I'm nervous. I'm not a youth in my prime any longer. I hope that I can . . ."

She placed a fingertip over his lips. "Don't fret. I'm not exactly in my prime either."

"But—"

"Hush." She kissed him lightly on the lips, turned and sashayed toward the screen.

Jonathan watched, transfixed by Ruby's generous hips undulating beneath the creamy beige skirt of her wedding gown. He swallowed, forcing moisture into his mouth as she disappeared from view behind the screen.

"I'm going to shed the confines of this beautiful gown," she told him as if they still stood face to face. "And then we shall climb into bed and snuggle. I'm quite exhausted too. It's been a long day."

"Yes," he speedily agreed. "Exceedingly long."

"If you will only hold me, I am certain that I shall be quite happy."

"Certainly I will hold you!" Relieved that his embrace was all Ruby required, Jonathan changed into his nightshirt and welcomed his bride into bed when at last she emerged from behind the screen.

Ruby's filmy garment quite clearly revealed her full melon breasts, the slight rounding of her tummy and full hips. By the time she reached the bed, Jonathan's body was afire. Hard and aching, he welcomed her into his arms.

An hour later, he still held his bride.

"You are a forest god," Ruby purred, nestling closer. "A satyr."

Jonathan grinned, feeling quite full of himself. "I hold you responsible. You reignited the young, lusty man in me, my dear."

A sharp snap came from the fireplace, followed by a crackle and the strong aroma of a smoldering pinecone.

"But tell me, Ruby, my love, do you always bring mistletoe into bed with you?"

"Mistletoe brings luck."

"You don't need luck when you have love," he said, bringing his mouth down on hers yet again.

# Twenty

"Kiss me . . . it's Christmas." The husky yearning of early morning desire infused Rand's quiet coaxing. His lips gently brushed Clementine's ear, sipped her sweet lobe.

Christmas morning dawned bright and clear. Beneath a brilliant blue sky, a dusting of freshly fallen snow glistened on the hard-packed earth, sparkled on the highest treetops. A fairy-tale world lay beyond, fresh and pure and cold. But Rand felt his world to be infinitely more beautiful. The carved marble fireplace warmed the room, and Clementine warmed his bed. Her Titian red curls fanned the milky white pillow case, inviting his touch.

He watched as she slept, watched her silky body wiggle in awakening. Her lips, moist with the pink blush of a baby rose, parted in a sleepy smile. "And soon you'll be saying, 'Kiss me . . . it's New Year's Eve.'"

"Followed by, 'It's the first day of the New Year . . . kiss me quickly.'"

Her laughing mouth met his. A light kiss became a lingering exploration. Warm and hard, Rand inched closer to his welcoming wife.

Princess growled softly from her spot at the foot of the bed.

Clementine broke away, raising her head to scold

the dog. "If you don't stop your growling, I shall banish you to the kitchen."

Annoyed that the spell had been broken, Rand braced himself on his elbows and shot the dog a murderous look. "At least she's not baring her teeth at me anymore," he conceded.

"She'll come to love you in time."

"I rather doubt that, but I'm resigned."

"Always remember, you are bigger than Princess," Clementine said. Her eyes sparkled like morning dew on clover.

Clasping his hands behind his head, Rand contemplated the ceiling. He wondered if there lived another man as contented as he, smothered in folds of soft down with the loveliest woman this side of Texas at his side. It had taken months, but at last he'd landed back in his big bed. Even better, he shared it with Clementine. Just a smile from her made his heart somersault like a child's ball rolling downhill. Over and over and over.

"When I stood beside you while Reverend Rowe married us, I decided to make the best of our arranged marriage," Clementine admitted softly. "I set out to win your heart, but I didn't know how much I would come to love you, or what a wonderful husband you would be."

Turning on his side to face her, Rand clasped both of Clementine's hands in his. Locking his eyes on hers, he raised one soft hand and then the other to his lips. "You won my heart, darlin'," he said, softly confessing. "I never knew the meaning of love until you."

Her slow, tender smile triggered a rampage within his heart. A roaring, reckless knocking rattled him to his core.

For some time, Rand had prided himself on being

a man of courage, a loyal friend, a good son and a skilled doctor. Now, with all his heart, he wished to prove himself the best husband possible every day for the rest of his life.

"Someday, I'll be the husband you deserve, Clementine. I shall never let a day go by without a kiss, without holding you, without telling you how much you mean to me."

"My pa truly did know what he was about when he arranged for us to marry. And Jonathan too."

"Hmm. We haven't seen my father since his wedding day. Do you suppose he's all right?"

The gleam in Clementine's eyes spoke volumes. "I do believe Ruby is keeping him busy."

"But they are expecting us for Christmas dinner?"

"Yes."

"Then perhaps we should stir ourselves."

Clementine cuddled up to him. "Oh, no."

"Don't tempt me, Mrs. Noble."

"Are you tempted?"

"By you? Always," he confessed with a grin. "But we have to go downstairs and see what Saint Nicholas left under the tree."

Her playful, dewy expression crumpled into a frown. "Ah'm afraid there is nothing under the tree. I spent all my money on mittens and mufflers for the church Christmas baskets."

"What money?"

"My return-to-Texas savings."

"You planned to go back to Texas?"

"I considered it, until I realized how much I loved you, and how miserable I would be without you. Then I had no choice but to stay right here and wait for you, no matter how long it took."

"If I hadn't been such a fool."

"You're back now, and that's what's important."

"Darlin', I wish I could make up for lost time. I regret each day spent without you. But I'm back at the Academy Hospital to stay."

Chuckling, she rolled her eyes. "Your tongue just drips with sugar. Ah have no doubts why you were so popular with the ladies."

Ignoring her jibe, Rand rolled out of bed and, taking Clementine's hand, tugged her toward the edge. "Come with me, my lady. My only lady."

Rand and Clementine wrapped themselves in warm dressing gowns. Then Rand led Clementine downstairs to the drawing room. Princess followed, sniffing suspiciously at his heels.

Millie appeared right behind them, bearing a tray exuding the delicious aromas of hot coffee and cinnamon buns. The old housekeeper had finally taken to Clementine. Millie confided to Rand that the new Mrs. Noble was always thoughtful and helpful when the arthritis slowed her.

One small white box, tied with a red ribbon, rested beneath the small tree. Rand retrieved the box and gave it to Clementine as he sank to the sofa beside her.

"Santa has been here," he noted, unable to suppress a grin.

"Oh, mercy." Her eyes widened as she gazed at the box. "What is it?"

"Open it and you will see."

Her fingers trembled as she pulled the bow and slowly opened the box. "My seahorse!" she exclaimed.

He withdrew the small ivory creature from its resting place within folds of pink silk. "You gave me the only item of value you possessed. You entrusted me with something no amount of money in the world could replace. The token of your father's love, your only

Christmas gift. No one has ever been so generous, nor demonstrated so much faith and . . . love in me."

Tears filled her eyes.

Rand held up the cherished symbol of love. "Your treasured seahorse is now held by a gold chain so you may wear it close to your heart."

"As I shall, now and forever."

No matter how hard and fast she blinked, tears of happiness streamed down her cheeks unabated. As soon as Rand had fastened the precious adornment around her neck, Clementine wrapped her arms around him.

Fearing he'd give in to the passion her nearness never failed to stoke, he gently disengaged. Standing, he pulled his plainly perplexed wife to her feet. "We have yet to look under the tree in the foyer."

"Why—"

"When Saint Nick sees a tree, no matter where or how many there are," Rand explained with a grin, "he makes certain to leave a gift."

Fingering the seahorse around her neck, Clementine's eyes grew misty once again as she regarded his outstretched hand. "Oh, Rand. You shall spoil me," she protested softly.

"That is exactly my intention."

With a soft sigh and an endearing smile, she slipped her hand into his and followed him to the foyer tree. Another small box nestled beneath it.

Bowing his head in a chivalrous gesture, Rand presented the black-velvet box to her. Inside, he'd placed her wedding band: the simple gold band his mother had worn. He'd had the ring enlarged and had another fashioned just for Clementine. Her ring featured delicate diamonds and glimmering emeralds that circled the band and surrounded the largest diamond he could find.

When she opened the box, she gasped and blinked.

Removing the box from her trembling hand, Rand dropped to one knee. He clasped her hand in his and looked into wondering eyes, gentle green eyes, as glorious as a sparrow's spring song. "Clementine Calhoun, will you marry me? Again."

Apparently speechless, she stuttered, "But—but—"

"Seven months ago, I was deprived of the opportunity to ask you the most important question a man can ask a woman. I want you to be my wife. Please say yes . . . because I love you with all my heart. I love every freckle on your nose, every little curl on your head. I love every tall story you spin, every song you sing. You are my one and only love."

Holding his breath, waiting for her answer, he rose slowly to his feet. His heart drummed, and the sound filled his ears.

Clementine appeared dazed. Barely breathing. Her lips quivered. "Rand . . ."

"Please, say yes."

"Oh dang!" she blurted, bursting into a dazzling smile. "Yes!"

Rand swept her into his arms, held her tightly, lowered his mouth and kissed her fiercely. A joy he'd never known fired through his veins, white-hot and lightning-light. He tasted her, loved the taste of her and yearned for more.

Loosening his hold, Rand voiced an urgent suggestion. "We need more rest. After all of this excitement, I think we should return to our bed."

Grinning, she nodded. "But first, come with me."

Rand followed willingly as Clementine led him upstairs and down the hall to the room he'd forbidden her to enter seven months ago.

He stopped short. His body tensed. "Why are we here?"

She opened the door, took his hand and gently led him inside the chamber.

"What the . . ." Rand's voice trailed off as he looked about in stunned disbelief.

The dirty chamber left to dust and to house the bones of broken dreams had been transformed. A bright, sparkling-clean and cheerful chamber had taken its place.

Ever since returning from Key West, Clementine had spent most of her days restoring the nursery. The cradle and the rocking horse gleamed with polish. The rocking chair boasted a bright yellow cushion. New curtains hung at the spotless windows, and a soft carpet covered the floor. She'd painted ponies, dolls and toy tops on the walls. In the process she'd discovered a talent for sketching she hadn't been aware that she possessed. During the long, lonely evenings, she'd fashioned stuffed animals. Giraffes, zebras and monkeys snuggled on shelves alongside books by Hans Christian Andersen.

"Do you like it?" she asked.

The crevices of his frown cut deep on Rand's forehead. "It's a child's paradise, but—"

"For our child certainly deserves the best."

"Our child?" he repeated, slanting Clementine a foggy expression.

"We're having a baby," she crowed, unable to conceal her joy a moment longer. "I knew in Key West, which is why I returned to Annapolis."

"Why didn't you tell me?"

"You were so excited about going to Samoa. I was

afraid if I said anything, you would miss your great adventure. The baby and I would be here waiting when you returned. I wanted you to have all of your dreams— a thrilling adventure and your son." Pausing, she pursed her lips. "Or daughter."

Rand's frown melted into a wide, heart-stopping grin. His blue eyes twinkled with love. "Oh, my darlin'."

"You understand I can't guarantee you a son."

The laughter of the best-looking officer and surgeon in Annapolis filled the room as he swept Clementine up into his arms and twirled her around and around.

"Dr. Noble," she gasped as her stomach began to spin as well. "I feel I should warn you, my belly has been a bit unsettled of late."

Rand put her down promptly. "I'm sorry. Are you . . . are you all right?"

"I would be if you kissed me."

"It's Christmas," he said.

His mouth covered hers, and in his kiss she felt a heart overflowing with love. In the distance Christmas church bells pealed. The joyful music resounded in Clementine's soul.

Throughout Annapolis the bells called parishioners to church.

"It's time to go," she whispered.


An hour later they left the house. Rand held Clementine's gloved hand as she stepped out into the light snowfall. Jonathan's butler Alvah held a horse at the end of the path.

"Oh, mercy." She dared not believe her eyes. It was her horse. It was Bay.

"Now there is no reason for your to return to Texas. Ever," Rand said quietly.

She could not speak. Her dear husband was full of surprises. Her lips quivered as she slanted him a smile before running down the path. Bay neighed softly as Clementine wrapped her arms about the horse's neck.

"How did you arrange this?"

Rand grinned. "Rather hastily."

"Thank you," she whispered tearfully. "Thank you."

Oblivious to the icy flakes melting on her nose and cheek, she crooned soft endearments to Bay.

"Clementine, we must go. Would you like to ride Bay?"

"No. This morning, I wish to walk beside you." She lifted her gaze to Rand, hoping he would see the deep love in her eyes, a love that would burn for him forever. "You're right. I shall never return to Texas. Everything I've ever wanted or needed is here. You."

The awful doubt he'd entertained vanished. Rand had fathered a child. He was as much a man as any man. But his intense desire to sire a son had subsided to a simple wish for a healthy child of either sex.

Rand hired a one-horse sleigh for the short journey to church. A woman with child should not exhaust herself. Following the service, they emerged from the church to find a gray sky and snow flurries. He wrapped the wool blanket around Clementine as the sleigh transported them to his father's house. Neither he nor Clementine could stop grinning. The merry jingle of the bells and the tickling sensation of snowflakes melting on their faces served to celebrate their joy.

Jonathan welcomed them with a warm embrace. Rand marveled at how kind marriage had been to his bachelor father. After little more than a week, the elder Noble looked as if he'd grown ten years younger. Ruby's earthy beauty and domestic talents lent a feeling of serenity to his father's house that had been lacking in the past.

"Can you smell the Christmas goose cooking?" Jonathan asked, rubbing his stomach.

"Is it ready to eat?" Rand teased.

"It will be by the time we enjoy a nip of eggnog," his father replied.

Rand hoped the eggnog might still his restlessness, but it did not. At his insistence, Clementine wore her new rings. Ruby appeared delighted with her friend's gifts, and the two women engaged in a lively private conversation until dinner was announced.

Every dish on the table invited praise. The children's excitement with a holiday unlike any in their memory bubbled beneath the surface. While Rand listened with interest to the wondrous gifts Santa Claus had left for them, he did his best to tamp down his impatience.

His newly expanded family numbered seven at the table. Next year they would be eight. Amidst the happy, noisy group, Rand realized he'd almost missed this grand holiday and gave silent thanks for the woman responsible for bringing him back.

After the children were excused to resume their play, the adults lingered over pumpkin pie. Anxious to put his plan into play, Rand lingered no longer than fifteen minutes. He turned to Jonathan and asked in a hushed voice, "Where is the champagne?"

"Well, I thought—"

Fearing Jonathan might inadvertently spoil the surprise he'd arranged for Clementine, Rand cut him off quickly. "I wish to make an important toast," he said, rising and gently tapping a spoon against his water glass.

Wearing a confused expression, Jonathan requested champagne be served.

As the glasses were filled, Ruby exchanged a questioning glance with her husband. Clementine appeared to guess what he was about and regarded Rand with a quiet smile.

"A toast," Rand declared, raising his glass. "To my father and my gracious new stepmother for sharing their love and the best Christmas in my memory."

"Hear, hear," Clementine added, raising her glass first to Ruby and then to the senior Noble.

"And to my wife for demonstrating, and for teaching me the meaning of, love." Rand raised his glass higher. "To the mother of my child."

Except for the hissing sounds from the fireplace, a thick silence suddenly blanketed the room. Rand grinned as Ruby and Jonathan looked at one another in surprise.

His father found his voice at last and shattered the silence. "A child?" he bellowed. "A grandchild?"

Grinning, Rand nodded.

The old man leapt up, hitting his knee on the table. He leveled a grimacing gaze at Clementine. "Are you having a baby?"

"Yes. Sometime in July, I believe."

Ruby rushed around the table to sit by Clementine's side. "Congratulations!" she gushed uncharacteristically, embracing the mother-to-be. "I am so happy for you! I know this child shall be the first of many."

"You *know*?" Rand repeated.

"*Many*?" Clementine echoed. "How many?"

Jonathan waved his hand in airy dismissal. "Do not be alarmed. My wife is a medium, not a clairvoyant. At least that's what she's told me," he muttered.

Rand noticed the wry exchange of smiles between Ruby and Clementine but said nothing. An officer risked ridicule if he indulged in baby talk with anyone but family, so he was grateful for the ensuing discussion. Puffed with pride, he answered Ruby and his father's questions.

When they'd exhausted the subject for the present, Ruby suggested adjourning to the parlor. There were more gifts to be opened and games to be played.

Although he could never trump Clementine's baby surprise, Rand had a surprise of his own up his sleeve.

In the parlor, they found Della playing with her new dollhouse by the Christmas tree. The boys played backgammon, Harley impatiently teaching Zeke as they played the game.

Della shyly approached Ruby. "Mother, would you like me to play the piano now?"

"As soon as we exchange our gifts. Della has recently learned to play several Christmas carols on the piano," Ruby said in a quiet aside to Rand and Clementine.

"She learned quickly," Jonathan added, as any proud father might.

The first gift to be opened was one to Rand from Jonathan and Ruby.

"*Around the World in Eighty Days* by Jules Verne." He read the title aloud. "Thank you. I shall enjoy this book very much." "And you'll find a good deal of adventure between the covers," his father pointed out with a sly smile.

Clementine excused herself for a moment but hurriedly reappeared carrying her banjo. "Harley, this is for you. It's kept me company on many lonely days and nights. Even if you never feel lonely like ah used to, music is one of the best friends you can have."

Harley's eyes turned as round as the head of the five-string instrument. "Thank you, Mrs. Noble."

"You're welcome." She cast the boy a beaming smile before turning to her father-in-law and handing him a leash. "I know how attached you became to Princess while I was in Key West. And I know how the children love her. So Princess is my gift to you. But be warned—she is a thief, and she still digs in the garden."

Della and Zeke jumped up and down, clapping their hands, their small faces wreathed in smiles. "Can we go get her? Can we go get her right now?" Zeke pleaded.

"What do you say, Jonathan?" Clementine asked.

"I'll have to ask my wife," he responded with a wink.

"Yes," Ruby allowed with a resigned twist of her lips. "Harley, will you go with them?"

Clementine watched the children bounce out of the parlor. Happiness bubbled within her, strong and vibrant. Her stomach felt steady for the first time in days.

"There is one more gift," Ruby said, rising to whisk a large box from beneath the tree. She carried it to Clementine. "I believe your name is written on the box."

"With mistletoe tied to its ribbon!"

Ruby only smiled.

"Is it from you and Jonathan?"

"No, it's from the three of us: Rand, Jonathan and me."

The three people she loved most in the world had banded together to purchase a gift for her. Clementine's heart reacted with a thump. "What could it be?" she mused, regarding the box. "It's so large. I . . . I don't know what to say. I'm not accustomed to receiving Christmas gifts."

"Say nothing. Just open it," Ruby prodded.

Clementine felt all eyes upon her while she slipped the mistletoe and ribbon from the package.

Holding her breath in anticipation, she lifted the

cover. One look set her heart to racing. Awestruck, her hands flew to cover her open mouth.

"Do you like it?" Ruby asked.

"I've never seen a more beautiful gown," she whispered in awed tones. "This must have been made for a queen."

"It was," Rand agreed. A mischievous twinkle danced in his eyes. "For you, my queen."

No clever reply came to mind. Overwhelmed, Clementine could only smile.

"Won't you try it on for us?" Jonathan asked.

"Now?"

"Yes, now, Clementine." In her usual no-nonsense manner, Ruby took charge. "Come with me."

When his stepmother and wife left the room, Rand looked to his father.

"Don't worry, Son. I've arranged everything just as you asked."

Although he attempted to relax, pins and needles skipped down Rand's spine. Beneath his father's amused eye, he paced the parlor impatiently, waiting for the women to return. When at last they returned, his gaze locked on Clementine.

She shimmered. She shimmered more brightly than any jewel, any star in the heavens. His heart slammed against his chest. Clementine approached him like a queen, graceful and proud. Gone was the wrangler walk, the determined gait of a young rancher. In its place, the fluid steps of a sophisticated woman.

The elegant, boned bodice of her pale pink silk gown came to a deep point over her waist, successfully concealing the start of a small round belly. Exquisite seed pearls embedded the matching skirt, with its small padded bustle and long, eloquent train. In every way, the gown complimented Clementine's fair skin and sunset hair. She wore the finishing touch around her neck. The tiny ivory seahorse dangled from its delicate gold chain.

Clementine stood stock-still, barely breathing, waiting for a reaction. She'd never dreamed of wearing such a magnificent gown. She'd never dreamed of having the love of a man like Rand. Certainly, she'd never dreamed of this moment, of being the center of attention and living a life of luxury with a loving family. She'd always expected a life of hardship and struggle.

Yet here she stood beneath a red-ribboned ball of mistletoe.

"Do you like it?" she asked.

Rand crossed to her side in two swift strides. "I like it very much," he said, planting a soft kiss on her cheek. "And I adore you."

The doorbell sounded before she could reply.

"Are you expecting other guests?" she asked Ruby.

"Only one other."

While Clementine basked in the light of her husband's eyes, Jonathan slipped from the room. Within seconds, he reappeared with his guest.

Clementine recognized him. "Reverend Rowe."

Rand took her hands in his. His loving blue eyes settled on hers. He lowered his voice. "I asked the reverend to stop by. When he married us in June, I must confess that the ceremony had little meaning for me, Clementine. It was more like a contract I fulfilled. This morning, you heard my heart speak when I asked you to marry me. Now I'm asking you, with a heart and soul full of love for you, to repeat our marriage vows."

Giddiness muddied her mind. "Another wedding?"

"Yes." He nodded.

"You wish to marry me again?"

"Yes. And this time I'll be marrying you for the right reason, the only reason. I love you, Clementine, and I want to spend the rest of my life loving you."

Tears from nowhere rained from her eyes down her cheeks.

"Is that a yes?" he asked with a devastating, crooked smile.

She nodded her head. "Yes." Her voice cracked.

Rand enveloped her hand in his and guided her into the reception chamber where they had been married in June. Ruby had festooned the intimate space with swags of white ribbon anchored with great white bows. Balls of mistletoe dangled from every available space.

Once again, Jonathan acted as best man, but this time Clementine had a dear friend in Ruby to bear witness as well. Holding Princess on her leash, Harley edged into the back of the room with Zeke and Della.

Clementine's mind whirled in light-headed happiness. She hardly heard what was said until the Reverend Rowe uttered the words she'd been waiting to hear.

"Do you, Clementine Rebecca Calhoun, take this man, Rand Jonathan Noble, to be your lawfully wedded husband?"

"I do! I most certainly do!"

# Author's Note

*Seahorses (Hippocampinae) are monogamous, and during the mating period they engage in a lengthy courtship.*